JOSHUAS COMING

2/3/08
Ms. Kelli,
Thanks for you
Support!
Believe 3 Know
ito coming!

Mt 21:22

[signature]
Your school
mate!

JOSHUA'S COMING

Rhonda C. White

To order additional copies of this book, contact:
Xlibris Corporation
1-888-795-4274
www.Xlibris.com
Orders@Xlibris.com

42946

DEDICATION

I dedicate this book first to Tara, Amy, Jenny, Debra, Jenn and all the women and men who have struggled with infertility. We are a fraternity of our own. No one truly understands unless they have been there. Next, to all the unnamed influences who will find their thoughts and ideas ingrained in the fabric of this tale. Thank you for pushing me toward God's destiny for my life. I hope you smile as you ascend these pages and if only for a moment are reminded of God's goodness.

Then the Lord replied:

Write down the revelation and make it plain on tablets so that a herald may run with it.
For the revelation awaits an appointed time;
It speaks of the end and will not prove false.
Though it linger, wait for it; it will certainly come and will not delay.

Habakkuk 2:2-3, NIV

Being confident of this, that he who began a good work in you will carry it
on to completion until the day of Christ Jesus.

Philippians 1:6, NIV

ACKNOWLEDGEMENTS

It would truly be unfair for me to go forward in the book without giving honor to my Lord and Savior Jesus Christ. It has become "cliché'ish" and trendy in this day and age to acknowledge God as the force behind accomplishments, with no true understanding of His power. Many drop Jesus' name to improve their status or how others perceive them. However, it is not until you truly know Him for yourself and know that He is God for real that you can effectively honor and praise Him as the one and only living God. He is responsible for the very air that I breathe and the relationship that I have with Him is priceless. I will never be able to thank Him enough for all that He has done and for selecting me to endure the storm that shaped this book. This story was birthed out of a ball of chaotic confusion and from the frustration and stress that is endlessly tied to infertility. Until you deal with the earth-shattering blow of the possibility of never becoming a parent, will you truly understand the monthly funerals that plague over 12 million couples of childbearing age in this country. The funerals that hold the dreams of a future with a family; a child to carry on your name, your characteristics and hopefully your morals. Nonetheless, I rise; we rise like a phoenix out of the ashes of the pain that barrenness and childlessness bring to provide hope to the hopeless and to restore the faith of the faithless.

I need to give much praise to the first man in my life, my husband and indisputable best friend. Without you Marc, I would not have made it through one of the most trying times in my life. Thank you for being my mate, my guide and even though I do not tell you enough, for being my inspiration.

My parents, Annette, Rufus, Yvonne, Ruth and George: Some of you I have had since birth and others I've attained through matrimony. You have equally poured into my life in different ways and at different times. I cannot thank God enough for how you have influenced my soul's growth. Thank you for all that you

7

have lived through so that you could instill your life lessons in me. I could not have been born to better parents. You have been my "life editors" since birth. Thank you for every correction, admonishment and every reproof. I know that each one was performed in love and was generated from a true desire to see me succeed. I am eternally grateful for the love and sacrifices you've all made over the years for me.

To my shepherd and his wife-Reverend Senator James T. Meeks and First Lady Jamell Meeks: Your courage and faith individually and collectively have inspired me to be fearless in my walk with Christ and in His plans for my life. Thank you for living true to His word in front of me.

To my favorite authors, J. California Cooper, Bernice L. McFadden and Diane McKinney-Whetstone: Each of you has a unique flair that I am absolutely in love with and your ability to paint vivid word pictures is breathtaking. I adore you all and want to be just like each of you when I grow up in "author world." In addition, to my special friend and author, Victoria Christopher Murray, you will never know the true impact that you have had on my life. Your kindness and prayer covering have been a true testament of what God meant when He said to let your light shine before men that they will see your good works and glorify your Father in Heaven.

I must also give a special thanks to two ladies, without them this book would not be complete. April Toi Bradley and Erica Cain, you both are genuine vessels that God used to encourage, push and sometimes threaten (smile) me to complete what I know He put in my heart to write. Thanks for the rich inheritance of accountability that you give me. You are unique inspirations and true gifts to the body of Christ. And a special thanks to Stanley Robertson: your repeated guidance and encouragement proved to be incalculable. Thanks for sharing your wisdom with me.

To Patricia Wallace, my editor and someone I now call friend. Thank you so much for your patience and diligence with getting this book edited and completed. You are an encouragement every time we make contact.

And then to all of my, as we used to say at Kentucky State University, lil' buddies, best friends, homies, aunts, uncles, cousins, siblings, godparents, adopted parents, teachers, associates, co-workers and other spiritual influences. There are way too many of you for me to name, but I offer you much gratitude and my sincere thanks for being a part of making me who I am. God has truly blessed me with a magnanimous life and to Him I owe all the praise, honor and glory.

Have I not commanded thee? Be strong and of a good courage, do not be fearful; do not be discouraged, for the Lord thy God will be with you wherever you go.

Joshua 1:9, KJV

RHONDA C. WHITE

"Deanna! I just can't take that baby crying like that! You've got to do something!"

"James I am trying to calm him down! What do you want me to do? He is just a baby!" Deanna slung her hips from side to side holding her precious ear-piercing gift in her arms, attempting to decrease his volume. Her five-foot, five-inch athletic frame had easily transitioned into a human swing after giving birth. The Carringtons' once beloved remodeled kitchen had turned into a battle zone of ill retreat in the last few months. The pounding in her head began again as if a choir director had pointed to it to sound on cue. This was what she wanted, right?

"What do you do all day long? Can't you at least get him quiet before I get home? I work hard all day so you can stay home with him and dang, I just need some peace! Is he hungry or what?"

"No, J-O-S-H-U-A is not hungry, I just fed him! The doctor said he's colicky and will cry like this!" Deanna could feel her temperature rising and her adoration for her husband falling as she watched him rumble through the refrigerator tipping over baby formula, looking for his six-pack of *Michelob Draft*. James had not acted like their four month-old son was his at all. Wasn't he a dream come true for both of them? Outside of complaining about their son, she couldn't even remember when he had spoken his name or held him last. She had full responsibility for the care of the baby while James went on with his life like they had not added to their family populace. The more she pondered, the more the baby cried. It was as if her pessimistic thoughts fueled the baby's irritation. She no longer saw an adorable bundle of joy, but an intolerable, dependent destroyer of life, as she knew it. She and James had been happy, once . . . before all the "baby drama" began. The pounding in her head became more intense. She instantly remembered the old saying, "Be careful what you pray for, you just might get it!" She looked up from her thoughts in time to watch the fading love of her life grab his twelve ounces of happiness along with his keys and slam the kitchen door behind him.

~

Time eroded away like a sand castle positioned too closely to an incoming tide. Each tide attempted to astound Deanna and squeeze the life out of her like she was a tube of toothpaste. She had experienced thoughts like this in the last few months, but never this strong. Could she really abandon her own child? The pounding was so intense she couldn't see straight. Joshua's crying had long faded into the background of her mind while the pounding stood up front like a lead vocalist. How had she gotten inside the gates of the garbage dump? She decided the pounding in her head had more power than she first admitted and quickly realized it had been responsible for leading her there. She couldn't remember driving the fifteen miles from her home to the city's disposal site. She wasn't even sure if she had stopped at one light on the way, but she was grateful that it was the dawning of a new day. Only a few people would have been on the streets that early. She glanced over at her child who had rolled back and forth on the floor of the front seat like a liter of bottled water on its side; still crying as loudly as ever. She had dressed him in his cutest outfit, the blue and white pin-striped baseball onesie with the matching hat that her mother-in-law had given him. She didn't expect anyone to find him at the dump, but the pounding had told her that he should still be presentable. Somehow, she had even found her way into the sundress that James liked her in best, the green and white one with the small palm trees on it, although now she realized she had it on backwards. She hadn't filled it out like she used to. The excessive weight loss she experienced since the birth of her child made the dress less attractive and more homely.

Well, none of that mattered now. Life just needed to be different and the pounding assured her this was the only way. She had considered suffocating the baby, but quickly pushed it out her mind; after all, what kind of monster would do something like that to her own child? She robotically rolled Joshua out of the passenger door and onto a heap of feces, trash and broken glass. She did not hesitate and she did not waver. She was sure she had done exactly what the pounding had told her to do. She firmly pulled the door closed and released her foot from the brake, allowing the vehicle to roll slowly

RHONDA C. WHITE

forward from the small hill it had been perched on. With that final action, the pounding drum in her head ceased. The percussion's finale allowed her to disappear gradually into her own silent existence, lifeless and numb, but finally at peace.

CHAPTER ONE

"If walls could talk, what would they say?"

The dawning of day in the Carrington home caused the cherry oak walls to brace themselves for a voyage down a belated pipe dream. By the year 2003, they had become familiar with that kind of agony. At one time the walls had been living, breathing beings with dreams of their own. These walls, by then, had stood through the joys and pains of the families that inhabited their spaces over the years and they could predict life's outcomes by the way the air sat in between them. Although by nature they were mute, the eyewitness accounts of history that they contained made them wise beyond their actual abilities. They spoke words of consolation to one another through the creaks and the settling of their matter on a daily basis. If they could only put a voice to their keenness they would have the ability to restore the broken hearted, rejuvenate the fatigued and encourage the hopeless.

Deanna begrudgingly drug her feet to the bathroom after being awakened from a terrible dream. The dream about abandoning the baby had been so vivid it scared her into thinking it was real. She had felt the perspiration on her forehead before she opened her eyes and just for a moment thought . . . . No, things were just as they had always been. Wow, she had read about women flipping out like that, but she knew after all that she was going through to get pregnant, it could never happen to her. Prior to going to sleep the night before, she had determined that the cramps in her abdomen were more intense and were continuing to get worse, but she still hadn't lost hope. A hope deferred maybe, but not lost. She knew that the severity of the pain could be an early indicator of her dream come true. As she sat on the porcelain throne waiting for her bladder to empty, she felt a large gush and instantly knew that what she thought was her second pregnancy was just a late showing of her monthly friend. The despair she felt at the beginning of what could be known as a "monthly ritual" was like a consuming darkness that sent her thoughts nose-diving into a bottomless pit, making it more than difficult to rebound from each month. She sat disgusted, frustrated and embarrassed since she thought for sure she was pregnant. What would she do this time with a hope deferred? And what about that crazy baby dream? Was God trying to warn her of something or was she just self-analyzing way too much these days? She had told a few friends and had assured her husband that what she thought were the early signs of pregnancy were the real McCoy.

She often related the perils of pregnancy, or lack thereof, to the Bid Whist card game that she loved so much. She was sure God dealt her a two-suited Boston hand this time, so now what? She had taken the challenge, played the hand and got set again. Her three-year struggle to become a mother and give her husband the one thing that she knew he truly wanted, seemed to be never-ending. The painful unabridged experience would once again shoot her faith in the foot and not even stop to ask if it needed medical assistance. Hadn't she gone through enough already? Hadn't she taken the miscarriage three months ago like a champion? Hadn't she concluded that God allowed that test to come so that her testimony about His power would be even stronger? Deanna had to admit to herself that even though she wanted God's will for her life, she was getting pretty frustrated with His timing. She wondered if she was putting more stress on herself than she realized. Maybe that's where the dream came from. There would be no way that she could ever suffer from postpartum psychosis and drive somewhere specifically to abandon her child. Not after she had been barren for what seemed like an eternity. Who knows, maybe the dream was just a result of the grilled tilapia she overstuffed herself with and enjoyed way too much the night before.

~

After another deep sigh, Deanna composed herself and slid back in bed next to her darling husband of eight years, who was sleeping soundly as if her motion had not stirred him. James had not changed much since high school.

RHONDA C. WHITE

He'd managed to maintain h
The only transition his body
head from the four-inch high-
really been married that long :
years? Wow, time had flown
clock was being wound up ove
keep the wrong time. Would i
endless ticks drive Deanna int
enough. After watching her hu
while the morning sun kissed
to breathe normally, but she v
satisfy James' desire to be a da

"Dang!" Deanna excl
what had seemed like :
and she was still co
of her period, he
nominee who
"I'm ti
work fo
even

James turned over like a rolled up piece of carpet waiting to be removed from a room to expose its original flooring. He saw his wife looking as solemn as she did on the day when he left for college and they broke off their puppy love relationship as high school sweethearts. He knew inherently what was wrong, but plunged into the deep waters of her thoughts.

"What's the matter babe?"

Before Deanna could hold back, a tear found its way down her cheek. "I started my period!"

Even though James knew the answer to the next question, he shut his eyes with disappointment and fatigue. "Are you okay?"

"Yeah," she said, even though she wasn't. She was so frustrated that every time she thought she had God figured out, He up and allowed something else to happen that wasn't supposed to be part of the plan. James grabbed his wife and held her close. He hoped he could hold her long enough for their hearts to intermingle and find a common peaceful resting place.

"Honey, it will happen, when God wants it to." As much as Deanna loved cuddling with her husband in the morning during a sunrise and hearing his comforting words, nothing could soothe the dull ache she felt in her heart every time she remembered that she had not met her goal of being a mother yet. She felt like the last runner in a track event. The difference was Deanna was running a race that she had neither signed up nor trained for. She lay in bed silently and listlessly as James returned to a light snoring sleep. Feeling lonely, she let her silent impatient tears befriend her and rock her back into a pained thoughtlessness and then finally into a morning nap.

...imed as she sat staring at the computer screen for
...everal hours. She was coming to the end of a long day
...nsumed with unfinished work. Usually on the first day
...r attitude could be compared to that of an Academy Award
...hadn't gone home with the Oscar.
...red of having to do all of this work at home! What do I go to
...r if I still have to pound out psychological evaluations way into the
...ing!"

James sat in the den watching his fifty-inch plasma Christmas present from Deanna while reading the sports section of the newspaper. He had turned reading and watching TV simultaneously into a true art form. He loved to drown his cares of the day in sports and news trivia. It was his opportunity to escape from the disappointments that the cold world could lay on a black man each day. However, he knew if he didn't check on his wife he surely wouldn't have the peace that he desired for the rest of the evening. Without missing a beat he yelled, "De, come here!"

She gladly jumped from her desk and went to sit next to her husband. He casually put his paper down beside him.

"Baby, what's really going on? You've been walking around fussing, grumpy, kicking the cat, yelling at your mom and just being down right nasty! And when I say nasty, I mean not in a good way."

He smiled a sly grin at his attempt to be funny. Deanna sat for only a second and then began to lay into him about how overwhelmed she was with her new job and all of her church responsibilities. She was tired of being everybody's scapegoat, but sarcastically said she knew that she had to keep "standing up for the Lord!" Deanna's words were rolling out like a midnight express train and faster than a speeding bullet.

"Whoa, whoa, slow your roll, maybe you're just trying to do too much. Why do you feel like you have to do the job of Secretary and President of the Intercessory Prayer ministry? What are all of those other chicks on the ministry for?"

Of course Deanna was not ready to hear one of her husband's quick fix it answers and began to huff. James leaned back, glanced at his paper sideways and tried to catch the high scorer in the Bulls' game during his wife's pause. His eyes reverted quickly back when he felt her stare burning the side of his neck.

"Oh, was this one of those times you just wanted me to listen?"

Yeah, she thought but she knew that all of the talking in the world to her husband, or anybody else for that matter, would not relieve the true anguish she was feeling. No matter how many words of encouragement she got, in the end Deanna still felt defeated and deflated regarding her failure of becoming a mother. She would get spiritually grounded, so she thought, ride the wave for a while and then fall right back into the frustration of not being pregnant. She had written articles about infertility for the church newsletter, talked to many ladies who were having those issues and even had a support group dinner for some of them. She had gone as far as to strike a deal with God regarding ten women that she knew were having difficulty conceiving. She prayed that each one of those ladies would conceive before she did. And even though the Lord had been faithful and blessed all but two of the ladies on her list, she was neither elated nor encouraged. None of those things seemed to scratch the itch that she thought being a mother would relieve.

In Deanna's wildest dreams, she never imagined that it would have taken James and her this long to conceive. The waiting had the hairs on the back of her neck constantly raised like she was in an eerie silent graveyard not knowing what was going to happen next. She was sure that God had told her four years ago during one of her morning devotions that it was time to get off the pill and prepare for motherhood. Had she mistaken her fantasies for His voice? Were they similar enough to confuse? She thought He had confirmed His plans in the scriptures she was reading about not being fearful. She remembered vividly the scripture in the book of Joshua. *"Have I not commanded thee, be strong and of a good courage, do not be fearful or afraid, for the Lord thy God will be with you where ever you go."* Deanna knew it had to be confirmation from the Lord about children since she had not thought at all about having kids. James had begun to mention it here and there, but it was still the farthest thing from her mind. She would jokingly tell him, "I'm still trying to decide if I like you, why would I want to have another you running around!" But in what seemed like an instant Deanna's mindset changed and she began actively preparing for conception and motherhood. She knew that if the Lord said so, this motherhood thing would be a breeze.

~

Even her fears about labor and delivery had been calmed when she participated in her three-year-old goddaughter's birth. Boy that had been exciting. At the time she was not envious or jealous about someone else bearing a child. She was not sure how she would take that experience now, though. Her girlfriend had made it seem like labor and delivery was a walk in the park. She called Deanna about 4:00 am and said that she and her husband were on the way to the hospital. Deanna met them there around 7:00 am. Her girlfriend had been admitted and was resting calmly. The wires attached to her belly made it look like she was being prepared like a broasted rotisserie chicken. The monitor would make large peaks and valleys every few minutes indicating that she was having a contraction. The only sign of discomfort that Deanna saw was her friend calmly grabbing the bedrails for a minute or so, which was followed by a brief rest. After a few checks by her doctor, the nurse told Deanna to grab a leg and hold on for the ride. Three strong pushes and a big "Huh!" later, Deanna's goddaughter was born. Watching life transcend from the spiritual into the natural had been a pleasant ride. It was so smooth Deanna realized that there really was no reason to be afraid. She knew every birth probably wasn't so simple, but with God on her side all could be possible.

~

After the birthing episode Deanna prayed honestly and diligently about how to begin the pursuit of motherhood. She did not want to do anything prematurely; everything else in her life had been planned out properly and almost perfectly. She had the husband of her dreams and a family out of this world. She loved her career as a school psychologist and her involvement in her church was fulfilling. Deanna had felt a strong sense of peace and felt that her relationship with the Lord was tight. One of the only other things that she wanted to do before becoming a mother was to become active again in her sorority, Delta Sigma Theta. She felt super guilty about not being actively involved in one of the oldest African-American service organizations in history; one that she had sweated blood and tears to become a part of. But between work, church and her marriage she just could not seem to find the time. When Deanna did something, she wanted to do it right and to the best of her abilities. She didn't mind finding shortcuts to her dreams, but when it was said and done, whatever she put her hands to needed to succeed. She looked up from her thoughts to catch the tail end of a diapers commercial displaying a mother and the cutest baby she had ever seen cuddling and snuggling with one another. She desperately wanted to have that scene play in her own home.

~

RHONDA C. WHITE

Like a previous champion entering the Kentucky Derby, she thought, in regards to having children that she would put up a little effort, mix in some Holy Spirit and "Walla," it was going to work. How hard could it be to conceive a baby? Women did it everyday, right? She put her emotional pedal to the metal and began researching ways to improve her environment for conception. She did everything some wise person told her to do, even taking herbal supplements like Don Quai, Red Raspberry leaf and Evening Primrose oil. She started prenatal vitamins and was dedicated to a healthy vegetarian diet. Her exercise routine, although it was brutal, including running up to 20 miles per week and weight training, was maintained to a tee. Her exercise regime was nothing for her thin 5'7" athletic-frame. She had legs like a gazelle and she had been running like one since she was a kid. Her period had always come like clockwork so charting her temperature and prime days of ovulation soon became refined skills. What could go wrong? Her plan was foolproof. She and her husband had both managed to stay, so they thought "baby free" through their wild college years in different states. They had matured enough in their marriage that an addition should not put too much strain on their relationship. They were ready. God just needed to do his part.

Little did they know that the strain of barrenness they would endure was more like the one felt when a four hundred pound woman walked on a tightrope. After a year of trying, Dr. Fluten, her well-educated, calm, African gynecologist finally decided that it was time to perform some preliminary tests. Deanna underwent a preliminary test called a hysterosalpingogram. In retrospect, she thought the name of the exam should be changed to "a history in pain o gram!" Even though she had been warned by other women about the pain involved in such a test and one of her friends who had experienced the procedure accompanied her to the hospital on that day, she was not prepared for the grueling twenty minute procedure. The physician essentially pushed dye through her fallopian tubes and uterus to determine if there was some type of blockage. Deanna felt like someone had continuously shot water balloons through her guts; a pain that did not resolve until forty-eight hours later. The medical staff that cared for her had been nice enough, but the torture that the "simple procedure" had put Deanna through made her want to stand them in a row and pimp-slap them across the face a couple of times.

A few weeks after that, James reluctantly agreed to do a sperm analysis. Boy was that a nightmare! Although male testing for infertility was less physically invasive, the emotional invasion was greater. James had to masturbate and bring forth a clean sperm sample for testing. Since he proclaimed that masturbation was not an option for him, they tried other measures. The sample was not to be taken after intercourse, which would have, of course made things much simpler. What was probably a simple procedure for most men turned into the challenge of the ages for James. In order to turn in a fairly new sample James and Deanna drove the thirty minutes to the hospital and attempted to "obtain the sample" in the parking lot. When that failed they slipped by the hospital security guard into the bathroom together and Deanna did her best to be the "hand meet" that she committed to be on her wedding day right there in the public washroom. She was sure that they were going to get busted with all the hustle and bustle that was going on in the washroom. If they had security cameras in there the guards were sure to get an early morning treat that day! How funny had all of that been? If barrenness didn't bring couples closer together what else could? Their lovemaking had never been stressed or strained, but they were not "on command" performers. Finally, they burst out of the bathroom giggling and embarrassed with a little more in hand than they had when they entered. Neither of the tests had proven anything conclusive so Dr. Fluten remained confident that conception would occur naturally. Deanna spent many days crying in his office asking all sorts of questions about when they would make their next move. Another year and a miscarriage later she sat still unsuccessful.

~

Deanna's cat Delilah managed to brush her tail against her neck, which brought Deanna back from her thoughts. Delilah's tail at times was as comforting as the smell of baking bread. James had long given up on consoling his wife and began flicking channels again. He seemed to never tire of watching ESPN, ESPN 2 or any other sports channel for that matter. Deanna couldn't blame him for giving up. How could he ever manage to comfort her when she was not even being remotely honest as to why she was experiencing such a roller coaster ride emotionally? That ride seemed to reside in a quiet empty space in her mind and it only made appearances at unscheduled show times. Her own insecurity made her feel that her husband was tired of hearing about her anguish in not having kids, but she knew deep down that he felt the pain as well. He was childless too. Frustrated, she returned to her work.

~

Steven Cook counted five breaths before he knocked on his supervisor's door. He felt sweat formulating in his palms, but shrugged off the nervousness that usually followed. He was not going to take anymore mess from this man. No, not today.

"Mr. Thomas, you wanted to see me?" Steven waited in the doorway for his boss to look up from his work. Instead of obliging, he motioned with his free hand.

"Yes Steven, please have a seat."

The small-framed, balding man dropped his pen and sat back, pushing his glasses up as far on his face as his eyes would allow. An awkward pause drifted in the air while Mr. Thomas rolled his stubby fingers back and forth formulating the right words in his mind. He was clearly nervous too. His normally pale skin had turned hot pink and the sparse mix of gray and auburn hairs that he managed to comb over his receding hair line began to curl up with the moisture formulating under them.

"Steven, I need to get straight to the point with you. You are a great employee and hands down over the years your performance has been tremendous, but as I tried to complete your quarterly performance review and I compared it with last quarter, I realized that your profits for the company have dropped considerably and I just need to understand what's going on here?"

Steven shifted forward in his seat. How could this man sit in front of him and complain about his work again? He had said himself that he was one of the best employees in the place. So what, he'd had a couple of bad months. Some of his co-workers had plenty of bad months, maybe not all in a row, but certainly his performance was no worse than theirs over the full year. It was the industry's fault, not his! Every time they saw an opportunity to push a black man back down, they did it! He was tired of not getting the recognition that he deserved for working his way up from the mailroom to one of the highest paid representatives in the company. What did they want from him, blood? Something inside Steven snapped and like a glass shattering in slow motion he realized that he could not take it anymore. He knew the next step after this poor review would be his walking papers. He would not let that happen. He had too many other dreams and ideas to make himself and his family rich to be burdened by this job any longer. It was holding him back anyway. He would not let Theresa and the kids down, but he could not take it anymore. He would just have to find another way to make it work! He just couldn't take it, not anymore . . . .

Steven realized even though he had to be wrapped up in his own thoughts that his boss had not stopped talking. He was still going on about how he had gone to bat for Steven before and he just didn't know how much longer he could stand at bat for him if he wasn't going to hold up his end.

"Mr. Thomas! Excuse me, but I need to interrupt you for a moment. I know that my performance has been inconsistent in the last few months, but you know as well as I do that the market for our industry is down across the board. Now I understand that you've been in my corner before, but I know good and well that many of my Caucasian co-workers have been experiencing the same plummeting records and nobody seems to be coming down on them. And another thing . . ."

"Whoa, Cook, don't even pull that race card on me! You know as well as anybody that I treat my team equally and fairly, across the board. I'm a man concerned about performance, not color. You know that many of my close friends are the same color you are and they have never once said that I've done something that was racially driven. So you back down on that one. Let's just talk about the job and your work!"

Steven stood to make his point. "But that's just it! It's always about race. I can't take my color off and deal with just the facts! The facts always include who I am as a man. Maybe it is not all driven by you but I know that the higher executives don't ridicule my counterparts as much as they do me. They run my performance over with a fine tooth comb while others get to slide by with mediocrity!"

Steven was feeling better already. He did not care at the moment where any of this was going. He was taking his manhood back. This job had robbed him of it for too many years. He could make it without them. He was going to be okay! God would not put more on him than he could bear. He made his mind up in an instant and he was empowered to do what he knew he was supposed to do long ago.

"You know what Mr. Thomas, I really don't need to hear a response. I am tired of all of this racial nonsense. You could tell me all day that it's not about this or that, but I know the deal. I have been black too long to not see clearly. This entire company is full of racist pigs and I just won't take it anymore! You will have my letter of resignation in the morning. I will not be back." Steven backed up slowly at first looking his shocked former boss straight in the eyes for the last time. He turned quickly on his heels and exited like a storm surge on the bank of the gulf coast. Mr. Thomas sat motionless for more than a moment. He had not expected that to happen, not from Steven

Cook. Steven's chair was still swaying from his quick stance and departure. He wondered what would become of Steven and his family now.

Steven walked out of his office building with his chest high, his shoulders reared back and his stomach turning somersaults. What was he going to tell Theresa?

~

Deanna's work was disturbed once again by the ringing telephone. Theresa Cook yelled almost to a point of intelligibility.

"Girl, I had to put that Negro out this time! You won't believe what he did! My kids are upset but, he just had to get out! I can't take this nonsense anymore!"

Theresa and Steven Cook had been friends with Deanna and her husband since they met in the couples Sunday School class at church three years earlier. Steven stayed in the doghouse for one thing or another, but mostly for messing up the family finances with his gambling and poor budgeting problems. The funny thing about Steven was that he was the nicest guy you'd ever want to meet-saved, in church every Sunday, great with their two children, but boy did he love to trick off money! Whether it was gambling or buying into some pipedream, he could use up their mortgage money before Theresa could even think of paying it. They were in credit card debt up to their eyeballs and every week it was a different story. Theresa was known to be a hothead and could get fire red mad in an instant at Steven, but she always managed to accept his apologies, which were often filled with flowers or jewels. The gifts seemed to make things okay again, but only for a minute. But this time Deanna sensed that it was a doosey and that their making up wouldn't be so sweet. Deanna loved her friends, but she just wasn't up for this week's ringside seat at the Cook fights. She knew that she would not hear the end of it if she abruptly ended their phone conversation so she buckled down and got into her "Ask Ann Landers" mode.

"What's going on now Theresa? Don't tell me he forgot to pay the bills again and your lights are off!" Deanna sat back and listened to Theresa's account of Steven's morning events. She sat speechless for what seemed like an eternity. And finding nothing spiritual to say, she asked, "Girl, how are you feeling after all of that?"

"I don't know how to feel, really. He's going to drive me to drink! I want to kill him for not thinking of his family at all while he was in there getting his boss told! How could a man who professes to know the Lord and can quote every scripture there is about leadership, jack every dime and job up he ever had? His momma tried to warn me when we met, but I was just too in love to see it. I resent my mother-in-law to this day for getting in our business all the time, but I know she is right. I just don't know what to do. I really feel like we need to have some time apart. We've been through ten years of this mess and Steve never seems to get that it's time to grow up. The rest of his family thinks he walks on water so anytime I try to talk to his brother or father about it they just brush me off."

Deanna was quickly reminded of the great relationship she had with her in-laws. She could even remember the time when her in-laws jumped all over James because of an argument they had which caused her to call the wedding off for a brief time. She could tell her parents or in-laws anything and they would still support them. They were supportive from a distance, though. They all made it clear that their relationship was just that, "theirs" and they could not come running to them every time something in the marriage went bad. Their parents' plot to keep them together had seemingly worked since neither Deanna nor James had spent one night apart from each other since they married, unless it was a planned excursion. They had their share of heated discussions and definitely had overcome some obstacles, but they somehow always managed to put their differences aside for the greater good. At least up until that point they had. "Well T, I know you have to be salty girl. I would be too! That's a lot to take especially with Steven's bad money history and all. But don't lose focus. You know you love him and want your family to survive. If Steve getting out for a minute is your answer, just make sure you're ready to deal with all that comes with it. Nobody knows the right answer but you and the Lord. Maybe you all should talk to Reverend Marshall and his wife. You know they have been through enough drama to be able to give you some Godly insight as well as some practical answers."

"Yeah, you're right. I just get tired of running to them with the same mess all the time. I wonder if they think all the teaching and ministering they do is a waste of time. We seem to end up back in the same boat on the same sea every year." Deanna could hear Lil' Stevie, Theresa's son in the background crying and she knew that their conversation was over. Deanna quickly prayed with Theresa and let her know that she would do anything that she needed her to do to help.

~

Deanna's morning nightmare popped back in her head as she shut the computer down for the night instead of finishing her reports. Her brain was fried and she knew that she couldn't be productive anymore anyway, plus she was still a little frightened of her own thoughts. How could a woman so desperate for a child leave him at a garbage dump? That odd reality drove Deanna's thoughts back to her friend's predicament. She had her own problems, but not having a child seemed minuscule in comparison to having to deal with bad finances, an unstable husband and kids who were suffering from that instability. She began to think of all of the things that she might do differently if she had an opportunity to be a mother as she went to share with James the new plight of their friends.

CHAPTER TWO

"Like the breeze of wind although it is invisible,
disappointment too has a way of blowing emotions and dreams to and fro"

Sunday arrived and Deanna momentarily felt a little better about the
whole "baby thing." She realized that she had put a lot of pressure on her
recent intimate excursions with James since they had been instructed by Dr.
Fluten to use protection for a couple of months after the miscarriage to give
her body time to recuperate. This past month had been the first time they
had tried to conceive since before the miscarriage and she had forgotten all
the anxiety that was brought up every time she put a big baby emphasis on
their lovemaking. Her thoughts wandered again like a doe in an unfamiliar
forest. She was reminded of the proverbial emotional roller coaster ride that
her infertility took her on from time to time. She allowed herself to go to
that dark and desolate place in her mind. She was sure it had been the devil
himself who picked her up for the date to Anguish Amusement Park where
the roller coaster was the main attraction. She could almost liken her dates
with him unto a true affair. She was not proud of the man she had chosen.
She knew he did not have anything good for her. He had been the one who
accompanied her on the ride in the front car, put her seat belt on and insisted
that she not get off. He was always a cheap date, not even gentleman enough
to open the door for her to let her out. He was one of those who would push
you out of the car door while it was still rolling and not call again until he
needed something. She just wished one day she would get tired enough of
emotionally dating the enemy and cast him back down where he belonged.
What was even scarier about their on-again off-again relationship was that

she knew she had the strength to leave him, but it was something about his immediate offerings, quick fixes and Mack-daddy lines that enticed her to leave momentarily that which she knew was the truth. He seemed to bamboozle her back into his arms frequently these days. Wavering faith had a way of lending itself to dances with the devil that made you rock to rhythms longer than you anticipated. Sometimes she wished God would just take her away from her own madness. She didn't want to die prematurely, but the relief that being solely with the Savior and without the trials that this life brought on was a welcomed relief. Those were simply selfish thoughts she played around with from time to time. Deanna knew her sole purpose in life and the reason that she went through all that she went through was not for her, but for someone else. Trips back from dancing with the devil took only a short time of reprogramming when she allowed God to be her reverse psychologist.

~

Deanna watched her husband as he dressed for church and realized that he could still make her feel like a perky high school girl when he looked at her in that certain way. He always managed to do little things that reminded her constantly of why she loved him so much, such as buying her candy suckers like the ones they shared back in the day, or bringing old movie rentals home for her to watch curled up on the couch with her cat. Audrey Hepburn had quickly become one of her favorite actresses. She had caught wind of Audrey's talents in the first movie she viewed with her in it, *Breakfast at Tiffany's*. She loved Audrey's charismatic style and how she said, "Darling" and "Marvelous." It was so strange how fate drew like-spirits together. Audrey, in real life, had difficulty getting pregnant and experienced miscarriages along the way before having two sons. Life had a way of dealing the same deck of cards to different players. It had no respect for gender, time, culture or status. Progressing back to her thoughts, she hated that she couldn't always show the strong front to her husband like she did with other people. Her friends and coworkers had almost drowned the life out of her by always asking her advice and opinion about things. She wasn't sure why she had become a pillar of strength for her co-workers. Maybe just the nature of her job made people run to her for advice. But with James, it was different. She could be a seven-year-old and cry, jump and scream. He seemed to still respect and love her all the same.

There was no reason for James and Deanna to be late to church every week but for some reason they always managed to slip in ten or fifteen minutes after service began. It was difficult to imagine that they would ever get to church before the sermon ended if they had a kid. There were definite blessings in being childless: they could travel as they pleased, didn't have to find babysitters at the last minute when the first one fell through, and they could still splurge on themselves occasionally without feeling guilty. Despite those advantages, Deanna still felt like the contrary would be better.

As they briskly took the church steps by two, they spotted Steven and his children slowly approaching. Steven looked like he had not slept in days and the children who were usually dressed to impress looked like they had slept in their clothes. Steven reached for James' hand and they did the guy hug thing where they shake hands and pat each other hard on the back not to exude any signs of sexual intimacy.

"Hey man, what's up," James said.

"Man I can't call it. I'm just trying to survive. It's been pretty rough these last few days. T won't speak to me other than to make arrangements for the kids and I've been sleeping on my brother's couch since Tuesday."

Deanna tried not to roll her eyes at Steven and kept occupied toying with the kids, straightening out their clothes. Their mother would have died if she knew that they were at church looking so unkempt. The kids, however didn't seem to mind.

"Yeah man, you know I'll always have your back and whatever you need, we've got you, but dude you gotta get your stuff together. You can't keep messing up and think T is gonna just take it. You got a good lady and I'd hate to see things boil over on account of some mess. You know we've counseled too many cats about the same stuff," James said.

Steven shook his head in agreement and sighed, "Well let's just hope that T can give me some of the good Lord's grace and mercy once again. I know I needed my job but it's hard to hear a man who has never been in your position, try and pull the race card over your eyes."

The main usher looked at them standing on the steps and motioned with her expression that they had better hurry in if they wanted a seat. The choir was about to march in and it was close to impossible to sit in a decent spot after that. The crew marched up the steps like an army battalion as Pastor Marshall yelled one of his favorite lines, "Has the Lord been good to anybody?"

The Holy Spirit had a way of punching Deanna in the face with a right hook of the Word of God. Just when she wanted to be mad at Him for not giving in to her childish antics, the Word would hit her so strong that she could do nothing but cry. Pastor Marshall's sermon just happened to be entitled "Get Ready For the Test!" His scripture reference was from *Matthew 6:33* and when Deanna heard the address she did not even take the time to find it because she knew exactly what it said and why she was hearing it again. "*But seek ye first the kingdom of God and His righteousness and all these things will be added unto you.* Now that's all that needs to be said," Reverend Marshall exclaimed.

He went on to talk about how we get tripped up because we put created things before the creator and that God was not having that. He said, "Our God is a jealous God and anything we put ahead of Him, He would make sure it disappointed us." He went on to tell the story of Abraham and Isaac and how Abraham had waited so long for Isaac to be born that he almost idolized him. God tested him by commanding him to make Isaac a sacrifice." Pastor Marshall had the congregation turn to their neighbors and say, "What have you put in front of God?" Deanna knew before she looked in James' direction that he was reflecting on their marriage and how they had put the thought of a child often times before God. Deanna smiled and said, "I know, I know." It seemed that every time Deanna experienced one of her down moments the sermon for that week had everything to do with what was going on. It was as if God himself had ordered up the sermon based on actual events from her life. Deanna was sure that many other congregants felt that same way but she wanted to tell God sometimes to "get off her porch!" She placed the sermon in her mental photo to make it a memory preserved. She valued it and knew she would need its strength again before long.

Deanna and James proceeded to Sunday School and Deanna braced herself for what she knew was ahead. Every couple in their class either was expecting or had infants and children in tow. Most Sundays Deanna could take it like a champ, playing with the babies and making small talk with their moms. Not too many people mentioned their infertility issues anymore, especially since they had the class pray for them after the miscarriage. A lady here or there would offer advice about how she and her husband had finally conceived but for the most part people kept their distance emotionally from that part of their lives. Deanna had heard everything about how to conceive from taking Robitussin® to increase vaginal secretions to having sex upside down during a full moon! Deanna wasn't sure if people genuinely cared or if they were just being plain nosey.

One of the older ladies in their class who she had grown to admire made sure only to come to talk to her every once in a while. Deanna appreciated her wisdom and the peace that she always shared. Deanna felt she had a calming melody to her voice. A voice that made words sing as she said them. She was a lady in her early fifties whose husband had been diagnosed with cancer. She managed to still come to class even though her husband had been bed ridden for several months. Carleen Adams approached her with discerning eyes as Deanna sat looking like she hoped she could just melt into the carpet. "Hey Deanna, how are you feeling today?"

"I am doing okay Carleen, just having a moment I guess, well maybe some minutes." It was amazing that she could so quickly close her spiritual eyes because of what she saw with her natural ones.

"Yeah I could tell you weren't your regular self, and the funny thing is you've been on my mind recently. I've been praying for you and your husband for a while now. I believe God is a keeper of His promises even when we don't see them," Carleen said.

"Well, I appreciate your prayers. I'm sure they are the reason I haven't lost it. The devil would have it so that I would throw in the towel, but then I realize that is exactly what he wants me to do." Deanna sighed. She often knew the right thing to say, but doing it was a totally different story.

"Well, the good thing about God is that He knows every mistake we will ever make and He has supplied all of our days with enough mercy to make it through. There are days, even weeks when I just get depressed about all of the things that I need to do. I have to keep a job and care for my husband, but I just press on. I know He has to give me the strength to make it, otherwise I would lose my mind."

Carleen always had a way of quickly comforting Deanna with her words even though they didn't talk much. Deanna respected the wisdom she obtained from mature ladies. When she talked to them it was as if she was viewing their lives from a front row seat in a movie theatre. She found value in learning from their mistakes and life lessons. Most of the time their advice was as solid as a rock unless you hooked up with the ones who were not trying to do things God's way and were too old to even think about changing. For whatever reason, Deanna had gained an intuition about those types of things and she could almost see people's intentions and moral values written on their faces. Sometimes her gift was a plus but in other instances it had proven to be a source of disappointment when she expected more from those who had achieved places of authority in the church. They had done all of the right "church things" to succeed but had not achieved the spiritual maturity required to really serve God in spirit and in truth.

~

She noticed that James was coming back to his seat with coffee for the both of them and devotion was beginning. She quickly asked Carleen if she wouldn't mind exchanging phone numbers with her.

The seasoned saint smiled and slid Deanna her card. "I was hoping you would want to do that. Can I leave you with this? Believe today, because all that hope you are storing up to use tomorrow may be wasted." Deanna sat in silence as she let Carleen's words bathe her in tranquility.

~

James and Deanna ended their Sunday on the couch watching football, allowing time to proceed at a donkey's pace without interruption. Deanna enjoyed the games but often got bored by the second one and fell asleep. James would tease her about not being a true blue football fan even though she fronted like she had mad football trivia skills. Her sleep was beginning to take her back to the bad baby dream when it was interrupted by the phone. She quickly opened her eyes and looked at James to answer, but knew that wasn't happening. His attention to the phone while he was engaged in television was like the quickness of a turtle, not a reality. She grabbed it on the third ring and was pleasantly surprised by her best friend's voice. A voice that had calmed her restless spirit many a day.

"Hey chicken head, what's cracking in the Chi?" Cairo said. He had been the only other black student in graduate school with Deanna at the University of Indianapolis and they had quickly become friends by "black only association." Their famous line was "birds of a feather will find each other and stick together in desperate situations!" Cairo and Deanna had been thick as thieves in grad school and their dependence on each other to survive had blossomed into a true blue friendship. There was something about being one of two blacks in a class of thirty-six Caucasian peers; no Hispanics, Asians or Arabs to be found. They were like two chocolate chips stuck on the side of a vanilla cookie. That type of unspoken pressure had a way of making a person feel like the weight of their race was on their shoulders. Most of the pressure was self-inflicted, but it felt like if you failed then you had failed your race and cosigned the majority's belief that blacks are less intelligent and less capable. Thank goodness Deanna and Cairo had one instructor, who happened to be white, who understood the silent struggle they faced and did his best to remind them of their capabilities and their value and worth as minority clinicians. His presence in both of their lives was still felt after being in practice for several years. She remembered that Cairo had been late registering for classes because of conflicts with his financial aide so he had not been present on the first day. Though they would stand as the only minority representation, it was always better to have two peas in the bucket versus one. They often spoke of how funny it was that black people had always seemed to become the sore thumb in the midst of a sea of white folks. Many white people had never had to experience trying to fit in just because they were the minority. They could easily slide in most of the time without the crowd knowing at all. On the other hand, especially in professional atmospheres, blacks were instinctively cautious about how they presented themselves. They became more mindful of what they said and especially how they said it. It wasn't something that was taught, it was something that was just known. Deanna, Cairo and many others failed to realize no matter how well anyone black, white or green presented themselves, people were still going to have an opinion about them, whether good, bad or indifferent. And most of the time those opinions were not based on who you were as a person but on that person's personal historical roots.

On the flip side of their cultural struggle, people thought it super strange that Cairo and Deanna had never been romantic with each other. They were attractive, young, heterosexual and full of hormones, but they had just been too cool with one another to jeopardize their friendship with something that others thought would be best for them. They had been through thick and thin together and after graduation they stayed as close as they could even though Cairo landed a job in Atlanta at a charter school for challenged teenagers and Deanna in the public school system in Chicago. Their separation from each other was only geographic. They were those type of friends who would not speak for weeks and then pick up just where they left off. Cairo was wild, single and still having fun with the ladies. Deep down inside Deanna knew that Cairo was ready for a committed relationship, but he would never admit it because of his own personal fears. He had been through so much with the break up of his parents after thirty-one years of marriage that she believed he

RHONDA C. WHITE

had lost hope in a true committed relationship. Cairo and James had gotten along well from the start. They never seemed to be intimidated by one another and Cairo could visit the Carringtons without Deanna feeling like she was stuck in the middle. In fact, they often left her unattended or with the young lady that Cairo had managed to drag with him. Deanna's continued prayer was that Cairo would grow closer to the Lord and return from his back slidden state so that he could find his "good thing." She didn't force her spirituality on Cairo though. He seemed to be making his way to the Lord on his own and her quiet example seemed to be making more head way than that of his "super-spiritual" aunts and cousins.

~

"Nothing chicken head, what's going on with you?" Deanna said.

"Oh just chillin', making my money and trying to stay out of trouble."

Deanna chuckled. "My psych reports have been piling up lately. It seems that every child in the system is being written up to be diagnosed with some disorder. My reports for the physicians are getting steeper and more intense each day as a result. Personally, I think the teachers are tired of being bothered with the kids so they push em' on me!"

Cairo chimed in, "Yeah, I know what ya mean. These kids down here are just as bad. I had to hem one of those knucklehead teenagers up the other day for trying to steal money out of my desk! These kids are crazy. I really feel sorry for them. Is your husband watching the game?" Cairo hardly ever waited for a response to his questions. "Tell him he needs to get a new team." As always Cairo's life stories and jokes could cheer her up and chill her out. Even though they did not talk much about the baby thing she knew that he cared and was supportive of them all the way. Cairo, after a long pauseless dissertation about his life, his loves and his wild escapades said, "Well I didn't want anything kid, I was just checking in. I gotta dinner date. This chick is sweating me so I better get ready and let her!"

"Cairo you need to get somewhere and sit down!" Deanna laughed.

"Yeah I am gonna get somewhere and sit down real soon. Don't worry you'll be the best woman in my wedding soon enough."

"Ha, I will probably have to be wheeled down the aisle as long as it's taking you to settle." Deanna said.

"Just taking my time, I want to do this thing right you know. So I'll holla at you all later."

Deanna said her goodbyes even though she wanted to get his opinion about them undergoing further fertility testing. She knew he would probably tell her to chill and let nature take its course, just like James. Men never seemed to be in a rush for anything except to watch the next play or the replay. Deanna went upstairs and started Sunday dinner. She was determined to get in the bed before 11:00 pm. No matter how hard she tried it seemed like there was always something else to do. Delilah followed her up the stairs and looked as if to say, "So when were you going to feed me?"

CHAPTER THREE

"Wisdom is the principal thing; therefore get wisdom:
and with all thy getting get understanding."

Proverbs 4:7, KJV

She wallowed in the few extra hours she would get to sleep in today. She had returned back to sleep immediately after James left. Her thoughts made tracks around the good-bye kiss his moistened lips left above her right eye as long as time would allow. She loved her some James. Who wouldn't love a fine, saved brother who went to work faithfully and even put in overtime?

It had been a long week and Deanna was certainly glad she had made it to the weekend. She was excited to have a couple of days off and not think about work and her church duties. She was also excited about their monthly group date with some of their married friends later on that evening. The group date had started two years before when one of the couples in their Sunday School class talked about Christian fellowship. She and James had shied away from hanging around too many people because they found them often to be on different pages spiritually or just too consumed with life. Not that she and James felt that they were more spiritually grounded than others, but they shared a freedom in Christ that not all people seemed to be ready for. They resorted to hanging out by themselves or with family, but when James heard Rodney stand up in class and say that he and his wife Cara were looking for some couples to hang with, he decided that they should check them out. James knew Rodney from little league baseball years before, but had lost contact with him until Rodney and his wife joined "The Peace" a year earlier. Their church, Salem Evangelical Church had been affectionately named "The Peace" by Reverend Marshall. Years ago when he started the church he knew that God wanted it to be a place where people could come and learn about Christ in peace.

~

Later that day, Deanna stood staring into her closet for something jazzy to wear. Her husband's return from work had found her still in the bed but she had managed to shower and finally pull herself up for the evening. That was one advantage of being motherless. Your time was your own, outside of your wifely duties. However, getting dressed these days had become a chore. She had gained a few pounds since she stopped working out consistently. Somewhere in her subconscious she was acting out what someone had told her. She couldn't remember who, but she was told that if she wanted to get pregnant she should stop working out and start eating meat again. Deanna knew that wasn't true. She knew of girls who had run marathons and did not even know they were pregnant. But as she stood there, she had to admit that it was probably the reason that she had stopped being so diligent in her workouts. Deanna liked to be toned and hated that only a few months of not working out had left the back of her arms loose and flapping like chicken wings. Just as she was picking out her red *DKNY* turtleneck sweater and *Seven* jeans, James came up behind her and gave her one of those hugs that meant more than hello. "You know you could leave those clothes off and stay at home with me tonight."

"Boy please, you would die if you couldn't hang out with your peeps!" Deanna chuckled and playfully tried to squirm away from James' massive arms.

"What cha talking 'bout girl?" "I would rather hang out with my Boo any day! Those Negroes ain't talking about nothing anyway!"

"Yeah right, you can't wait to hear the new gossip. Sometimes I think you are worse than a woman with that and you can't hold water!"

"Well I haven't said anything about Steve and T yet. I really feel bad for them, you know. I just don't see how they keep getting into the same kind of trouble over and over again. I guess it really comes down to being a heart issue. Like Pastor always says, "You can hear the Word over and over again, but until you are truly ready to apply it, your actions won't change," he said.

Deanna agreed, trying her best not to add her two cents to the already "Messy Cook Drama." She did best when she kept her comments to herself

RHONDA C. WHITE

and the Lord. She had been trying not to be so opinionated about everything. She knew she could be too critical and was sure that her strong criticism was one of the barriers in her spiritual growth and the reason that some of her friends shied away from her during their struggling moments. Deanna was hell bent on telling the truth even when she knew that sometimes her friends would prefer she just agree with them for the sake of comfort and validation. Deanna felt like there was a place for that, but she also valued truth and honesty and benefited most from people telling her like it was. The truth often hurt her, but in the long run she had always benefited from someone who could look her in the eye and not sugar coat their comments. She guessed that trait had been inherited from her momma. She knew her growth spiritually and mentally could be contributed to those people who had loved enough to show her all of herself and not just the parts of her that smelled good.

She remembered her eighth grade teacher had been one of the first ones outside of her family to let her have it. One day Deanna had seemingly gotten beside herself and Mrs. Goodan let her know that she was smelling her own underwear and she didn't even realize it stunk! Whoa, that had been a blow coming from a woman who had been encouraging to Deanna all throughout the school year, so she took those comments to heart after Mrs. Goodan explained them to her and did her best to try her hand at modesty. The rest of the school year was uneventful and Deanna moved on into other experiences that challenged her emotional growth. That experience would be a stepping-stone for her into being honest at all costs. As Deanna found her way back from her thoughts she caught James looking at her as if he knew she had something else to say, but instead he went to the guest bedroom to iron his clothes. Deanna waited for her curling irons to heat up and thought about how strange it would be for the Cooks not to be in their circle of married friends. She knew that the stability of her own marriage was partly due to having solid Christian friends to be accountable to. After all, the Cooks had been the ones to mediate between she and James when they experienced their episode with Angela.

~

A few years ago Angela, James' so called "friend" had done plenty to damage the trust in their relationship. Although no physical evidence of infidelity was revealed to Deanna, the fact that James felt comfortable sharing his dreams and aspirations with a woman he was not married to had been enough to send them to the Cooks for some counseling. Deanna had to relearn how to trust James after that and it didn't happen over night. She struggled from time to time with believing that he had severed all ties from that relationship so easily. James simply made a phone call in front of Deanna to Angela and told her that they could no longer communicate in the same fashion because it was interfering with his marriage. After the call, they would be going along fine and then out of nowhere something would trigger the anguish of those past emotions. She often felt that the "emotional affair" between Angela and her husband was as bad as or equal to them actually committing adultery. Deanna believed that a man could sleep with a woman faster than he could share his heart with her. To her it took more effort for a man to be transparent than to pull his pants down. James had vowed not to ruin her trust again and they had slowly tried to establish the stability of their relationship through continued prayer and open conversation. Still from time to time when James' cell phone rang, Deanna felt that strange feeling of deceit again. She had finally come to the conclusion that she was going to have to trust the God in James again if she was going to have a successful marriage. She knew T had been integral in her ability to push through the bad days and look to Christ for peace. She only hoped that she could provide that same peace to her friend during her storm. Sometimes she wondered why God pressed so hard on His children, but she was always reminded that all things did work together for the good of them that loved the Lord.

⁓

"Who was that?" Deanna inquisitively and cautiously asked after hearing James' cell phone vibrate.

James gave her a frustrated and anxious look. "It was Brian, the guy I told you about from work. His wife had a baby girl, 10 lbs 7oz," he said.

Deanna was grateful to have been looking in her closet again. She knew she should be happy for others having children but somehow it seemed to cause a deep, sustained burn in her throat like rubbing alcohol on a fresh cut. In that week alone she had bumped into at least five pregnant women in various places and they all seemed to have a special glow about themselves. At times she wondered if she was the butt of a cruel joke. She was reminded that the enemy not only wanted to make her frustrated, but that he wanted to kill her.

She had nearly lost all composure at church last Sunday when a young lady that she didn't know too well, walked up to her and said, "No baby yet?" All

Deanna could do was smile and take the spoken dagger that had been thrown her way. She knew that the girl meant well, but did she have to say it as if to taunt her? She knew she needed to talk to someone fast. She believed in the power of the Word of God, but she knew that something was blocking her from receiving the comfort that only God could give. Many Christians looked down on the use of psychology but Deanna held the belief that God could use anybody or anything for healing and deliverance. She also knew that just like people experienced physical illnesses that required medicine, some people experienced mental illnesses that required prayer and intervention. She was going to have to put her own profession to work in her life if she was going to be at peace with the cards she had been dealt. First thing Monday morning she was going to call her insurance company to see what services were available to her.

⁓

The dinner was fun and depressing at the same time. Although no one wanted to talk about the Cooks without them present, the aura of the evening seemed to be only about them. Rodney and Cara had bumped into Steven at church and he shared what happened. The other two couples had been unaware of the separation but were just as shocked and hurt at the news. As much as the couples tried to turn the evening into the fun-filled comedy hour that it had always been, it did not seem the same without their friends. Deanna sat and wondered how much more the Cook marriage could take. T seemed hopeless and Steven seemed helpless. God was able but He needed something to work with. She just hoped and prayed that one of them would wake up before the nightmare ended and decide to take some proactive measures to save their family. Surely, the dam of their marriage would fall with one more drop of disappointment or pain.

As Deanna and James reached their black Infiniti FX35, an early birthday present for Deanna, they both turned and shared goodbyes with their long-time friends. If their friend circle was going to get smaller by default, they planned to do their best to maintain their own marriage and be accountable to the marriages that God had given to them. They did not plan to let another couple that they were friends with separate or divorce without doing all that they could for them spiritually and emotionally. After all, it was their duty as Christians to sharpen one another. Deanna and James made that vow that evening and they planned to keep their promise.

⁓

On Monday, Deanna quickly learned that finding a black female psychologist who she didn't know professionally was more difficult than she thought. There were only a few of them in the Chicago area and Deanna had bumped into most of them at conferences or worked in connection with them on one occasion or another. Finally, after several frustrated attempts through her insurance website, Deanna located a therapist in East Chicago, Indiana who could see her at the end of the week. Deanna was encouraged, frightened and frustrated all at the same time about her appointment. Had she truly lost control of her well-put-together life? And even though she hadn't mentioned that bad baby dream to anyone, it still haunted her silent thoughts from time to time. The devil sure knew how to lay it on thick when he wanted to. Was she slowly moving to the caboose of her "got it together train" which was slowly derailing into a pit of hysteria and failure? One minute Deanna was on her way to being at peace and in the next minute, after seeing a pregnant woman or getting her period, she would become this spoiled frantic little child. She did not want anybody to comfort her. She did not want to be strong. She did not want to pray or seek what God desired from her. She was afraid to admit it, but she was just down right angry with God. Why did He make promises that He wasn't willing to keep within a fair time frame? Deanna knew that God had it all together, but her double-mindedness about His plans for her life, and specifically children made her apathetic to Him and His plans. She remembered one of her favorite television pastors saying what she often said to God, "You know You are big enough that You would not even have to blink or get off Your throne to bless me!" Wow, if that was not how she felt now. "Mrs. spiritually mature", "Mrs. has all the answers for everybody!" How had she allowed herself to fall this far so fast? In one week she had gone from floating to flatness. Her joy was gone and she was not interested in trying to find it. She knew she was allowing the devil to win by getting angry and feeling defeated, but somehow she found comfort in her sadness. She wanted to grieve and mourn about the child she missed conceiving month after month. Did anybody really get it? It was like having a regularly scheduled funeral. She knew she was not the only one who had been through it, but for some reason the comfort in knowing that she was not alone just didn't seem to help. Boy, she knew that her therapist would have her arms full.

After fighting through traffic on I-94 that Friday, Deanna finally turned into the parking lot of the small-framed house that had been renovated into an office building. She rehearsed over and over again her opening line. She knew already what questions would be asked and she was ready to get to the outpouring point where she knew healing began for most of her clients. It was odd that she had been so willing to take on practicing what she preached. For so many clinicians it was difficult to take their own medicine. Deanna knew she was desperate and she did not care how nasty the medicine was because she was willing to hold her breath and take as many doses as necessary to heal her wounded heart. She hoped that Sharon Miles, LCSW was ready for the doozey that was going to walk in her door. She entered the narrow waiting room that was empty, with the exception of two weathered brown leather couches, two tweed chairs that looked like the ones the *Brady Bunch* had in their living room and assorted magazines including *Time, People, Jet* and *Popular Mechanics*. The waiting room was the communal area in the building used by all of the professionals who had offices there, which ranged from attorneys to real estate agents. Deanna could smell the stench of old cigarette smoke ingrained in the tweed chair that she sat on. She could not stand smoke. She smoked for seven years and at the time did not seem to mind infringing on other people's clean air space. But once she stopped, it was almost nauseating to be in the same room with what Deanna had labeled "carcinogenic clouds."

Deanna really needed to go to the bathroom, but since no one was available to direct, she sat as still as she could and read an article in *Time* about the crackdown on the sell of imitation designer bags, or knock offs, as they were called on the street. She noticed that the office labeled Sharon Miles had a large green "In Session" sign on it. Deanna looked at her watch and wondered how long she could prevent her bladder from exploding when the door creaked open and a large silver-haired woman walked out and turned to a hidden voice saying, "I will see you next month." She turned toward Deanna, gave a polite nod and trotted out the front entrance. Sharon Miles, a young, strong coffee-colored woman poked her head out of the door, introduced herself and welcomed Deanna in. She was so embarrassed that her first encounter with the woman she hoped could help soften the load that life had laid on her had to be, "Hi, where's the toilet?," but she asked anyway. Sharon smiled a cool uninterrupted smile and directed Deanna to the ladies' room.

When she returned Deanna found Sharon's office to be simple but comforting. The "famous couch" was an oversized black leather contemporary model that was soft and enveloping. Deanna sank back in the fluffy pillows and fixed her body into a relaxing position. She wanted to appear ready to pour out and receive emotionally, but her nervous scale had elevated well above ten and she could not hide the cold sweat rings that were emitting from her nylon shirt.

"So," Sharon began, "Why are you here?" Deanna wanted to say, "Because I am crazy," but began telling Sharon about her infertility issues. Sharon asked about her and James' health history, but then more specifically about their relationship and family life.

"So describe how you feel you are handling your difficulty getting pregnant." Sharon said.

Deanna huffed, "Not so well, I guess. I feel as if my life is full of counting days. I count ten days from the time my period starts, then the seven days in which I will possibly ovulate, then the next ten days are usually spent determining if my breasts are staying sore and if I'm cramping because I'm pregnant or because of my period. I feel super unsure of myself and what's even more scary is that I feel unsure about what God's plans are for my life."

"Well, let's talk more about that. How is your spiritual life?" After explaining to Sharon where she thought she was spiritually, they talked more about her marriage and consequently decided that she was dealing with poor self-esteem issues due to the fact that having a child had been one of the major things that she hadn't accomplished yet. They discussed how everything was magnified now because of the delicacy of her emotions.

"So tell me a little about the miscarriage you experienced three months ago." Ah, Deanna thought, the time had come to spill her guts about one of the most dreadful events in her life next to her parents getting a divorce. Deanna had faced most of the tragedies in her life head on. The storms had been rough but she always felt that God had pulled her through. On the other side of the storms, it never seemed as bad. She knew in her heart of hearts that God had always been faithful enough to pull her through, but what if it just wasn't His will for her to be a mother the way she expected.

"Well," Deanna began. "I discovered I was pregnant while on a girlfriends' trip to New York for my birthday. I really hadn't expected to be pregnant even though my period is more regular than an elderly person on prune juice. One day passed and I thought, I must have miscalculated my expected start date, but I wasn't really too concerned since I was engrossed in shopping and having fun sightseeing in Manhattan. When my period didn't show by the time we returned on Sunday, I knew something was up, but I just wasn't ready to get too excited. A week passed and Old Martha still hadn't shown and I was terribly excited. I knew I was pregnant and Valentine's Day was around the corner. I thought what a good way to surprise James to give him a positive pregnancy test for Valentine's Day. He couldn't believe it. It took him the whole day to ingest it and once he grabbed hold to it you could see him move from sheer delight to his serious "analysis mode." His brain wheels were turning. Now that our dream was about to come true, how were we going to afford a child? Nonetheless I was overjoyed and stayed bubbly all week. James was ready to spill the beans to the world, but I wanted to savor the moment and besides, I was also a little cautious since I knew the possibility of an early miscarriage. Another week passed and we began to buy pregnancy magazines and my breasts began to swell. It seemed like even the wind blowing hurt them. I remember the Sunday before the miscarriage the thermostat went out and James was going to make sure his wife and baby were warm. He attempted to light a fire in the fireplace without opening the air vent. Smoke was everywhere within seconds. The funniest thing was watching James take lit and smoldering firewood outside with a shovel. We had blackened snow all throughout the front lawn. Needless to say we got the thermostat fixed and all was well for a few more days. I continued to go to the health club as usual. Running has always been a major part of my life so I thought nothing of doing my regular routine. I went shopping and wore high-heeled boots as usual. I wasn't tired at all and I remember being excited about being able to park in the expectant mother's space at the grocery store.

We went out to dinner with friends that night and when I went to the bathroom I noticed some spotting. Not much but more than I wanted to see. I returned to the table a little concerned but did not share my discovery with the group. When James and I got home that evening I told him what was going on and he assured me all was well and that I should just rest. When I woke the next morning the spotting had turned into a light stream and I panicked. I remember letting fear take over like it had been in charge all along. I immediately called my doctor and his nurse told me to do more of the same, rest, put my feet up and relax. By 4:00 pm the light stream had turned into the Red Sea and I told James that I needed to go to the hospital. I began cramping like I had eaten something spoiled, but in retrospect, I think that was more of fear bringing his friends to the party. On the way to the hospital I made calls that I hadn't wanted to make earlier to my parents and in-laws. I had to share joy and pain in the same breath. My mother met us at the Emergency Room door and we sat for what seemed like an eternity. Tears enveloped my face as friends called to pray with us every other moment. Many of them were shocked because we hadn't shared the news before then, yet all of them shared their support and love for us. I distinctly remember not wanting to turn to God myself because I was too afraid of what I thought He was going to say about my baby. Had I just prayed to be pregnant and not to deliver a healthy baby? Could my Abba Father be that cruel and harsh based on semantics alone?

I wasn't ready to face up to the fact that He said that He would be with me wherever I went, even through this. Every medical provider at the hospital was sensitive and supportive.

One in particular sticks out in my head. He was the young man who administered one of my ultrasounds. He spoke in a foreign dialect and I swear to this day that he was an angel. Alone in his work area, that man ministered to me as if the Holy Spirit himself sent his comforting arms to surround me in God's love. He sang the entire Psalms ninety-one to me: *He who dwells in the shelter of the Most High will rest in the shadow of the Almighty. I will say of the Lord, He is my refuge and my fortress, my God in whom I trust. Surely He will save you from the fowler's snare and from the deadly pestilence. He will cover you with His feathers, and under His wings you will find refuge; His faithfulness will be your shield and rampart. You will not fear the terror of night or the arrow that flies by day, nor the pestilence that stalks in the darkness, nor the plague that destroys at midday. A thousand may fall at your side and ten thousand at your right hand, but it will not come near you. You will only observe with your eyes and see the punishment of the wicked. If you make the Most High your dwelling—even the Lord who is my refuge-then no harm will befall you, no disaster will come near your tent. For he will command his angels concerning you to guard you in all your ways; they will lift you up in their hands, so that you will not strike your foot against a stone. You will tread against the lion and the serpent. "Because he loves me," says the Lord, "I will rescue him; I will protect him, because he acknowledges my name. He will call upon me and I will answer him; I will be with him in trouble. I will deliver him and honor him. With long life I will satisfy him and show him my salvation."* As the tears flooded my face and the reality of God's sovereign will seeped into my unwilling but knowing spirit, I began to let go of my plans for this baby and say "not my will but Thy will be done."

Deanna sighed as if the episode was only yesterday. "The doctors advised me to remain on bed rest at home and to see my own doctor on Monday for further medical care. It was too early for them to tell if the baby was going to make it or not. How could a person go from pure delight to agony and suffering all within a matter of hours? The rest of the week was filled with rest, blood tests and plenty of company as I waited to expel death from my body. My mom practically moved in with us and she was a great help. I think James was being strong for me, but inside I know his bottom was falling out just like mine. My mom kept him grounded or at least distracted for the time. By the end of the week and after many passages of blood, I had gathered my emotions around the fact that this was truly a miscarriage and that the short pregnancy had ended on a sad note. Waiting to expel death from my body had prepared me for the morbid news that I was sure to receive. I was ready to accept my journey back to life as I knew it when on my final doctor's visit he informed me that he was not comfortable with my hormone levels or the size of my uterus for seven weeks of gestation. He suspected an ectopic or tubal pregnancy and wanted to admit me into the hospital late that evening. James and I stared at the doctor in disbelief. He sat calm, but stone-faced. We were definitely not expecting that and fear struck a cord in my heart once again. I had to deal with the loss of a child no matter how small it was as well as a threat to my own health. I had not been admitted to the hospital for any type of major testing, let alone surgery, since I was too young to remember so the probability of that was just not cool.

James and I went to dinner that night and sat in awe of the devastation that our small family had gone through in such a short time. I mean, all we wanted was a kid right? It wasn't supposed to be this complicated. James drove me to the hospital and stayed with me until his poor back couldn't take the unyielding wooden visitor's chair any longer. After he left, I was left alone with only an IV and its pole as my friend. There was no chance of me sleeping with nurses and technicians coming into my room every two hours. Fear had also propped himself right up on the bedside table and did a good job of keeping me wide awake as well. He continued to play the "what ifs" over and over in my head. What if it was a tubal pregnancy and it ruptured before the surgery the next morning? What if they had to take my tube? How would that affect my chances of getting pregnant again? What if something went wrong with the surgery and I didn't wake up? Boy, fear was bobbing me back and forth that night and it became more and more difficult to find the comfort of God's hand even though I knew it was just a prayer away. The morning found me with a swollen hand from the IV and an empty, growling stomach. I don't think I was anymore happy to see my husband than I was on our wedding day when he arrived that morning. My mom followed shortly after and their prayers and scripture reading comforted me until I had to leave and make a solitary journey to the operating room. I waited for at least an hour before it was my turn to go under the knife. I focused on a large number two that was printed on the wall before me. I said to myself that it must mean it's just Jesus and me. I kept praying that the Rapture would occur and that He would come back and rescue me, but the anesthesia did instead. I remember the burning sensation I felt as I was administered the drug and then the lights went out.

When I woke in the recovery room, I was groggy and confused. I could hear everything and everyone moving around me but I couldn't respond. Finally, my doctor quickly said that I was okay and that he was going to speak to my family. I remember yelling in my mind, hey it's my baby and my body, tell me first, but nothing came out.

When I could speak I kept asking what time it was, trying to calculate how long I had been under. If it had only been thirty minutes or so I knew my tubes were fine and that I had just had a D & C. But, if it had been longer, then I was expecting the worst. The feeling began to come back to my abdomen area and I decided that it only felt like I had been cut and nothing had been removed. As the pain set in with the arrival of my full senses I replied, "Yes," when asked if I wanted a shot of morphine. I was taken back to my room pretty quickly where my relieved husband and mom shared with me that all had gone well and that no ectopic pregnancy had occurred. I was administered what they call the abortion drug in laymen's terms and sent home to recover at my own pace. I remember thinking, how am I supposed to recover at any pace from the loss of the child that I never had? My anger at my doctor was quieted when I found out later that at least two women that I knew had experienced ectopic pregnancies and ruptures of their tubes due to late detection. These women had not experienced any pain at all before the ruptures and one did not even know she was pregnant. The rest of the week went by slowly and uneventfully and I returned to work two weeks later on light duty. My doctor said to give my body a rest and wait three months before we started trying again. I wanted to start trying right away but James allowed the doctor's advice to grip him like a vice and he was not budging. I realize now that he probably wanted to take a break from the whole "baby thing," and think about other stuff. The wait was more than likely good for us, but here I sit now just as confused and disappointed as I did the month after we initially started trying."

~

Deanna had not wanted to share that much but it seemed like when she started talking a hurricane pushed her out to talk sea and she could only return to shore after she had exposed her deepest emotions about the miscarriage. She knew from her own practice that the mind had a way of hiding things from itself and then expelling them when the pressure became too intense for it to hold any longer. It was the brain's source of checks and balances. Sharon expressed her condolences regarding Deanna's pain and validated her

RHONDA C. WHITE

feelings of loss and despair. One of the main points that Sharon made was that it was so important to acknowledge sorrow and grief. Those emotions were not something that you could stuff away and not deal with. Left alone and unattended they were able to cause illness, emotional distress and cause personal wars. She suggested that Deanna start journaling her feelings about what she was going through. People who tended to want all of their ducks in a row needed some place of outlet and escape. Deanna knew that was an awesome idea and she laughed inside at how she had given many of her students that same suggestion when they were going through difficult times. They decided to continue to see one another and Sharon strongly suggested, after a discussion with James, that they seek medical attention from a fertility specialist. She felt that she and James were too young to be discouraged so soon and especially without seeking an expert first. Deanna felt somewhat relieved after seeing Sharon. She felt the heat of the light at the end of the tunnel but unfortunately, she still couldn't see it. She needed to allow God the opportunity to bless her even if it was not in the way she expected. Beyond that, she needed to be willing to give time, time. Her problem was that her life-clock was ticking way too fast and too loud these days.

CHAPTER FOUR

"Tears are the silent language of grief"

Voltaire

She cried those upside down tears before the day even began. Tears that ran from the side of your face in no particular pattern. The tears that were tired of falling in the same direction and chose another vector out of boredom. Her tears inherently knew that drama was ensuing and they fell as the warm up act. Like the smell of rain that warned of its coming but did not give a specific time, trouble had scented the air.

~

"James, I am not sure why she wants to see you by yourself this week!" Deanna had spent the last ten minutes trying to convince James to visit Sharon alone as she requested. She and James had been to see Sharon together on a couple of occasions and the sessions had gone well. But now Sharon wanted to talk to James individually about his life and feelings about infertility without her, and James was not having it.

"I just don't see why I have to see her. I am doing okay with the baby thing and well you were the one . . ."

"Oh just go on and say it, James. I was the one who was tripping and had all the problems about not having a child!" Deanna yelled from the kitchen. She was fuming now. Even if she was the one who had initially sought out counseling to deal with her emotions, the sessions had been good for their marriage and had exposed other areas that they also needed to focus on in regard to trust and communication. She could not believe that James was being so immature and selfish about seeing Sharon on his own. He had seemed comfortable enough when it was about them, but now that the tables had swayed some, he was backing down and out. "Well you know what, you call her and cancel for yourself. Last week when she mentioned it, you didn't seem to have a problem with it. I refuse to clean up your mess this time. If you don't want to go, you deal with it!" Deanna was slinging pots all around the kitchen now as she prepared dinner. She heard James blow hard through his nose and say, "Just forget it!" She heard his work shoes scuffle down the hall and she knew he was retreating to his "other woman" as she called it, his *Play Station 2* game. James turned up the game louder than usual and began attempting to beat his last score on *NBA Live*. Deanna wished she had enough guts to go up there and throw the game out the window, but she knew no matter how saved James was, he would have thrown her out the window right behind it.

~

She had just decided to call T to check on her when the phone rang. Carleen's soft, but commanding voice greeted Deanna and she chuckled to herself. Well, God certainly knew how to get her straight, she thought. Certainly her conversation with T would have turned into an "I can't stand my husband" session, but with Carleen she would have to remain at least reflective on how grateful she was about having a healthy husband, even if he was too stubborn to know what was good for him. "So, Carleen how have you been?"

"I've been doing pretty well. This has been a good week in the Adams household. John was able to get up and walk around some without feeling too weak and he was able to eat some of his favorite food and keep it down."

See, Deanna knew that without trying, Carleen would make her feel horrible about not wanting to even be in the same room with James. Here this lady was excited that her husband was walking and eating and she wanted to kick hers in the knee and make him throw up if she could!

"But I did not call to talk about me. I just wanted to see how you were and how you were holding up these days. I haven't been able to come to Sunday School recently because John's nursing agency is short staffed and I've been missing you. I want you to know that I see so much in you. I know things are tough right now because you can't seem to figure God out, but He does have good and prosperous things for you and your husband, just wait and see. It amazes me that a woman so young has the wisdom and the faith you have," Carleen said. Who was this woman talking about and where was she? Deanna thought. She had been playing a broken record entitled *Faith to Doubt* for the last several months and she did not understand how Carleen saw so many great things in her.

"Well Carleen, I thank God that you see something in me that I definitely don't feel or see right now. I appreciate your encouragement and I know I need to seek the Lord continually about His plans for my life instead of only reminding Him of mine." The women prayed a quick prayer and Deanna asked for forgiveness for thinking ill of her husband a few moments earlier. She knew that all of her barking, complaining and jumping in the floor was not going to change James' mind about counseling. If the Lord wanted Him to go alone, he would be there. She let it go and finished cooking as she and her mentor got off the phone. She wished all of her times of surrender could be that easy. She and James had begun to talk more often about deeper things but they also had started arguing and disagreeing more often. She knew that often before things got better they got worse, so she was ready to buckle down for the ride. She was curious as to why James was so hesitant to attend a session alone and felt in the back of her mind that there was something she didn't know about or quite understand. She finished their dinner and toddled up the stairs to feed and apologize to her husband, even though she had been the one to apologize last time.

~

Deanna and T met for lunch after church the following Sunday and even though T looked weary and worn, she was a sight for Deanna's sore eyes. It had seemed like months since the two friends had gotten a chance to hook up. Most of their conversations had been short and focused on what T should do regarding her marriage. And, although Deanna wanted to be there for her friend, she had to admit that she needed T just as much now. The counseling was still going well and Sharon had been a lifesaver, but Deanna needed her friend to lean on, someone she knew loved her and would accept her whether she was right or wrong. They met at one of their favorite restaurants, The Flossmoor Train Station. The couples had fallen in love with the restaurant after meeting there one year for someone's birthday. The duo ordered drinks and spinach artichoke dip with tortilla chips to start. Deanna had the portabella mushroom sandwich and T ordered the coconut shrimp. Both ladies were doing something that they hated, but needed to do—they found comfort in food. They both loved the rich flavors that the food choices offered at the station and they planned to race each other to the bottom of their plates and leave with their bellies bulging out above the top of their stretch jeans.

"So T, what's been going on girl? I miss you something terrible."

"I know girl. I have been out of commission trying to find a second job and a new school for the kids."

"You are taking them out of Salem Academy?" Deanna asked bewildered.

"Yes, I have to do something to make my ends meet closer together. Steven does not even look like he's trying to get another job right now and I can't cut it alone. I wouldn't care if the brother got a job at McDonald's flipping Big Macs. You know that Negro has to be crazy if he thinks I can stand one more minute of his paying his pipedream bills and not paying our telephone and gas bills!" Deanna could tell from her friend's expression that this was more than a normal Cook conflict. She could see that the fire in T's eyes had gone out and only the Lord could restart that flame.

She dared herself to ask T about her spiritual life but did not want her friend to retreat into her own emotional world. T seemed to be able to easily transfer her anger at her husband towards God. Even though she would never admit it, she was frustrated that a man who said he loved the Lord could be so disappointing to her and his family. She often said that if Steven's relationship with God was so tight and he could still do the fool like he did, then she was unsure if she wanted to get any closer to that kind of Father. Deanna decided to go another route and asked about the children. She wasn't ready to defend the Lord even though He could stand up for Himself. She was having a hard enough time trying to figure Him out for herself. "So tell me about Court and Lil' Stevie. How are they holding up?"

"Well, you know Ms. Thang thinks she is grown and knows what's going on. I promise you, that seven-year old is going on twenty-two. She keeps asking why daddy is sleeping at her auntie's house and she has become extra talkative in school. I had to go up to talk to Ms. Jones at least three times in the last two weeks. You know Ms. Jones don't play and she can tell that things aren't right. She is used to Steve and me ganging up on Courtney when she gets out of line and not seeing just me. Courtney has an excuse for everything and every time she gets in trouble it's someone else's fault. I know she got that from her father." T displayed a coy smile but it was short lived. "Lil Stevie is very clingy and wants to sleep with me every night. The used-to-be independent five-year old, has reverted to sucking his thumb and the other day, he wet my bed. Girl, I was about to commence to whipping his little tail and then I remembered the state of my marriage. How could I expect my baby to understand or even cope with the fact that his dad has not been around? It's hard enough on me so I really have been bending over backwards to try to make them comfortable. But that has not been easy either since I'm all consumed with me. I just don't seem to be holding it together either. My hair is falling out, hence the multi-colored do rag." Deanna wondered why T had covered her pride and joy. T never missed her hair salon date and her usually long flowing locks were a testimony to that. "I think I had better get some braids or something soon because I just can't handle my hair right now." T mumbled.

"And what is Steve doing? Is he helping with the kids?"

"Yes, you know he is not going to miss a beat trying to be a part of their lives. He comes over to do homework every night with Courtney and play a few games with Stevie. He puts them to bed and I put him out." T finally let out a desperate and much needed laugh.

"Does he try to say anything to you?"

"Of course he comes in with the sob story junk and tries to tell me that he's working on some things to get our money straight. The first time he said that I said what money do *we* have for you to get straight? It sounds like you want to get my money straight. Last time I checked you had nothing coming in, hence no income!" Deanna had to laugh then. She loved Steve like a brother but she could not understand how he insisted on messing up his finances. He and James sat down many a day to discuss a budget and to put his bills in order. The Cooks would have some semblance of financial peace for a month or so and then he would fall into some opportunity to make money fast and blow all that had been established in a matter of days. "And you know he has been doing everything to try to get him some! He brought some flowers over the other day and I told him to cash them in for the light bill! I ain't giving up nothing! Sistah girl is on lock down!"

As their appetizers and drinks arrived Deanna was reminded of how T had told her how easy it was for her to get pregnant. She said if Steve even looked at her crooked she got knocked up. When they got pregnant in college, they decided together to have an abortion. It had been a hard decision for Steve but T had convinced him that there was no way they could afford a child and continue in school. Then they had experienced a miscarriage right before Courtney and right after her. Deanna thought about what it would be like if Steve and T had five kids. She was about to jump off in the deep end of her emotions about the baby thing when she was quickly brought back from her thoughts by T. She started sharing what Tyra, her crazy coworker, had done last week in the middle of their staff meeting. After they devoured their meals Deanna abruptly asked T, "So what are you gonna do about your marriage?"

"Honestly De, I don't know what to do. I'm tired of counseling, which is ineffective because Steve seems to let what he hears seep in only for a moment. I'm tired of all the lies and the feeling of insecurity I get whenever he lets me down. If he would just get the money thing right we might be able to make it. I came from parents who worked together to get what they wanted. They paid their bills and were able to buy things together even though they didn't have much to work with. Their marriage was a true testament to what two people can do when they really put God first. I think that is what makes me feel even worse and so disappointed in myself. I feel like I fell for the oke doke when I married Steve."

Deanna felt her professional side taking over and before she could think she blurted out "Well T, you know you have had some bad experiences in the past, even with other guys. You always talk about how your first boyfriend was abusive and you felt trapped in that relationship until you moved away. Do you think maybe there could be some things you might be able to work on while you and Steve aren't together?" T raised her eyebrows and huffed as she grabbed for the last of her drink. T's silence was an indication of her anger. She sat for a moment and finally said she didn't want to talk about that any longer. Deanna felt nervous about opening that can of worms, but she knew better than anybody that God allowed things to happen over and over again so that we might learn a valuable lesson and grow from it. She didn't want to hurt T, especially now, but she knew T had some issues just like she did. Deanna was grateful that the rest of their conversation was about what was going on at church, James and his job and about the latest fashion trends. Deanna managed to successfully steer the conversation away from anything about her pregnancy woes. She and T had talked so much about it that she was tired of rehashing the same pot of stew. The ladies ended their lunch date in front of the station with a hug and a plan to call each other for prayer on Wednesdays again like they used to.

~

It had been two weeks since Deanna and James last spoke about their counseling sessions. Sharon thought it best that they take a break for a couple of weeks since James was not interested in attending a session alone. Deanna remembered being almost in tears when she spoke to Sharon over the phone about James' refusal to come alone. She had broken down and called Sharon after she realized that James was not going to cancel his appointment. Sharon had assured her that it was okay and that it often took men longer to share their soul with someone else. Deanna knew in James' case that it was not true. When he wanted to, he would talk up a storm and share too much sometimes. That had been one of the reasons why she fell in love with him so many years ago. He was totally different from other guys she had dated. Unlike them, James was always ready to give an explanation as to why he did what he did or why he felt passionately about one thing or another. That is why Deanna found his resistance so strange. As much as she loved him and wanted to trust him completely, she always felt that there was something she did not understand or could not quite put a handle on. She hated feeling the way she did about the man she loved so much, but something in her heart would not let go of the insecurity that rested in her subconscious. She would have to commit more time to prayer in regard to her emotions. She knew that God's Word said that things that were done in darkness would eventually come to the light. She didn't think James was lying to her, but maybe he wasn't being transparent to himself. Only the Holy Spirit could intervene. The Spirit's comfort still did not ease her curiosity.

CHAPTER FIVE

"What do you do when the air stands still and the fire doesn't warm . . .
Keep living"

Deanna smiled to herself as she waited for Courtney and Lil' Stevie to be dismissed from school. She saw Stevie running to her car excited that "Auntie De" had come to pick them up. Deanna volunteered to help T with the kids since she transferred them to the public school a few blocks from her home. T was getting home later than usual since she took on more hours at work. Deanna's day to get the kids was Tuesday. She loved to spend a few hours with the kids, helping them with their homework and feeding them dinner. This was her opportunity to fill the void that she thought only children could massage. She knew that her friend was doing the best she could financially for her children since Steven still hadn't found work. It had been three months since his last paycheck had been cashed. He was doing some odds and ends work, but nothing that could truly pay the bills. Deanna was afraid that T's apathy towards Steve was getting stronger. She knew that soon there would be no hope for their marriage. When T was ready to shut off emotionally, she did. She could totally disconnect herself from a situation and move forward faster than anyone Deanna knew. Maybe she and James needed to have Steve over to see where his mind was. She would discuss that with James as soon as she took the kids home that evening.

~

"Lil' Stevie, where is your sister?" Deanna pulled the seat forward as the scrawny little boy with wire-rimmed glasses threw his book bag on the seat and popped in. He was a proud little kindergarten student who loved to brag about all that he had learned in school.

"I don't know Auntie De, but I got to be the leader in class today. Courtney was standing over there with some of her friends before." Lil' Stevie pointed towards the entrance of the school and she saw "Ms. Courtney" easing down the steps with no hurry in her motion. Deanna could see attitude all over Courtney's face and she prepared herself for the whirlwind that was opening the car door. As the winds from the winter weather blew in, Courtney's emotional weather seeped in the car as well. Anything that was warm and toasty was now cold and frigid. It was amazing that a child so young could command such a presence about herself. Courtney was wearing every bit of her frustration on her face about transferring schools and she did not care who knew it. This was going to be a doosey of an afternoon if Deanna did not nip this thing in the bud immediately.

"So hello Ms. Courtney, looks like you are not doing so well. Is that true?" Courtney fixed her mouth into a downward "u." "I am okay Auntie De."

Deanna knew that was Courtney's attempt to diffuse a long conversation, but Deanna was not falling for it. She wanted to make sure her friend's children knew that they could talk to her and that she understood their pain. Deanna had gone through the divorce of her parents alone and afraid. Although she was a little older she remembered feeling isolated and, more specifically, responsible for breaking her parents up. They seemed to always be fighting about her. She did not realize until she was older that she was not the problem. She was just a subject that could be used readily by her parents to engage in battle. Children suffered so much in a separation and divorce. Nobody won in a divorce, but so many generational curses could be set up in children who observed their parents in combat with one another. Those scars often never healed. And, although parents did not mean to make their children casualties of war, the resulting pain was inevitable. Deanna was determined to help her play niece and nephew stay healthy emotionally.

"Courtney it looks like you have something on your mind. Maybe we can talk about it later if you want. In the meantime do you guys want McDonald's or do you want to make tacos at home?"

The kids both exclaimed together, "Tacos!" Deanna knew the answer before they even spoke. She and the kids had that in common—they loved Mexican food. They enjoyed preparing Mexican fiestas together. They stopped by the store and picked up some last minute items for their tacos and proceeded home.

Deanna prepared the ground meat and beans and the children sat at the kitchen table finishing up their homework. They all looked up from what they were doing when the door flung open and a breeze of Calvin Klein's *Truth* met them way before they spotted James. "Hey Uncle James," the kids yelled from the table as he entered the room and set a beeline for his wife. After kissing Deanna on the cheek and hearing the children giggle, he turned to them and said, "So what's up? How are my favorite niece and nephew doing?"

"We're fine Uncle J." Courtney spoke for the both of them.

"Uncle J, after dinner I think I can beat you in some *Tekken 3*. I've been practicing." Lil' Stevie shouted happily.

"Oh yeah, little man, I doubt it but I'll let you take a shot after dinner."

The foursome finished their meals and as soon as James and Lil' Stevie put their plates in the sink they darted simultaneously to the guest bedroom. James had the ability to go from responsible adult to a carefree kid in 2.5 seconds. Deanna chuckled to herself and turned to face her niece. She did not let a moment of their alone time waste. "Courtney, if you want to talk about anything you know that I am here for you." Deanna thought she would try a casual approach with the mature child. She knew that her parent's conflict was affecting her in a big way and she did not want Courtney to dwindle away in her own pit of depression, anger and frustration. Courtney huffed and came to the sink to help with loading the dishwasher.

"Auntie De, I don't know what I did to cause my mommy and daddy to break up. It seems like I can't do anything right. I try to be a good kid even though I know I talk too much. I guess I just don't get it."

Deanna was reflective of the child's comments. She was reminded of feeling the exact same way when her parents fought. She was even reminded of times when she felt like if she killed herself, then they would not have anymore problems or anything to argue over. She decided that she would share some of her life with Courtney in hopes of securing her feelings and helping her to realize that her parents' split had more to do with them than it had to do with her. She had learned that kids had a knack for seeing right through people, so transparency had become her best friend when dealing with them. "Courtney, I know how you feel. My parents got divorced when I was sixteen. They had trouble way before that and it seemed like I was always a part of their arguments. I felt like no matter what I did, I had to choose sides. Even though my father and I didn't really get along at the time, I was very sad when my mom and I moved away from him. It wasn't until much later that I realized I was not responsible for the failure of their marriage.

Their marriage problems started way before I was even born. It was tough for me for a long time and I still have some problems as a result of them not being together." Deanna grabbed Courtney into her arms hoping to console her from her tears as they rushed down her face.

"Courtney you are a sweet girl and believe me, you are not the reason that your parents are having trouble. They both love you very much and will always want what's best for you and your brother. Sometimes they may argue about you all or about the money that they need to buy things for you, but it doesn't mean that it's your fault. They both would do whatever they had to do to make sure you and Lil' Stevie are safe and healthy. Do you understand?" Courtney rubbed her weary eyes and shook her head to indicate that she understood.

"But Auntie De, can't they just work it out? I don't want to be without my mommy or daddy and I don't understand why God is not listening to my prayers."

Now Deanna huffed. Explaining that delay was not denial to a child, let alone anyone else at this point was not something that was going to be easy. Deanna wanted to crawl into someone else's arms and ask the same question. "Well honey, I guarantee you that God does hear your prayers and He is answering them too. He doesn't always answer our prayers in the way that we think is best. God does love you and He does want what's best for you, but He can see some things that we can't see. Sometimes he doesn't answer right away for our own good." Deanna said that to herself more than to Courtney. Courtney's emotions seemed to be calmed some by her answer and they both were torn from their thoughts by a big scream that came from the guest room. They knew that James had either let Lil' Stevie win or that he really had practiced and had beat James fair and square. Lil' Stevie was having his own victory party and summoned both of them to the room for the affair. Deanna and Courtney ascended the stairs and joined in on teasing James about the big defeat. James sat quietly and smiled at Lil' Stevie's winning performance. Deanna could only wonder how much James wished that it was his own son that was showing out over their time together. They had not talked about their future son "Joshua" as they had named him in awhile. Deanna was afraid to open the door to that conversation since the need for individual counseling had gone nowhere.

A few hours later, T called to let Deanna know that she was home. James went outside to warm the car and the kids packed up their belongings for the short trip home. T waved through the door as her troops marched into her home and Deanna departed feeling like she had made some headway in how

Courtney was feeling. She was surely going to make T aware of how Courtney felt as soon as she could get a chance. She thought it was important for T to be able to reinforce the fact that their split was not her children's fault. But for now, she needed to discuss with James how or if they should consult with Steven about his marriage.

~

Steven stopped by on Saturday evening. He seemed to always know when Deanna was making one of her famous pound cakes and he was always ready to be the taste tester. "Ooooh De, you put your foot in this one." Steve mumbled as he devoured the two slices of pineapple-flavored cake that Deanna had cut for him.

"Dang Steve, should I cut you another piece? You act like you haven't eaten in weeks," Deanna said, laughing at her friend. He looked like he had not eaten well in a while. His semi-pot belly was slimming as if he had caught hold to a dynamic diet. Deanna thought that wasn't such a bad thing, but she knew that Steve loved his food, so his losing weight was a definite indication that something was up.

Steve commented, "Yeah, I could eat. What else y'all got? You know I have to fend for myself these days."

Deanna turned to stare at the sink of dirty dishes. "I just ordered a pizza and James is on his way home with it. We've got some other junk here but I hadn't planned on cooking tonight. You can stop by tomorrow for dinner, though. You know I'm good for cooking, well, at least one time per week." Deanna turned towards the door as her husband trotted in with the aroma-filled box in tow.

"Wha's up baby boy?" James gave Steve a high five and then wrapped his arms around his wife.

"Can't call it man, just living day to day." Deanna wanted to immediately jump on Steve about why he hadn't found a job yet, but she thought it safer to follow the lead of her husband. Men had a tendency to shy away from aggressive comments from women for whatever reason. They ate their pizza in peace and chugged their bottles of IBC root beer. Deanna squirmed on the kitchen barstool trying to indicate to James his need to start the conversation as they had planned. However, James continued to submerge himself in small talk with his buddy about politics and sports. Finally, Deanna had enough and she jumped up and began to clean the dirty pizza plates as if to hint to James that she was not going to wait on him any longer. James grimaced and finally faced Steven.

"So man, what's going on with you and T?" Steven's face turned almost an opaque color and he drew his hands to his forehead.

"Man I don't know. She won't talk to me and I don't know what to do. I've been doing some contract work here and there, but nothing that's going to keep food on the table. T ain't trying to hear anything from me until I get a job. I'm tired of sleeping on my sister's couch, but she is not budging."

Deanna couldn't hold it any longer. "Well have you tried to talk to Reverend Marshall again? What about a financial counselor?" James gave her the eye that said, "Why don't you hush!"

Steve replied, "Yes, I've gone to speak with Rev. He told me that I needed to get a job and that I had to stop using the word as a drug, meaning that I only use it when I'm down and need a fix. He said that I needed to start living what I was professing. As far as the financial counseling goes, I've looked on the internet for some things, but I haven't been successful in finding any good resources." Deanna thought to herself. That internet is what gets Steve in trouble all the time. He finds all of these places to invest and send money to make these quick deals and they turn into dust. He needed to stay away from the internet, in her opinion.

"Steve have you ever thought about going back to your old job? I know it's not the best thing in the world for you, but at least you would have something steady."

Steve rolled his eyes at her like a woman. "Girl please! I would starve before I went back like an Uncle Tom to that man to beg for my job back."

"Yeah man, but your wife and kids are starving for their need for a father and husband! Have you ever thought about putting your pride aside for one moment to think about them? And what about doing some more counseling?" James had scored one on him. However, Deanna was ready to pounce on him about the pride thing. Pride had to be the reason that he had not wanted to go to counseling. How could he tell someone else to sweep around their front door and he was not willing to sweep around his. Deanna decided to leave that for another match.

"Yeah, I guess you're right. But T won't even think about going to counseling with me. She said she is tired of hearing the same stuff and not applying it. I think she is serious this time about us splitting up. The tripped out part about it is that she won't admit that she has some issues too. She doesn't say anything about having money problems when she's out there buying all the Prada and Gucci she can put her hands on!"

"You know what dog, you are right. But if things are that bad then you have to be the man and put your foot down. If you're not being accountable about your essentials, meaning your lights, mortgage, telephone and gas, how can you expect her to be?" It was obvious that James was frustrated with his friend. He did not understand how a man who professed such a strong relationship with Christ was able to practically throw money out the window.

"Steve I'm going to be straight up with you. I love you and T the same, but I have a feeling that this is not going to be a time when you can just swing in like Prince Charming and win her back. She's pretty serious with moving forward with a legal separation and eventually a divorce. Especially if you don't make any moves towards getting financially sound." Deanna sighed after her small speech. T had not shared all of that with Deanna, but she was sure that it was inevitable if Steven didn't shape up.

"Well, maybe I'm tired of her mess too," Steven retorted. "She's not coming out of this without a stain either. I know I have stuff to work on, but what about her?" James was tired of it and he realized before Deanna that their convincing was not working. The Cooks were bent on blaming each other for their problems and no one wanted to accept responsibility to make some positive changes.

"You know what man, you are right. But until you and T decide for real that some changes have to be made and make them, you will continue to waddle in the same pool! We're here for both of you, but we cannot continue to sit here and act like everything is okay. We'll continue to pray for you man, but we cannot choose sides."

Steven breathed in deeply and stood to walk to the door. James followed him to the front porch. "Man, so how have you been holding up for real? I know it's got to be hard to be without your wife."

"Yeah dude, I am softening her up though. She almost gave me some last night." Steven's eyes brightened for the first time since before their dinner. James gave a half smile. He knew that the Cooks having sex was not the answer to their problems, but he also knew that a man in conquer mode was not giving up until he had won what he started out to accomplish. Their conversation ended with prayer and the hug that only real men could give one another.

~

"So what do you think will happen to them, James?" Deanna met her husband at the door with her words before he could close it.

"To be honest with you, I don't know. I feel sorry for the kids. I wish they could get their acts together, but we can't want it for them." James approached his wife and grabbed her hands. "Haven't we talked enough about the Cooks tonight? Let's talk a little about us."

"Oh, so Mr. Carrington, what would you like to talk about?"

"I can show you better than I can tell you." James kissed his wife's forehead and led her upstairs to their room. Although their desire for one another had been concealed in the past weeks, it only took a spark to remind them of their passion hidden inside.

~

The sweet silence in the room engulfed them as they fell away from one another's bodies like magnets when they lost their charge. Passionate love could caress a couple in a way that no other experience could. Even watching the sunrise, smelling fresh cut flowers and watching children play in sand could not amount to the emotion that could be felt by two human beings after they have successfully satisfied one another's mind, body and soul. The sounds of their breath rose and fell in sequence as if it were on a respiration sea saw. His heart played the drums for her once again as she lay draped along side his body. This space had always been a source of comfort to Deanna. His heart drum had a way of relieving her soul. They took her on a syncopated journey and hypnotized her restless thoughts into submission. The exhaustion from their lovemaking wore off into the sheets of their king-size bed.

CHAPTER SIX

"Holding closely to what hurts me
Tightening fingers, stubborn soul
Wanting peace but err' forgetting
It only comes by letting go."

Kerri Mason ©2000

It was amazing how fast things could change from day to day. As the anniversary of her miscarriage approached Deanna began to feel that deep draining dull ache that would not seem to go away. Strangely enough she found herself not wanting to be with her husband sexually anymore. It had been over six weeks since they had come together and she didn't care. Every time they had a conversation about "the baby thing," it turned into a heated argument. They could not talk about further fertility testing or anything remotely close to adoption without one of them storming out of the room. It was a shame how fast they could move the Holy Spirit out of their conversations. He would sit and wait like the gentleman He was and only hope that she or James would be mature enough to invite Him in. When that didn't happen, He remained on the sidelines, disappointed and grieved.

~

Deanna stopped the counseling sessions prematurely when James refused to go on his own. That was still a puzzle that she had not put together. She blamed her early cessation of the sessions on James, but she knew in her heart that she was giving up. Because James had not given her a legitimate reason for not going to counseling, she could tell that the old feelings of distrust and insecurity regarding their marriage had crept back into her life. It did not seem like her desire to have kids was even there anymore. It was somehow easier not to even try. She guessed there could be no failure if no trying occurred. Their lovemaking had turned from something exciting and adventurous to a monotonous, methodical chore when it happened. Deanna knew that they were married for more than procreation, but until they climbed over that hurdle it seemed to her that their relationship would remain stagnant. Deanna hated to face that reality but the truth was evident. She even overheard James talking to one of his boys about how paranoid and insecure his wife had become. He said that he felt like he had been duped since he thought he had married a strong confident black woman. He said that she had become obsessed with having children. Wow! Deanna felt her chest caving in as she sucked in the comments that her husband made. Had her emotional roller coaster caused that much heartache and pain in the man she professed to love? She thought for a moment. Where was his strength? Why wasn't he comforting her? How could he say such terrible things knowing that all she wanted was to fulfill a dream of his? He went on to say how she had shared with him her biggest fear that she would not be able to conceive. His biggest fear, however, was that he may not get his wife back after all of this. He believed that they needed to go on with their lives even if children were not in the picture. Deanna knew she could not talk to him just yet about the pain he had inflicted in her unknowingly. She felt helpless and afraid.

~

As Deanna read the church bulletin during Sunday service she noticed that a sister church of theirs was starting a women's rap session series. Curious about the offered topics she took down the number and decided to give the committee chairperson a call. What could it hurt? James and Deanna managed to make it throughout the rest of the service with hypocritical smiles and decided to skip Sunday School and go home early. James had some extra work that he needed to finish and Deanna decided not to argue with him about how that should not interfere with their church attendance. She was sleeping a lot lately because that seemed to be a place of peace for her. This would be as good a time as any to take a nap. She knew that there were several warning signs popping up in their marriage and in their spiritual lives, but she did not want to find the strength to address them.

~

Deanna called Faith Baptist Church on Monday morning and requested a listing of topics for their women's rap session series. The young lady on the other end stated that she would send Deanna a copy of the full schedule, but she was willing to share over the phone what some of the upcoming topics were. Deanna did not expect to find what she was looking for but decided to give the lady a chance to do her job well.

"Let's see. We have a variety of rap sessions going on in the next two months. The sessions have been designed to address topics that may not affect all women, but certainly some of them. We have a session on sexual purity, living with an unsaved spouse, how to balance marriage and ministry . . ." The young lady went on and on and Deanna was about to allow her mind to drift off when she thought she heard, "how to live with barrenness."

"Excuse me, did you say, how to live with barrenness?"

"Why yes I did. That session will take place two weeks from now on a Tuesday evening from 7-9 pm. Is that something you might be interested in?"

Deanna perked up and leaned forward in her chair. Well, if it was what she thought it was she was more than interested.

"Could you tell me a little more about that one please?"

"Yes, that session will be facilitated by Mrs. Susan Turning. She is a young lady who is dealing with infertility and wants to share her testimony about how to live victoriously through the disappointment associated with not having the children that you expected to have." The young lady paused as if to give Deanna time to let her comments sink in. "If that is a session that you are remotely interested in I can put your name on the list to reserve your spot. You can always cancel if you choose at a later date not to attend."

Deanna felt like someone had blown fresh air into her lungs. She knew that God said that He would never leave nor forsake her, but sometimes she stayed down so long that she wasn't quite sure how true that scripture was to her. But this might just be the catalyst that she needed to grab hold of God's plan for her regarding children.

"Yes," she replied. "I would like you to put me on the list as well as send me out the information regarding the other sessions."

"No problem. That package will go out with tomorrow's mail." Deanna got off the phone and returned to her work with a little more energy than she had before.

~

Tuesday could not come fast enough. Deanna was excited about attending the rap session. She knew that this was going to help redirect her back to where she needed to be in Christ. Her marriage's strength was built on their individual relationships with the Lord. When they were not on point spiritually, they could almost bet that their marriage was going to be in the doghouse. Before Deanna approached James she wanted to get back to a comfortable place in Christ. She also wanted to give the Lord enough time to work on James. She was glad that God knew when she needed help getting back to Him. Deanna took off work early so she could go home and prepare dinner before she left for the session. James seemed to be excited that she was attending the session and for once in a long time they had a decent meal without any tension. Deanna finished straightening up the kitchen, returned a few phone calls and prepared to leave. She kissed James on the cheek and made a mad dash for the door.

~

Faith Baptist Church was quite a ways from where Deanna lived. She did not mind the drive because it gave her an opportunity to enjoy the city. When Deanna got half way to the church she felt her cell phone vibrate. She looked at the caller ID to see that it was Cairo. She smiled at her friend's perfect timing. She and Cairo did not speak often but when they did it was as if they had not missed a beat.

"Wha's up man?" Deanna chimed.

"Wha's up with you? I just talked to your husband and he told me that you were in the streets. Girl, don't you know how to sit down? I thought I taught you better than that." Cairo chuckled. He stayed busy and knew that it was usually Deanna that was trying to get him to slow down.

"Hey, I am so glad that you called me. I miss you dude!" Deanna didn't want to sound mushy. She knew that Cairo hated that, but she did miss the comfort of having someone who knew her inside and out. James usually filled that void, but he had not been there lately.

"What's wrong? I know when you start talking about you miss me something is up." Cairo knew her like a book.

"Well, I guess I am a little depressed about the baby thing and James and I just aren't seeing eye to eye about it lately. I overheard him telling somebody that he was disappointed in how I had been acting . . . ."

"Whoa, pump your brakes! I thought you and James were being really honest about where you stood about children. How did things go south so fast?"

Deanna sighed. "Well we were doing a pretty good job but when I started going to counseling and . . ."

Cairo quickly interrupted his friend. "Hold up. When did the shrink start going to see a shrink? You must be really mentally banged up. I'm sorry buddy. Do you need me to make a road trip? You know you and James can grease my pockets with the dough you are giving somebody who I know is only half as qualified!" Cairo always had a way of making her laugh even when things were pretty serious. Deanna felt better already knowing that the world was not going to end because of her current crisis. She and James were not the first and would not be the last people who would deal with infertility. She and Cairo talked more about his job and his brother who had recently been diagnosed with HIV. Deanna pulled into the church parking lot and fortunately found a space right in front of the church.

"Cairo, how do you think women feel who are past the child bearing age and never have the children that they wanted to have? I mean I know you are not a woman, but seriously, tell me what people do when their dreams aren't fulfilled and they can't do anything about it?" Deanna knew she sounded crazy but she needed to hear an honest opinion from someone she loved.

"De, you are really having a tough time. Don't start thinking like that. You will have a little bambino soon enough." Cairo hated to see his girl like this. She was the strong one of the two. When she was not on point it scared him. She was one of the most together people he knew. Her relationship with God was inspiring. He knew that one day he wanted to have a relationship with Christ that emulated hers. When she was unstable his whole world became unsteady. He did not think that Deanna would ever know how he gained strength from her strength. Cairo did his best to make Deanna laugh and promised he would make a visit to "Chi" real soon. The dynamic duo made plans for a quick visit with one another in two months.

~

Deanna could not help but be a little proud of herself as she climbed the steps of the church. She was taking charge of the pain that she was experiencing as a result of being childless. Deanna always felt better when she was being proactive. She could not understand why people found comfort in sorrow and complacency, even though she had done a pretty good job of it lately herself. Deanna could only stay in those places for moments at a time. They were too intoxicating and always made her feel like she was suffocating. Even in her weakest moments Deanna found herself fighting against her emotions. She was always looking to break into a new place of freedom. She would be insane if she became a lady waiting in despair too long.

~

Deanna was shocked that she had made it all the way to the north side in record time. For once she was not rushing into a place twenty-nine seconds before the event. She wished that her normal "on time" meant to arrive fifteen minutes before something started. She admired people who had it together enough to make that their normal routine, but for now she had to be satisfied with being on what many had coined CP time or "colored people's" time. It tickled Deanna that the culturally diverse, yet primarily Caucasian church she was in seemed to have adopted the CP tradition when fifteen minutes after the scheduled start time the session hadn't begun. There were only a few ladies situated strategically around the room. Some looked like they had thought long and hard about the best place to sit. It seemed like they wanted to be in a place where they could catch all of the good information, but not be in too deep to disappear if the information did not pertain to them. Deanna found a spot at a table with a woman who looked to be in her forties. The lady with a fair complexion, sandy blonde hair and black wire-framed glasses looked up from the book she was so heavily engrossed in long enough to give a friendly smile that said, "you are welcome to sit here." Deanna began to pull her chair back and even though she was trying her best not to be disruptive the chair had other plans. The heavy wooden chair with its orange vinyl arm rests and seat made a long lurching noise as it moved to its new destination. Deanna could feel the eyes of the other rap session participants on her back. She nervously sat down and scooted up towards the hardwood table that matched the seat that had made her grand prelude. A young lady who seemed to be in her late twenties with straight jet-black hair and a long athletic figure transitioned to the front of the room. Her smile and presence seemed to add a dose of peace to the disjointed scene immediately. Her first request was that those who had spread themselves way too thin across the room join her at the front of the cafeteria.

"There is no need for us to be so far from one another. We might have to borrow each other's tissue," she said. This young lady seemed so calm and collected, there was no way she was the facilitator of the session. She had to be the mistress of ceremonies or the announcement reader. You couldn't deal with infertility and have that cool of a spirit, Deanna thought, or could you?

"Well ladies, it looks like we will be a small group so let's get started. I'm Susan Turning and I will be your facilitator today for the talk on infertility." Deanna sat back in her seat, comfortable and ready to be poured into.

"Let me start off today with a song by Wes King." Tears immediately came to every eye in the cafeteria as the guitar filled song played on Susan's massive boom box. "*I never thought I'd miss someone I've never met.* That is exactly what infertility is like. You can never really understand infertility unless you've been there or exposed to it first hand. It has been said that nurses who work with women dealing with infertility have the same stress level as nurses who work with cancer patients." Susan allowed the impact of her statements to sink deep into the skin of the participants.

"I know that we have a difficult topic on our hands tonight. I want to share my story with you and when and if you feel comfortable, please jump in. I was shocked like many of you were to find out that I would not be a mommy, or at least not the way I thought I would. I grew up like most little girls with my dolls and my dreams of becoming someone's mother. Unfortunately, after five years of marriage and four years of unsuccessful trying, I found out that due to a rare disease that I had been miraculously cured from as a child, I probably could not conceive. My husband and I went through so many emotions once we realized that our dreams would not come true the way we thought they would. I remember begging God about having a child. I believed and still do that God could do anything, so how hard could it be for Him to give me a child. I tore through the Bible to find scriptures and people who God had blessed in their barrenness with children. I studied Sarah, Rachel, Hannah, Samson's mother and Elizabeth. My lists and study journal got full of bittersweet stories about women in the Bible and their triumphs with children. I knew that there is no respect of person with God, so surely His word would surpass what my doctors had told me and bless us. I could not go to baby showers and pregnant women, whether they were strangers or not, sent me into a frenzy. I literally broke out into hives one evening after going to a baby shower that I could not get out of. One of my first cousins had expressed her understanding if I could not bring myself to come to her shower, but I heard the pain in her voice. My mother would not allow me to back out of a family event like that one. I held it together at the shower for about two hours using excessive inappropriate laughter and excessive cleaning at the shower as my coping mechanism. The guests could not get done with their food before I snatched their plates and utensils and ran to the kitchen to clean. Many of the guests were family members and they knew my pain and allowed my uncharacteristic behavior to continue. By the time I got home that evening I had large red raised spots all over my back and arms. My eyes were not only swollen from crying, but from the reaction that I was experiencing. I think I was allergic to pregnancy, someone else's pregnancy that is." Every lady nodded in understanding of Susan's story. If they had not experienced the exact problem they could definitely relate to it.

"So, enough about me. I will be glad to share the rest of my experiences with you all but I want to give you an opportunity to talk. Let's throw a couple of words out there and I want to get your honest reactions to them. The words are barrenness, hope and surrender." Susan sat back in her seat and awaited a willing participant. Of course, Deanna was ready to share her soul with the room of strangers, but she decided to sit back and survey the lay of the land and see what the other women who unknowingly shared a common bond with her had to say. A well-dressed large-boned woman wiped her eyes with a crinkled tissue, shifted in her seat from one side to the next and cleared her throat.

"When I hear the word barrenness I feel fear, isolation and anger. I feel fear and even though I know fear is not of God I just don't feel whole because I haven't been able to conceive. I feel isolated because it seems that every other woman I know is pregnant and either doesn't want the child or did nothing but look at her husband and got pregnant. I also admit that I am just plain angry. Angry at the doctors and at people who say insensitive things knowingly and unknowingly. I am mad at my husband because he doesn't seem to understand and lastly, although I am embarrassed to say, I am most angry with the Lord. I know He knows what's best but I don't understand how me having a child is not what's best for us." The lady turned her face towards the window to the side of her. Her attempt to hide her pain only exposed the river of tears streaming down the ridges of her smooth, round face even more. Her tears flowed off of her into the souls of each woman in the room.

The strange thing about the struggle of infertility is that it instantly connected the souls of those involved through the perils of the pain. Women enduring the empty calamity could be likened to potholes that had been repaired with asphalt year after year as a result of the snow and salt reopening them. Several streets in Chicago in the less exotic areas of the city had many of these sites that gapped along the shallow and overused travel ways. Each one of these women could represent a section on those streets-each month being repaired by the Holy Spirit after the painful experience of menstruation. The hole had been repaired only twenty-eight or so days earlier and they found themselves once again adjusting to the same painful episode. Susan acknowledged the willing talker's pain and assured her that she was not alone and that she too felt the same way for many years. She indicated that she found herself disgusted and frustrated with God's plan and His timing.

Before Susan could finish her statement completely, another lady who looked to be in her early fifties who was sitting at the end of the room stood and walked toward the nucleus of females. She walked and spoke simultaneously. "Well, uh I don't know if I should be here exactly but I am suffering from a different type of barrenness. I have found myself without children as a result of never getting married. The dream that I had to be a wife and a mother died several years ago along with the death of my biological clock. I had a double funeral. But what I guess I never realized, even though I have been successful in so many other ways, and the blessings of the Lord have truly been upon me was that I had not been able to fulfill my childhood passion of being a mom. Time somewhat did a job on my hurt and the void and the numbness that I felt in my late thirties and forties in my heart healed by default. I can relate to the need to surrender. I once heard a preacher say that surrender was the hardest form of worship and I can attest to that fact. What makes surrender the most difficult is that it leaves you vulnerable and uncertain." Several nods and spoken "ahs" confirmed the informal sorority's agreement with the wisdom that had just been shared. Deanna had never thought of a woman who had not been married as one who was struggling with infertility. She thought about how she had probably been as insensitive to those ladies as other people had been to her. She would never view singleness the same from that point on.

Deanna had chilled her comments on ice long enough. She felt like if she didn't share something that she would burst. "I think the hard thing about hope is that when it is deferred it makes it easy for one to doubt. Hope deferred makes you question your faith and your belief in what God's word says. I am a control freak and because I have not done all that I can in regard to finding out about why we are infertile, it makes my ability to surrender that much more difficult. I believe in some warped way that as long as I am doing something I can hold God to His promises. Its like that old saying goes, "God helps those who help themselves." My marriage is suffering along with my personal sufferings. I know in my heart of hearts I do believe God, but I also feel that if I let go of my dreams that it means that I'm giving up on the possibility and opportunity to be a mother. Each day I'm challenged by how to combat the implanted lies that the enemy successfully shares with me. I often compare this experience to being on a roller coaster with many peaks and valleys representing the drastic changes in my emotions from day to day and week to week. The most horrible part about the ride is that it is a continuous trip that often leaves me emotionally nauseous and physically drained. There are many days when I just want to sleep it all away. I cry at times at the sight of a pregnant woman or the report of someone who is pregnant. I stay more frustrated and disappointed at myself for not being a big enough Christian to handle the load that has been put on me. I often fail to believe the comment that He won't put more on you than you can bear. I want to feel whole enough again to believe God no matter what. I don't want to be a spoiled child anymore who stomps her feet and has a temper tantrum in the floor because she doesn't get what she wants. In my earthly and narrow-minded thinking, I feel that if God would share with me what His plan is, then I could digest it regardless of whether it gave me heartburn or not and move forward with my life. If bearing a child of my own is not possible or a realistic goal, then I am ready to move on. I would adopt or care for foster children in a minute but I can't feel safe proceeding with that if the possibility of my own child is still present. I am ready to get off the unexpected ride at the non-amusement park of my life."

Whoa, where did all of that come from? Deanna thought. Had she been holding her tongue captive for so long about her true feelings that when it was given a peek at freedom it ran like the slaves on the Underground Railroad? Had she said too much? Was any of it true? Did she really feel as empty as her words sounded? Deanna began to feel angry and ashamed all at once. She wished she could reel in the rod that the words she had just spoken so freely from her lips to a room full of strangers were on. She looked down in defeat, self-pity and doubt. How could someone who helped so many people gain emotional stability and freedom from mental bondage be so bound herself? Deanna looked up when she felt a warm touch on her left shoulder. When she turned and looked into Susan's eyes their kindred souls locked arms and embraced as if they needed to hold on for dear life. Deanna felt a release in her spirit like never before. She knew that God was wrapping his love around her through one of his children. Deanna held on tight like a child frightened of the boogie monster. The other ladies in the room consoled her with their glances and tears. They all were experiencing life on a road less traveled, one that no voyager wanted to experience. Infertility to each one of them in some way had been the most horrible trip they had been on, one where luggage was lost, reservations had been cancelled and traveler's checks had been stolen.

Deanna knew that surrender had to be next on her spiritual agenda. And as much as that whole concept hurt, deep down in her soul, surrender's journey would be the only way to gain some sense of tranquility. Deanna desired to have the peace that passes all understanding once again and she knew that it was waiting on the other end of surrender. It had not left her presence. She had walked away from it when she decided to take the plans for her life into her own hands. What a dangerous way for a Christian to live.

~

As tears dried and noses were drained, the other ladies in the group began to pour out of their bosoms the stories and experiences that barrenness had brought to them. One lady suffered from secondary infertility. She had a seven-year-old son, but had not been able to conceive since then. Another participant had experienced several miscarriages and was dealing poorly with the grief associated with the loss. Although their experiences were somewhat different, they were all quite the same. Their souls had been locked together in a chain link fence of despair that day. They joined a sorority by default, one that they wished no one else had to join. The remainder of the session was filled with discussion about ways to be proactive about infertility: adoption, foster parenting, coping mechanisms and counseling were among the topics of choice. They ended with a time of prayer, praise and worship. Deanna found some resolution and peace among the strangers and even though she knew that it was God in the midst, there was nothing like having Him wrapped in some skin that understood your personal pain. Her friends and family had been supportive, but there was only so far they could go with her down the desolate road she was on. The group discussed meeting again and Deanna left Faith Baptist Church with an old friend named peace.

CHAPTER SEVEN

"Burning embers ward off the pains that lurk in the darkness of one's soul"

As winter turned into spring, Deanna felt her life turning right along with it. She did not know what to expect, but just as the trees and flowers began to bud and blossom, she felt in her spirit that something new was on the horizon. She usually had good intuition and could determine the scent of the experience she was about to undertake. She could smell the sweet flavor that the perfume of a good encounter would bring. She could also smell the foul-smelling stench of an event that was about to dramatically change her life for the worse, but this time her nostrils failed her. She did not know what to think as she reflected on the present state of her emotions and was reminded of a line from the movie, *The Color Purple* in which Celie said towards the end, *the more things change the more they stay the same.* Although Deanna felt like she was moving closer to a state of emotional surrender, she would inevitably experience a moment of depression when her monthly visitor showed up at her door. She couldn't help but hope right before her menstruation came that this might be the time that God decided to bless her with conception. It was getting easier to wrap her emotional arms around the fact that that day may never come, but the sting of that reality had not lessened with time.

In one of Deanna's feeble attempts to be proactive regarding her life and motherhood, she made another appointment with her doctor. She would see him next week and get some questions answered and a timeline generated for what they should do next on the infertility totem pole. She was amazed that Dr. Fluten was still so calm about it all. She believed that he really thought that they were going to conceive on their own. She hoped James would go with her. She knew that he had to have questions that he wanted answered, but either because of pride or stubbornness, he would not ask on his own. She desperately wanted to be able to share with her husband what she was going through, but the area of babies and conception had been a no fly zone for them for several weeks. They had finally put their weapons down in surrender to one another as long as it had nothing to do with the baby thing. Although both of them knew that avoidance was not the answer, they felt that it would suffice for the moment. They were tired, frustrated and fatigued. Their emotional legs had run a crude marathon and they desperately wanted to be at the finish line, whether the prize was a baby or giving up in peace. Deanna, in an effort to keep their dreams alive, sent out an email to her family and friends about praying for their conception: *Hey family, All of you know that James and I are seeking the Lord's favor regarding becoming pregnant. It has been a long, topsy-turvy battle with infertility. Although we would not trade the experience for the world due to the growth and deliverance that we have received, enough is enough! We are excited about what God is ready to do but we need your help. Sometimes when you wrestle with God you need to tag someone else to stand in the gap until you gain your strength back to keep on fighting. We have received confirmation after confirmation recently that God is ready to bless us, but that He wants us to push until we get our breakthrough. We love God no matter what, child or not, but we are excited that just when we become content with our lives, He reminds us that He wants to keep His promise to us regarding a baby. What we are asking is that if everyone who loves us and wants to see a miracle occur in the near future to pray for us on this Friday. Please pray as many times as you think about it regarding the following: Wisdom/discernment regarding God's will for us as parents, for conception to occur, for health and peace for us and the baby, against the spirit of infertility and miscarriage. Also we would like everyone to pray together at noon (central time) regarding the above requests. If you have been looking for something to believe God for, here is your opportunity. When this manifests, we want you to be able to say it was because God hears the prayers of the righteous. I guess we will need to pray for baby-sitters too, huh? God is real guys and just like we are doing this in faith, I believe that He will answer your prayers too!! He is too big not to show Himself righteous! God is not a man that He should lie nor a son of man, that He should change His mind. Does He speak and then not act? Does He promise and not fulfill? Numbers 23:19.*

She wanted the enemy to know that the power of prayer worked. She figured if she got other people on the job that her resilience would be renewed. She did believe in the power of prayer, right?

The Carringtons knew they needed a vacation. They needed time away from their structured lives in order to regroup and recover from the strain that barrenness had placed on them, the game that they had not chosen, but instead had chosen them. They were excited that April had been the month selected for them to go away to Fiji. Cara and Rodney had a time share that allowed them to take a couple or two along with them to various vacation spots and the Carringtons were overjoyed that Cara and Rodney felt comfortable enough to ask them to tag along this time. Although Rodney and Cara Alexander did not spend a whole lot of time with the Carringtons, their friendship with them had proven to be tried and true during times of trouble. Their relationship was as comfortable as a pair of old working boots.

The Alexanders had been right there for Deanna and James when they experienced their miscarriage. They were not just a couple that had the "I know how you feel comfort," but they were people who had experienced baby tragedy first hand. They struggled two years with infertility, which was followed by a bittersweet pregnancy. Cara delivered her 2 lbs. 3 oz. bundle of joy prematurely. Kala remained in the hospital for over three months when she finally received a clean bill of health. It was only a miracle that she survived. She looked like a stickpin doll on many of the pictures that had been taken of her with all the pumps, needles and lines coming from her fragile body. All seemed to be well and Kala began to grow up like most other premature babies, spunky and full of life. It was amazing that most premature babies shared a commonality of being a spitfire on wheels. It made sense because they needed that to survive all those months living outside their mother when they were supposed to be inside. They needed that will to survive to swing back at the blow that life had swung at them. Life wanted them to strike out, but their wills often would not let them. Then we outsiders expected them to calm down as they got older. How could you expect that from a child whose will had kept her heart beating and blood flowing? Shoot, life was too precious to them to waste one moment not living it to the fullest. Sadly, Kala began to experience seizures again like she had during her days in the intensive care unit. Her seizure experience led to a coma from which she would not return. Rodney and Cara made the hard decision to remove Kala from life support. She had become the shell of a body. Inherently they knew that Kala was better off being with the Lord, but it did not make the sting of losing their precious daughter any lighter. They had shared how hopeless and let down they felt through the whole experience. They had trusted God until the end and had to accept His sovereign will no matter how disappointing it was to them. Kala had sashayed in and out of their lives as quickly and as quietly as wind blows during a quiet storm. Part of them died with her and they both desperately wished they could take her place. They believed that she had been the strongest of the three and the plan for her life was to survey this world for only one moment and report back to the Lord on what could or needed to be changed. Unfortunately their baby trials did not end there. They suffered through the agony of two years of secondary infertility and finally came to the conclusion that their parenting plans must take a different route.

Cara shared with Deanna in one of their conversations that the experience of secondary infertility had been more frustrating than their first experience. She felt like she questioned God more frequently and pressed Him even more about why they could not conceive and bring a child to term again. She reported how she even felt like God owed her something for dealing with the death of Kala and not turning away from Him after He had allowed her pride and joy to be snatched, stomped on and drowned in a deep pool of pain and misery. She shared how she had wanted to have arms long enough to box with God. She told that it was not until she hit rock bottom that it was revealed to her that she had idolized motherhood so much so, that she had placed the thought in front of her Heavenly Father. As much as she wanted to be mad at Him, she knew that the lesson had been one that she could not have learned until she had gone through the storm. There was something about going through something. You could talk about it, have an opinion about it and even judge someone else's actions while they went through it, but until you walked that line yourself, you would never know what you would actually do.

They packed up their "trying to conceive bags" and began a new travel in pursuit of adoption. God had mercy on them and the process was a quick, painless one. They had been told that international adoption could take almost two years from start to finish, but only a few months after the legal process was completed, they found themselves on their way to Rwanda to pick up their new four-year-old son, Kigeri. They decided on Rwanda because of all that they had heard about the genocide that had taken place in the country in the early 1990's. It had broken both of their hearts simultaneously to hear of the slaughter of almost one million people over a civil issue. They were determined to relieve some child of the heartache of being orphaned by being ripped from his or her family due to social epidemics or from the continued unrest in that nation. It was amazing to both of them that even in a country where people's color was the same, there could be fighting and division due to class and hierarchy. Adopting from Rwanda was their way of supporting a country that had been abandoned by so many of the super powers in years prior. The child that they received may not have been directly involved in the genocide, but certainly had parents or grandparents who would have been living right in the midst of the trials. The package that they picked up after their fifteen-hour flight would be the balm that massaged their hearts from the loss of Kala. Kigeri had been abandoned by both his parents and was living at an overpopulated orphanage run by the American Red Cross. Naturally, Kigeri did require some time to get adjusted to life in America, but three years later, other than the tribal markings he received at such a young age, you could not tell that he had not been born in Chicago. He learned the language quickly and fell right into the perils of childhood in a country of waste and excess.

One year after Kigeri came to live with the Alexanders, Rodney's seven-year-old nephew came to live with them because his sister terminated her rights to parenthood when she overdosed on heroin and died a tragic death. She was found in an alley behind a drug house on 63rd and Loomis. Yes, tragedy had been the Alexanders' last name for several years, but God had seemed to smooth the path and adjustment and peace had followed like a rainbow after a storm. They were one big, happy family now and they seemingly had recovered from the deaths that had shadowed them like a dark rain cloud.

~

"Babe, we need to go do some last minute shopping for this trip because you know a brother got to be looking good while he's on the beach!" James had no problem at times tooting his own horn. Sometimes he could be as vain as they get. But what amazed Deanna even more was that James was unable to use that same energy and confidence when it came to more important things. He was indecisive, inconclusive, and vacillated when it came to making major decisions. She wasn't sure if it was fear of failure, rejection or a combination of both. Her continual prayer was that one day he would truly see himself as God saw him. She wondered if the mystery that continued to hover over his head like a smoldering fire had anything to do with it. She was reminded again like it said in Ephesians 5:13, that light exposes the character of everything. She prayed that she was strong enough to ride the wave no matter what size it was when it came to pass.

"Yeah babe, I was sure that you would need something else. I knew you wouldn't leave the Fiji ladies without anything good to look at." Deanna smiled as she thought about the summer clothes that she would need to pull out of the crawl space. She always hated to pull that stuff out. It seemed like it was such a tedious job to go searching through all of the clothes that she had tossed in her summer bin last season. James always warned her that she would have a difficult time sorting through all that stuff that she hurriedly threw in the bin. She hated to have junk lying around. She would much rather have it thrown in a closet so she did not have to see it. James was so different. He wanted every closet neat and in order, but he could rest easily with stuff lying neatly in piles all around the house. Peace in that area had only come to the Carrington home when both of them adopted a little of each other's philosophies as their family motto.

Time flew like the turning pages of a book and the Fiji fun crew was well on their way. The sun met their personal madness at the door of the 747 Boeing that carried them to paradise. Their trip was a much needed rest filled with dancing, good food, swimming and lots of sunshine. One night as the ice melted in their drinks at dinner their conversation changed from the normal sport, politics, church gossip and entertainment to something that would strike a cord in Deanna's heart. Rodney began to speak of a gift that he knew he had received from the Lord, but was somewhat cautious about because he didn't quite know how people would view it.

"Honey, tell them instead of making them guess." Cara had a way of encouraging her husband even though she was a woman of few words.

"Well, I have known for a long time that I have the ability to interpret dreams. It seems strange but until I read about Joseph and how he was able to be freed as a result of his abilities to interpret Pharaoh's dream did I realize that the gift was not anything to be taken lightly. Plus, you don't hear of people interpreting dreams unless they are fortunetellers or psychics. I guess I didn't want anybody calling me Cleo, the lady from the infomercials' nephew." The laughs emitted from the table in a four-part harmony.

"Nah, dude that is deep! I know I've had several dreams here lately, especially since I have been maturing in the Lord, that I can't quite understand. The last one was really strange," James said, as he shifted in his seat and took another bite of bread.

"Well, I don't know if you want me to listen to it or not, but the first question I have to ask you is, if I interpret it, do you want to know what God has to say no matter what?" Deanna and James glanced at one another and their look answered the question louder than words could. James had shared the dream with Deanna and they were both anxious to find out what God was trying to tell them. Deanna spoke up for the two of them.

"Yeah man, we want to know the truth even if it hurts." Deanna took a sip of her drink as if to swallow the potential pain that might be attached to the truth of the dream.

"Well," James spoke up. "Everybody at the table was in the dream except Deanna. It was a vivid, colorful dream. I swear if I was not sleeping I would have believed that it was real. I found myself at your door looking to see if you were home. Cara answered the door and said you would be home in a minute. I went in and started playing with Kigeri. The strangest thing was I had three colorful fresh-water fish in my hand that looked like I was taking home to put in a fish tank. You came home a few minutes later with another guy whose face I couldn't make out and then I woke up." A dull silence came over the table.

"Wow, man that is deep," Rodney said as he looked deeply into the Carringtons' eyes one set at a time. "I certainly will pray about it and let you know what happens." Rodney grabbed Cara's hand as if to put a period on the end of the conversation. The mood went from serious to silly in 0.5 seconds and the quartet finished the evening by happening upon a free concert. They danced to the live melodious music of Harold Melvin and the Blue Notes until the sunrise told them it was time to rest. True friendship never got tired though, it just continued through the winds of change. It had been like breathing, constant and steady.

~

A seed of hope was planted in the Carringtons that night. In subtle ways God was showing them that He heard their prayers and was willing to answer them His way and in His timing. The challenge for them would be to keep those God moments close at bay in order to use them as a defense when the devil tried to steal their joy by reminding them of their dreams that lay dormant.

~

The last Sunday of their trip brought sadness into both James and Deanna's lives in different ways but for the same reasons. Would the reality of returning to life as they knew it cause them to return to the same sting that infertility had shared with the both of them? Were they strong enough to endure the disappointment that each month would bring? This vacation had definitely halted their sedentary thoughts, if only for a moment. As the crew waited in the small, humid airport for their Chicago flight to arrive, they reflected on the fun they had over the last week.

"Oh yeah, I forgot to tell you. I got an understanding about your dream, man." Rodney had a way of changing from comedian to counselor with a spin of the wind. He turned toward James but spoke to the entire group. Everyone turned to him with a sort of startled look, like where did that come from? Rodney did not notice and he went right on with his speech. "Here it is. God was telling you that you and De could have the son that you wanted. That was represented by you playing with Kigeri. The guy who was with me represented Jesus and His desire to get closer to you. You couldn't determine who He was because there was something blocking your relationship with Him. The fish represented three sins that were in your lives causing the blockage. Two were De's and one was yours. Sorry De." Deanna pursed her lips as if to say, "it's always me." "Anyway, the reason that the fish were colorful, fresh-water fish was because these sins were ones that God had made you aware of but you had not addressed them yet, thus keeping them at bay in fresh water." Deanna and James stared into space roughly in the same direction. Their individual thoughts were joined at an emotional hip. Could God really be ready to bless them, but yet they had not been listening? And what were the sins that they had not addressed? Had they both been so neglectful and disobedient that they had missed the hand of God in their lives? They certainly had some praying and fasting to do. They hoped that they were both able to put their resentment towards one another aside to open the door to the fulfillment of their dream of having Joshua.

CHAPTER EIGHT

". . . Lord, I believe; help thou mine unbelief."

Mark 9:24

"Honey, I've been doing some thinking and praying and I believe I need to change gynecologists." Deanna had thought long enough on the subject without hearing from James.

"Why De, what's wrong with Dr. Fluten?" Deanna treaded from that point at a snail's pace with her words since she sensed the initiation of irritation in James' voice.

"Well, I think it's been long enough and nothing has happened yet. I feel like I need to know what's going on with us. Aren't you the least bit concerned that we haven't conceived in close to four years?"

"You know what, yeah I'm concerned but only to a degree. You have to let God do His work. I can't say that I am not frustrated but I know God has His hand on us and that it will happen when it happens." James' pause allowed Deanna to jump in.

"I agree, but God has called us to watch and pray. How do I even know what to pray or look for if I don't know if anything is wrong?"

James huffed, "Deanna you're not going to be satisfied until you go see someone else so I don't even know why you asked my opinion. But I can't see how you would drop a doctor that you have been with for so long. At least don't you think you should go see what he says?" Deanna could not understand why James was so resistant about anything that had to do with the baby. She wondered at times if he still wanted a child. She made up in her mind that even though she already knew Dr. Fluten's stance, she would go to see him just to please her husband. She turned back towards James when she heard his lips smack open.

"On another note, . . . um? Have you been thinking about the two sins that you need to deal with?"

It took everything in Deanna's power not to retaliate with her facial expression. Didn't he need to be worried about himself?

She calmly replied, "Actually I have, and I guess it could be a number of things, but I have narrowed it down to three or four, though. What about you?"

James sniffed and focused on the wall behind her. "Nah, God is still silent about it when I ask Him. I just don't know." The uncomfortable silence that followed did not lend itself to furthering the conversation. Deanna moved quickly from the dining room table towards the phone to make her date with Dr. Destiny.

⁓

Three light taps on the door announced the entrance of Dr. Fluten into exam room number two where Deanna sat nervously shaking her foot. Dr. Fluten's concerting look indicated to Deanna that he already knew what her unscheduled visit was about.

"So what can I do for you today, Deanna?"

"Well doctor I was just wondering what kind of time frame we are on in regards to investigating further into why we are having such a hard time conceiving."

Dr. Fluten quickly interrupted, "There is no time line Deanna, you'll get pregnant when its time, nothing more!"

Deanna couldn't believe the shout in Dr. Fluten's voice. He had never seemed so frustrated with her before. Before Deanna could prevent them, her friends named tears began to well up in her eyes. She had prayed about being a big girl this time, but somehow Dr. Fluten's lack of patience had thrown her for a loop. Where was James when she needed him? He said he was going to try his best to make the appointment. A third person could have at least softened the vocal blow that Dr. Fluten delivered.

"But Doctor I am thirty-six years old! There is no way that I am supposed to wait around now and see what is going to happen next. A woman thirty-six should be tested after six months of unprotected sex if she hasn't conceived, according to the medical literature I've read. It has been well over a year since the miscarriage and nothing. James and I are willing to adopt and I need to be able to go on with my life if having my own children is not an option." The tears were flowing like a river runs deep, but they did not seem to penetrate the decision that Dr. Fluten had made about her case.

"So you are not pregnant when you want to be so you think there is a problem? Why are you thinking about adopting already?"

Deanna couldn't take it anymore. Her voice raised two octaves above her normal pitch. The new tone and the tears mixed together did not make for a harmonious resonance. "I am just telling you that this is getting very frustrating. I know I got pregnant on my own once, but I have not again in over a year. Couldn't there be something a little wrong with that picture?"

Dr. Fluten turned his back on her and flatly said, "So what is it that you want from me?"

All she could see was the white blur that his coat made through her tears. Oooh! If Deanna could only share what she really wanted him to do and what she wanted to do to him, she would probably feel much better. She could not believe her doctor of eight years, whom she had trusted with her very life, through her first surgery, was making her feel so inapt and small. "I want to do some further testing to see what, if anything, is going on with us so that I can make a better decision about our future." With the climax of her words, Dr. Fluten left the room without a comment. Deanna sat stunned. Her thoughts about seeing a new doctor were confirmed in that moment. So many people had tried to encourage her to get a second opinion before then, but she had not seen the point. She and James were confident that Dr. Fluten knew his stuff and they were willing to ride the wave with him. But, finally Dr. Fluten had shown a side that she was not willing to tolerate. She was not crazy and she knew that there had to be someone out there who would take a more serious look at her case. As her mind wandered back to the baby garbage dump dream she had several months earlier, Dr. Fluten's nurse interrupted the saga by giving her a card with instructions for her to follow up with a reproductive endocrinologist that Dr. Fluten had recommended. She looked sadly at the nurse and took the information. The card would only serve as a going away present from Dr. Fluten. Whether he knew it or not, this was the last time that Deanna would enter into his office voluntarily. A girlfriend at church had recommended her doctor to her long ago. She had ranted and raved about how thorough he was and she guessed it was now time to find out for herself.

~

RHONDA C. WHITE

Deanna set the appointment to see Dr. Banner on Monday evening. She did not bother telling James about the appointment she'd made. She knew that she had to eventually have an open and honest discussion with her husband about their marriage and how they had been treating one another. They were beginning to wear their "church faces" at home, being kind enough to one another to get by. Something had to change. They would not survive like this. Deanna knew the struggle with infertility had put their marital emotional state in jeopardy but she never thought it could manage to excel to this level of detriment. God must have known what he was doing by not blessing them with children. There would be no way that their current relationship could be a good environment to nurture children in. She had been thinking tirelessly about the sins she had to face since her conversation with James. She had an idea about what God was trying to tell her in the dream that Rodney interpreted. Her sins, "the culprits" as she had named them had been around for a while and she knew that she had neglected addressing them on purpose when she really got down and dirty honest with herself. It was a painful selfless road that she would have to endure, but beyond having a child, she needed to be right with God. It was time to rend the veil of deceit in her life and unmask the hidden ugly sins that kept her entangled in her own turmoil.

~

Dr. Banner's office was shared with two other physicians. The office was unremarkable but it was filled to the brim with patients chattering about their babies, illnesses and families. Deanna checked in and tried to busy herself with three of the 300 magazines piled on the wall racks to her right. She had surprisingly made it to the office on time. Recently her difficulty with time had decreased. She couldn't explain it, but she was grateful. She was tired of being one of those women who was rude and careless with other people's time by being chronically late. After several minutes of solitary sitting, she wondered if her newfound doctor had been diagnosed but untreated for the same untimely disease she'd suffered from. Finally, a small-framed Hispanic nurse called her to the back.

"I'll need to take your weight and blood pressure first. Also, when was your last period?" Deanna could perform this part of the doctor's visit all by memory. If there had been a degree in "ob-gyn patientology" she would have mastered in it.

"Unfortunately the doctor is stuck with a patient delivering a baby and will be delayed. Once we finish with the preliminaries I will have you go back out and sit in the waiting area."

Deanna wondered what had been the back up. Not one of Dr. Banner's patients had been called forward until then. She imagined she couldn't be too upset since he was doing what she would want him to be doing with her soon.

"So tell me why you are here?" Deanna wiggled on the patient table, which had become her trademark for entering a conversation about infertility.

"Well, my husband and I have been trying to have a baby for over three years now and we have been unsuccessful. I had a miscarriage over a year ago but nothing has happened since then. We had some initial testing done, a hysterosaliogram and a sperm analysis, which were inconclusive." Deanna's eyes weakened and began to let her down by filling up with liquid. "I had been with my previous doctor since before I got married and he was not willing to investigate any further into what was going on with us."

The nurse continued to busy herself with taking Deanna's history. "Were your tests performed at this hospital?"

"No, we were seen at Ingalls Memorial. I can try to obtain those records if need be."

"No worry, the doctor will probably want to do his own testing. How did you find out about us?"

"One of my friends at church referred me to Dr. Banner and she gave him and his whole crew excellent reviews." The nurse beamed and her discerning eyes blinked incessantly for a moment.

"You know, I know exactly whom you are talking about. How is her baby? We haven't seen him since he was a few months old."

Deanna relaxed and spoke cheerfully about her friend. "They are both doing well and he is just the cutest baby you'd ever want to see."

The compassionate nurse finished writing in Deanna's chart and directed her back to the room of wait. "The doctor just called. He should be up in about 30 minutes or so," said the same nurse who had taken Deanna's vitals. Deanna already felt more confident about her change in doctors. Whether James understood it or not, a woman needed to feel comfortable with who was probing around in her.

Forty-five minutes later Deanna was escorted to a patient room. She felt her bladder nervously fill as she sat and waited hopefully for her new friend and confidant to arrive. Dr. Banner's short, stocky stature met Deanna as she glanced from the novel she was reading. His self-assured smile and calm demeanor were a sight for Deanna's emotionally fragile eyes. She hoped upon hope that he would bring her some concrete answers. She breathed a silent prayer and awaited their initial interaction.

"Well, as you can see," he said, pointing to his name badge, "I am Dr. Banner." The doctor's corny smile soothed her nervous tension. "What brings you to see us today?"

Deanna wondered if that was the first line all doctors learned in medical school. She began her story from chapter one and Dr. Banner listened intently like it was the Sunday Night Movie. He asked her what seemed like 400 questions before he sat back to assess his findings.

"Well, Deanna I am going to be honest with you. I am not going to waste your time. Your age is not in our favor and I know your goal is to have a baby and that's what I want to help you do. I want to run a few tests—hormones, ultrasounds, etc. And I guess we need to test your husband again, as well. But what I am thinking is that we should probably try you on a drug called Clomid for a couple of months, but if that doesn't work, I want to send you directly to a specialist. Or, I can refer you right now if you would like. Either way I would want to get started soon. The fertility specialist would want some of the same tests done that I want to have done anyway, so if that is okay with you and your husband I would like to start there."

Wow, Deanna thought. How could the light at the end of the tunnel go from a flicker to a flash in one conversation? A weight was instantly lifted from her head. She was not crazy after all. It was smart to at least investigate what was going on. And Clomid? She had never known that she was a candidate for it before. Her periods had been regular so she had been told that she was ovulating normally. Dr. Banner explained that Clomid is a drug used to jump start ovulation from third gear into fifth gear and that it is usually used in conjunction with other forms of infertility treatments like artificial insemination and in-vitro fertilization.

"Doc you have just blown my mind. I feel good about your plans. I will discuss them with my husband and get back to you as soon as possible."

"No problem Deanna, and if your husband has any questions, here is the number to the direct line to my office. Feel free to have him call me." Deanna could have jumped past the reception's desk and the lobby in one leap to get to her car. She was finally being heard. A medical professional had taken her concerns seriously. She did not know if Dr. Banner understood the magnitude of him doing his job at that moment. She did not know if any of his plans would yield her prize, but she was satisfied in knowing that he at least wanted to try. The next hurdle would be getting James to comply with the doctor's campaign . . . .

CHAPTER NINE

"A man and his emotions tussle like wild animals
competing for their next meals . . . ."

James found himself flustered again as he zipped in and out of traffic going home on I-294 South. His mind wandered back and forth like a ping-pong game, moving from one compartment of thoughts to the next. He had crafted the art of being able to carefully close the door on one compartment of his mind before he moved to the next. Men and women's thought processes were so different. Women tended to think globally or in a more dispersive manner with everything being connected and related, while men had the ability to think on things separately and independent of one another. This unique male ability often kept James isolated and secluded from his wife and others. He did not plan to leave emotionally, but at times his thoughts unexpectedly crowded his mind so much that he felt like if his brain could choke, it would. Those times were infrequent, but then there were times when he used his escaping to his advantage. He found himself agitating his wife with his silence just to get one up on her. Deanna was such a refined debater, determined to win at all costs. He felt like he needed to keep some points in his private stash when her verbal competitiveness got the best of him. A crooked boyish grin found its way to his face as he thought about his feisty wife. He had always thought so much of her. Her strong confidence and endurance through trials had drawn him to her. He was mystified and intrigued by the essence of her being. Her vigor had been like an enticement that pulled him through the storms of his own life.

Even when they were not a couple he could remain stable because he knew that she was somewhere doing the same thing. James was reminded of what Will Smith said on a talk show a few days earlier. He said that he loved Jada because she was 100% woman and could go from ghetto to White House etiquette with ease. James felt the same about his own wife because no matter where they were, Deanna had a way of fitting in and making the best of the situation. She knew how to be a rough neck and an elegant damsel all in the same day if need be. His love for her had bound them even through the winds of change. But Deanna's recent instability had been a real puzzle to him and he wondered if her show of weakness was the reason why he had pulled away from her emotionally in the last few months. Was he disappointed in her humanness? Had he put her on a pedestal that she couldn't maintain when the poop hit the fan? James knew God had a way of making anything that you put ahead of His greatness disappoint you. James was disappointed that he thought Deanna was idolizing motherhood. As he thought more however, he realized that he must have been doing the same thing by putting her higher than she should be. They had gone through thick and thin together, but for whatever reason he never felt like he could share all that he needed to with her. Hell, he didn't feel like he had shared all the perils of his own life with himself. Why did he think it would be different with De? It was an eternal void that he felt never seemed to go away no matter how much he detached himself from it. It was a never ending nightmare that he continued to run from. A dangerous cat and mouse chase.

When it came to being able to dig deep into his emotions to reveal his true self, James had always come up a failure. He guessed that's why it was always easier to talk to women that he was not intimately involved with. When the tension of sexual intimacy was lifted, he did not feel threatened or intimidated. But he wasn't fooling himself either. There was a thin line between simple friendly attraction and true sexual magnetism. One tip of the bucket in the wrong direction could mean danger. Angie, his long distance co-worker, had caused him to jeopardize the sacred trust of his marriage. He knew she had wanted more than he was willing to or could give. Angie was a short, sassy, biracial sistah who was almost cute in James' "Attractive Ladies Scale." Most of their conversations had been innocent initially, but in the last pages of their previous friendship they moved closer to dangerous waters and James found himself having difficulty treading in them.

It had been next to disastrous when Deanna found out about his secret friendship when she did something out of the norm and looked at their cell phone bills. He found relief in not hiding it any longer. He had made several calls to Angie in Dallas where she worked in their company's corporate office. Their distance had been another safeguard for James, or so he thought. He couldn't deny the attraction that he felt toward her and even though their relationship had been surface in nature it had been soothing to his soul.

James had successfully lied and played down the friendship with Angie to Deanna and she had let it go based on his consent to be honest about any future business contact he made with her or anyone else of the opposite sex. He could tell that she didn't mind him having female friends, but what she did mind was the deception that seemed to be involved. The obvious warning sign he did not heed. Months went by with him and Angie getting closer than ever. Eventually the "friendship" barrier broke and James gave way to the safeguard around his heart. Fate had a wicked way of setting things up. Angie had sat waiting patiently in the wings for James to respond appropriately. His ego had taken a licking with this infertility deal and he needed, so he thought, all the support he could get. He knew in his heart that a job like that should only be left for his wife, but he found himself slipping into the subtle traps that the enemy set in order to kill, steal and destroy his covenanted marriage. Every time he wanted to reveal the true identity of his camaraderie with Angie to his wife he got colder feet than a groom on top of a wedding cake in the freezer.

Finally, the proverbial poop hit the fan and Deanna found a suggestive email to Angie in James' personal electronic mailbox. Deanna told him that she hated to pry into his personal life, but that something more than intuition had pushed her in the back and prevented her from retreating. James knew immediately that the pushing had been by the Holy Spirit. The Spirit had not been too keen on James not practicing what he preached in his Sunday School marriage class about honesty and integrity. Every thing done in darkness had to be revealed by light one day. Once Deanna exploded her new findings all over him like a ton of firecrackers, smoke bombs and M-80s on the Fourth of July, he had no reply. He walked around like a silent zombie taking quick opportunities to glance in her direction hoping to pull her into the conversation that he wanted to have, but was not willing to initiate. She had refused his feeble attempts by moving into her own mode of silence. He had not been used to that retort. They waged a small game of nonverbal tennis filled with silent serves and muted returns. The breakdown of communication in a relationship was like a dam holding back that which naturally wanted to move forward. Stubbornness had been the referee for their noiseless match and as usual he had not called it fairly. They both galloped and retreated to coping mechanisms that had failed others numerous times before. Those faulty mechanisms in marriage were like worn and tattered shoes that you knew needed to be thrown away, but were too comfortable to part with. To James' surprise the rest of that evening went on without a sound. He was awed at her silence. She was usually not silent when it came to matters of the heart and he was afraid that her new found friend could be the devil in disguise.

His current life came forging quickly back as he blew his horn at a semi-driver who thought he owned the expressway. Why did people have vehicles if they refused to drive them fairly? James seemed to find himself more frustrated than not at the poor state of Illinois drivers. His belief was that if you have enough money to pay for a vehicle then you should have enough money to know how to use it safely! It was easy for James to explain to himself the current state of poor driving around him, but what he could not or refused to explain to himself is how he had gotten himself back entangled with Angie, after all the counseling, tears, hurt and the pain it had caused. How could he have done the same thing to his wife and his marriage again? What was really going on with him? He had not wanted to, had denied it for months. He turned his back on her attempts to reconcile, but finally had become weakened by the intrigue a rekindled relationship with Angie created. Danger had a way of soothing him. He could not even explain it to himself, but the confidence he gained from entrusting his thoughts and emotions to someone else had been seemingly successful in restoring the wounds that the present state of his turbulent marriage made. He believed things would get better with time and that he and Deanna would one day see eye to eye again, but for now he needed to escape, to change directions and be in a place for a moment where he didn't have to make life changing decisions. As sad as it was, Angie was like an emotional VIAGRA® pill to him. Just being able to hear her voice and know that there were no strings attached to their conversations, nothing that he had to be accountable to, lifted him to an emotional high that no circumstances could pull him down from. Angie had walked in his office earlier that day on a routine service check for the company. Her not sharing her visit to Chicago had been a welcomed, but scary surprise for James. He decided to have an innocent lunch with her at a popular restaurant in the Hyde Park area. No worries, this was just a business meeting. No one had to know, including Angie, that he was falling fast for her.

James started chattering out of nervousness after they had been seated for only a few minutes at the secluded table for two. "So Ang, Ms. Corporate America, how is work going for you?"

"Well, it's just been the regular stuff going on, the political crap of our company can be a pain at times but I manage. Sometimes as a woman you have to fight a little harder to get the respect that you deserve." Angie's well endowed chest enveloped her tweed burgundy and gray business suit. James tried his best not to focus on the obvious, but his manhood would not leave him alone. He could play tricks on his mind for only so long before he knew that he would be in trouble. He was glad that Angie didn't live in Chicago permanently. If he could get through her stay safely then he knew that he was strong enough to make it and maybe even break things off when she returned to Dallas. Well, what did he have to break off anyway, they were just friends right? Angie leaned in and took an inviting sip of her drink. She did not hide her attraction to James ever. Even when they did business together she managed to drop voluptuous hints about her true intentions. It would be nothing for her to brush her arm against his side or casually grab his hand and hold it longer than she really needed to during a business deal. She did not have to spend as much time with James regarding work issues on the phone or otherwise, but it had been a good excuse to get next to him.

The arrival of their food was a needed distraction. Their conversation had moved to an intimate silence that if not broken could lead down a road that only one of them was 100% ready to take.

"So what about you, how are things here in Chicago? Anything new?" James answered carefully. He knew that Angie was well aware of his marriage and he was sure that she was alluding to the current state of it, but he was not willing to discuss that with her. As he formulated his words in his mind he noticed that she certainly did not mind eating in front of him. Sister girl was getting down. She was gulfing her glazed pineapple chicken down like a drill sergeant was leaning over her back. Was she even breathing? He had never seen a woman kill a plate like that before. She had not missed a beat even when she dropped some of the glaze on her jacket. A small burp emerged from the depths of her abdomen and she was still able through continuous chewing to spatter out a quick "excuse me," and kept going. He sat in awe of how the woman could get down like that. He had not taken one bite of his steak yet. He knew his food was getting cold but he could not help being entertained by her display of gorging. He had almost forgotten the question that she asked until she finally looked up and questioned his lack of response with her elevated eyebrows.

"Oh yeah, things are alright I guess. Work is really tough. I'm trying to decide if it is really cut out for me. You know I'm a man who likes to be out interacting with others. This job makes that kind of difficult. Although I enjoy what I do, it doesn't lend itself to me interacting with new people with new ideas." James hoped that answer satisfied her curiosity for the moment as he swallowed hard a bite of the salad that had been placed before him. He reluctantly ate the roughage drizzled with Catalina dressing. He could hear his wife reminding him of the need to eat more vegetables. It was funny how food could remind him of where he really should be. When was the last time he had taken his wife out to lunch? He couldn't remember even hanging out with her much since they had returned from vacation. His thoughts were interrupted by Angie's direct proposition.

"Well, Jimmy, I need to know something. I am only here for two more days and well, I just want to get straight to the point." Her lips seemed to be drenched with a combination of desire and the remnants of oil from her salad. "You know I've been digging you from a distance for several months now and I want to know how can I be down? I mean, you pushed a sister to the curb a while back but here I sit determined to get what I want. I am an independent woman, but I need what I need."

James had a hard time keeping a straight face. Angie had just proven that she needed what she needed by the way she had scoffed down her food. In a way, it even alarmed him for a moment. What might she do to him given the right opportunity? "Ang, you're putting me in a hard spot. You know that Deanna and I are trying to work on things." He lied. "It's really hard for me to even start looking into other things. It wouldn't be fair to you." He was trying pitifully to douse the fire igniting between them.

"I'm not asking you to be fair James, I'm asking for you and I to hook up to ease a little of the corporate strain. I know you are a good brother and I ain't trying to step on another sister's toes and I don't want to share. I just want to be there when you need me. I'm not here that often so how could us hooking up really threaten anything?" Wow, James thought. How had he gotten himself in this mess? Not only was Angie aggressive and direct, she didn't seem to have any real scruples when it came to the covenant of marriage. But how could he talk? He was the one married, sitting in a restaurant with a woman who wasn't his wife, contemplating moving one step towards total deception.

"Angie you don't play fair. I can't deny that I have feelings for you but I just don't know. I mean our work would be jeopardized and my marriage, I mean that's a big step." James sat forward and nervously completed the rest of his meal now faster than his cohort had done previously. He could feel her eyes poking holes through the top of his bald shiny head, but he would not look up. The tension was rising in the room and if he could lean back and fall into the Nestea® pool he would. He did not want Angie to think he was a punk, but he was trying his best to push that still small voice out of his mind that was saying, "run!" He kept engaging in the emotional fencing match with his brain as he finished his meal.

"Look, this is the last thing that I'm going to say about it. I'm staying here." Angie slid the address of her hotel and electronic key toward James in one motion. "I will be back at the hotel around 9:00 pm. No hard feelings if I don't see you, but I promise you that you won't regret it if you show." And with that Angie turned her attention to the crowd changing in the restaurant. They had sat unaware, well past the lunch hour. It did not seem like she wanted James to respond so he didn't. She ordered a slice of double chocolate cake from a passing waiter and quickly changed their conversation back to one about work. Oddly, it was as if she had not even mentioned anything to the man in front of her about stepping off into the deep end of sexual insanity.

CHAPTER TEN

"What do you do when the walls of duplicity close in on you?"

He pulled into the driveway of their dream home. They had never imagined that they would land in Tinley Park in the home that they had discovered across from a country club they visited for a friend's wedding years earlier. James had noted the twinkle in Deanna's eyes when they turned around in its driveway after mistakenly passing up the club's entrance. He knew then that he would do everything in his power to purchase that home for his wife. He and Deanna had scouted the house harder than the Chicago Bulls had Michael Jordan. The plush five bedroom, three-car garage home with the front drive lined with hostas and multicolored lilies in early spring had been a rest haven for them. But instead of rest and peace, the appearance of his home caused panic to rise in his heart.

Thoughts wandered in his brain like particles floating in the waters of a still bath; forever listlessly moving in and out of their own cosmic spheres. Would he ever come to a point of understanding regarding his boggled unawareness? Why did he continue to run to chaos for comfort? What sense of peace did he find in the perils of detrimental decision making and careless mistakes? Mindless chatter echoed in the archives of his head, revealing the void all the more. The vacant lots there were filled with abandoned cars stalled with thoughts of chaos. He slowly pulled into his garage space and carefully placed the address and key to his prospective escapade into the glove box. He hated that he even had the gall to bring it into the hemisphere of their home. He wanted to make the right decisions, but his mind's inability to turn from the challenge of wickedness was taking over. Where was God when he needed

Him most? Why wasn't He speaking out loud like He had in biblical days. He was instantly reminded of the scripture in I Corinthians that said that there was no temptation that was irresistible and that you could trust God to keep the temptation from becoming so strong that you couldn't stand up against it. James couldn't figure out if he was standing or sitting right then in his mess. Before he could find an easy space to rest in his mind, Deanna swung open the service door to the garage. Dang, was she clairvoyant or what? How could she know that he was planning to potentially mess up their marriage even further? Women, he thought, you can't live with them and you can't live without them.

~

She didn't give the brother a break before laying into him.

"James we need to talk now! I can't take this any longer! We have been walking around like zombies for what seems like ages and something has got to give! I've been walking on egg shells with you because every time I say something to you about what's going on, you go off. Come on man, what's up?"

James could see the hidden panic in her eyes. He felt it too. He always did when they were unstable, but he was not willing to allow it to overtake him this time. He had his mind on other things and so he decided to attempt to defuse the argument before it got started. He managed to take a short glimpse at his wife and quickly looked away. He couldn't bear to lie to her eyes. He stared at the bicycles and gardening tools affixed on the wall, attempting to concentrate on his next line.

"Look De, I know we need to talk but now is not the time for me. I have a lot on my mind. Work is really crazy right now. I don't know if I am coming or going. I may even have to go back to the office tonight to catch up on some work. I just need a little more time to digest it all. I mean, going to these doctors and all was not in our original plan. I don't know if I am ready to hear some doctor tell me that we have something wrong with us. Could you stand to hear that something is wrong with your body, or better yet, that we did something when we were younger that caused us not to be able to have kids? You are always the one talking about how medical doctors are trained exclusively to prescribe medication or perform surgery, so why are you so gung ho to do things their way? We were believing God for a miracle regarding a child and now we are considering spending thousands of dollars on something that we know that God can do for free."

James had managed to get both of them into the house and into the den as he was talking. Deanna huffed and sat back on the couch. She was famous for rolling her Betty Davis eyes when things were not sounding quite right to her. For a moment he thought he had gone too far and blown it.

"Can we set a time maybe in a few days to sit down and iron out our plans, together? I promise I want to get things straight." James allowed a pregnant pause to redirect Deanna's frustration toward his water-filled eyes. Even with all that was going on, he really did feel bad about how he and his wife had been getting along. James removed his glasses for effect. "I have been avoiding it. I know I have. It's just so much. I know we'll get through this babe and God is on our side." James internalized his words, wondering how could he even bring God in this? Was he one of those low-down dogs that he and his boys had always talked about?

~

The turmoil she heard in his voice pained her to no end. How could a person who appeared to be as solid as the Trojan horse evaporate into crumbled blue cheese in an instant? The enemy thought he had a foolproof game plan when he messed with Christians. He knew that if he could put a cloud of doubt in front of their physical eyes, then their spiritual eyes would be blinded and bound. Mental chaos had a way of causing a physical breakdown at every metabolic level in the body; joints ached, gastric juices waged war against one another and the heart attempted to continue to beat by jumping over the cracked patches that sadness and depression caused. At least Deanna knew that was how she had been feeling. The mysteries of her husband's mind would have to be placed on the back burner for now. He needed her to be patient and like a wild horse that had finally been tamed, she submitted to his will. James reached over and grabbed his wife with both hands and held her tight. He didn't want to hurt her. He couldn't, not again, but his mind needed to rest. He needed to go someplace where he did not have to make decisions that changed his family's destiny.

"I know you cooked already, but I really do need to go back to the office. I had to come home and get my laptop. I'll just grab something on the way back. I shouldn't be long." James kissed his wife's forehead and patiently walked to the door to ward off any suspicions about what his mind was trying to get him to do. He was reminded of how his boys back in college had labeled a kiss on your girl's forehead as the kiss of betrayal. He hoped his wife hadn't felt betrayal on his lips.

Sunday approached and the Carringtons proceeded to their married couples Sunday School class and shared mini-reunions along the way with people they had just seen days earlier. The week that Christians experienced out in the world could make the comfort of like-minded individuals that much more special. Unfortunately, at times the refuge people sought in church was often not found. Church folk could be cruder and less sensitive than those of the world all in the name of Jesus they would say. Even though James stayed on Deanna about talking too much, he often was the one who indulged in the pleasantries of male camaraderie in the Sunday School's hallway. He waved Deanna on and delved head first into a conversation with a few other guys about his new motorcycle purchase.

As Deanna made her way into the class she walked straight into a punch to the face of spiritual warfare. A few of the wives in the class were congregating in the front of the room congratulating one of the newer wives. Their Sunday School teacher turned the female around to face Deanna and said "Oh De look at what God has done!" She reached down to pat the swollen abdomen of the young lady, glowing with pregnancy pride. Deanna did her best to regroup as quickly as she could in order not to offend the excited "barren-less" woman. She muffled out some cheap congratulations with a smile and quickly moved to the side to take care of some of the intercessory prayer ministry business that was due that week. Deanna at that moment touched and agreed with Hannah from the Bible. Her story told about how her adversary provoked her into despair in the first book of Samuel. She knew her teacher understood her struggle and was not intentionally trying to hurt her. However, she also knew full well that her adversary the devil was always trying to sucker punch her with someone else's blessings. Over the years, the pain of hearing another couples' expectancy news had not gotten any easier for her. Even though she was genuinely happy about what God was doing in other people's lives, her unanswered prayers were a constant reminder that she felt like the last person chosen on a team to play dodge ball. Deanna hoped she had done an adequate job in masking her despondency. She certainly didn't want to spoil the young lady's moment or make her feel like she couldn't share her excitement with her. She knew that only someone who was going through the same thing would understand what she was feeling at the moment. She was grateful that her husband, despite their current differences, had always been there for her. Where was he when she needed him? As if God answered her question, Mr. Carrington dashed through the door in his excited on-fire mode. She was relieved to see him, but at the same time she also felt a weird quirky feeling in her stomach. That uneasy feeling she got when she knew something was not right. They still hadn't talked and James only had one more day of stalling to hold onto before she cornered him again. Regardless, she decided to enjoy class and forget about her women's intuition.

~

As Deanna and James ascended from the back of the room where they had gone to pray about Deanna's mishap, they watched Carleen slowly approach them like a graceful doe. They sat down as she pranced over and stood before them, a pillar of strength. Deanna and James sat in awe of the expression of vigor that the woman displayed before them. They had just heard the prayer request that she gave the class about how her husband was doing better physically, but that he had been on an emotional roller coaster ride lately. Carleen had admitted that she couldn't blame him. How strong could you be facing death at any moment when your original plans were to grow old with your spouse and see your grandchildren marry? It had to be challenging to believe God's promises in the midst of all of that gloom. Her prayer request was no longer for his recovery, but that his soul be restored from the anguish of not knowing when the end would come. She believed in her heart of hearts that John would get back to the place of peace, however what she wanted now was an increase in faith for herself. Carleen sat down next to Deanna and appeared to unload more than just her body weight into the seat. She grabbed her young friend's hand and a moistened track formed on the right side of her face.

"How are you doing, sweet ones?" She glanced toward James and pierced into his eyes as if she had something important to say to both of them, but especially him. She prevented her thoughts verbally several times before she was able to speak a full sentence. She seemed as if she really was intent on James receiving what she had to say. She had learned that sometimes men had difficulty taking advice or direction from a woman so she was careful with her words. Not that men did not respect or reverence women, it was just that she had found at times receiving from women seemed to go against their natural way of thinking. As Carleen hesitated with her comments, she finally asked them if they wouldn't mind coming to her house for dinner one evening. She had been hard pressed to share something with them, but it appeared that she had decided that Sunday School was not the appropriate place to delineate the message.

"I would love for the two of you to stop by, maybe for dinner. John is physically better these days and would be up for a visit from you all. I know you really didn't get a chance to know him before he got ill, but these days he is welcoming the company of fellow believers. It seems to keep him focused." Despite the hesitancy that both James and Deanna felt about going to visit a terminally ill man that they did not know very well, they agreed to go. One thing they had learned was that when God was ready to speak, they should be prepared to listen no matter who He used to speak through. Carleen obviously had something to share with them and they were not willing to miss an important message from the Lord even if they were not spiritually right themselves. The trio made a date for the visit to occur on Thursday and then settled back in their seats to hear the Word for the week regarding marriage. Even though Deanna loved her class, she couldn't help but wonder why it seemed that most of the lessons had to do with what the wife should or should not be doing and only touched briefly on the role of the husband. She was sure that it was just her own narrow thinking and convictions jumping on her at once and she decided that women inherently needed more verbal cueing to stay on track, especially her. Submission was such a humbling position, one that a proud woman like herself would probably challenge until the day Jesus came back. She concluded that she wanted, no, desperately needed God to speak to her 37 hours per day, if possible!

CHAPTER ELEVEN

"Tears are summer showers to the soul"

Alfred Austin

As James pulled up to the circular drive of the Adams' home, he wondered why he had agreed to come visit this man. He didn't know him that well anyway and besides, he had never stomached death well. He found himself at a place of understanding about his salvation and eternal security, but the actual act of dying was still more than an eerie mystery to him. He realized that his hesitancy with coming had been the reason for his current episode of crankiness with his wife. He often felt like he made sacrifices for her that he wouldn't make for himself. He knew that was the way he should love her, but it sure didn't always feel good. He glanced at Deanna from the side of his right eye. Why did he have to drive them everywhere they went? She had taken the whole princess thing way too far. Early on, she had insisted that he put gas in her car and he rebelled against doing it for several months until he realized that the headache was not worth the peace he received once he did it. She constantly complained about the gassy smell on her hands and the men who always seemed to be lurking around the pumps. She always seemed to jump in the passenger side when they were going places together as if he never wanted to ride anywhere. One day he was going to sit on top of her and see if they went anywhere! Boy, marriage was a trip!

Deanna had managed to remain quiet for the remainder of the ride since her feeble attempts to engage in conversation with him had gone nowhere. The Adams' wooden ranch home in Crete, Illinois appeared to have a heavenly midst hovering over it. James couldn't tell if he was imagining it or not, but he was too stubborn at the moment to involve his wife in his thoughts. They proceeded from the car in silence, individually putting back on their church faces to cover the mask of frustration and hopelessness that lay underneath. Their attempts, however, were going to be futile because they knew that Carleen had a way of piercing right through the both of them. Who knew what her husband could see through? Facing death could make you more sensitive to God's voice. Before they could reach the doorbell, a blue-gray haired woman opened it with a pleasant smile on her face. For a moment Deanna and James thought they were at the wrong house. The lady greeted each of them with a warm handshake and informed them that she was John's sister. She told them that she would let Carleen know they had arrived.

Relieved, they walked into the comforting, warm refuge that the Adams called home. The smell of fresh gardenias added to the feelings of peacefulness that greeted them as they walked through the foyer. The front room was decorated in cream with beautiful ivory front furniture and plush cashmere carpet. Deanna and James immediately felt like they should take off their shoes. They knew how some people could be about walking on light-colored carpet. They hated to be asked to remove their shoes, so they began to do so before the dreaded request was made.

"Please don't feel obligated to do that." Carleen's voice met them in the midst of them stumbling to untie their shoes. Her smile was rich and beautiful as always. Her coffee-colored skin seemed to shine in the rays of the setting sun that peeked through the foyer's skylight. "We want our company to always feel comfortable. Life is too precious to waste it on worrying about tangible things. The floor was meant to be walked on. If I didn't want to clean my carpet I shouldn't have bought it."

James immediately knew he had met up with his kind of couple. What was the use of having things if you could not enjoy them? The undue pressure that people put on each other could be incredible at times. Carleen's comments even made him glance over at his wife who had the same grin of comfort on her face. Even when they were not talking to one another they could agree.

They followed Carleen down a narrow hallway filled with pictures of her and John with their children and grandchildren. Many of the shots were of them involved in all kinds of sporting activities like skiing, rafting and hiking. James laughed inside as he thought about how atypical it was for a black couple to be so outdoorsy. He enjoyed play more so on the inside so he was slightly shocked when someone of his persuasion moved out into foreign territories. The pictures were not very old either. It looked as if the

Adams were heavily active up until John's diagnosis became a reality to them. He remembered how Deanna had told him about their experience. John had been feeling pretty good and was a real advocate of men going to the doctor for regular check-ups. He had received a clean bill of health up until he fell while they were on vacation last spring. What started out as a check-up for a sprained wrist led into a MRI and CAT scan of his whole body when the treating physician happened to come across a small lump under his right arm. The doctor assured John it was probably nothing, but the Adams should have known that devastation was waiting for them to open the door and be invited in since the doctor insisted on them having the diagnostic tests done right there in Denver while on vacation instead of when they returned home. John kept the faith and continued to enjoy the few days of their vacation after the diagnostic imaging visit. When they returned home the following week, James' primary physician had been forwarded the bad news. What had begun as a cancer in his lymph nodes had spread to his liver and gall bladder. The cancer was so aggressive and so far gone that medicine could only offer some palliative treatments to make what his doctors thought were his last months more viable. Carleen screamed like bloody murder when the doctor came in with the news. Her frustration heightened more at the fact that John had been so diligent with his healthcare and she not as much. "Why not me!" she screamed. She was the one who had to be reminded several times about her annual mammogram and pap smear. She was the one who was taking medication for her high cholesterol. She often teased John that he would be the one to bury her first since he probably wouldn't die until he was 150, still eating green grass and shrubbery for dessert! His health decline made her more concerned with her own health. Not for her benefit, but for his. How could she care for her husband who had been given a short time to live if she was not better herself? She felt like John had probably done so well up until then because he had been careful about what he ate and how he exercised. Life had a funny way of dealing with obedient and disciplined people. Maybe it used those people as examples for those who did not have concern for their own lives.

Carleen's saddened eyes met James in the midst of his thoughts. He vowed to himself that he would do better by his own health. How many times had his wife begged him to make more wise choices about his food intake? Until that point he felt like as long as he exercised and kept his size 34 waist that he was okay. John's life had proven his theory wrong. Carleen grabbed both of their hands and looked intently into their eyes. "I know things have not been right between you two for a while now. And I know it has a lot to do with the infertility issues. James, just so you know Deanna and I have not talked in a while, so this has not come from her." Carleen tightened her squeeze. "You both need to know that God predestined this storm for the both of you. He wants to make you all stronger, not weaker. Do your best, babies to hold onto His unchanging hand and remember Reverend Marshall's favorite scripture, Romans 8:28: "*All things work together for the good to them that love the Lord.*"

How could she do it every time? James thought. She seemed to have the inside scoop on their marriage and she never failed to hit them square in the midst of their mess. He hoped that she could only see through his first veil of fraud and not beyond into the deep waters of his psyche, which he didn't even understand. He didn't know her like that nor was he ready to share even with himself what was truly going on. He had done a seemingly good job of camouflaging the depths of his pain thus far and he was not willing to give up acting in that play just yet. For him, that would be devastation revealed, anguish discovered, shame displayed and possibly even his marriage destroyed. No, he wasn't ready for that.

"Now before you guys go in to see John, I want you to know that we have been in serious prayer for the both of you. We are getting up in our age and it seems that at times the Lord will confirm things in the both of us and we would not be responsible saints if we didn't share what we feel the Lord has shared with us. We don't want you to think that any of this is any hokey pokey stuff but, we want you to be prayerful about what we need to say. We believe that our comments will be confirmation for what the Lord has been telling you."

The mystery overwhelmed them simultaneously. God had sure been into telling them things lately. It was a surprise, though, seeing that they had not been on one accord with God's plan or each other lately. Carleen interrupted their collective thoughts, "Also I don't want you all to be nervous about seeing John. He really doesn't look that sick other than he has lost some weight and is a little weak. He doesn't mind if you ask him questions about the cancer or anything. He feels that the better he can get his story out there, the more lives he can help to save."

The deep sighs that were expelled by the Carringtons proved to be a sign of relief for Carleen. "Now John's sister is a fabulous cook and she prepared a wonderful meal for us. She has been a gem through all of this. She inherently seems to know when I need her most. You guys go in and have a seat and I will go get John." James and Deanna were met at the dining room door by a plethora of wonderful aromas. Their mouths watered at the thought of a good down home meal. There was nothing like cooking done by wise hands. The table was filled with melodious colors and rising steam. The pot roast was bathed in light gravy and the scalloped potatoes swam in colby and cheddar cheeses. The string beans were lined neatly next to what James' grandmother called "iced potatoes." The corn sat buttered and ready to be devoured. It was as golden as the sun. The fresh baked rolls stood alone in the middle of the table waiting to be blanketed in sweet honey butter. They would have to go straight to the gym when they left from there. There was no way that they were going to miss any part of that meal.

James caught his wife staring at him and for a moment he felt sorry for her. Why did he have to be so cruel? She only wanted what was best for them. He wished he could be totally hers, but his complicated life always seemed to get in the way. He quickly looked away, not wanting to give the impression that he was into her again.

John entered the room smiling and cheerful. His rolling walker made an aching noise as if it was tired of being used. James chuckled at the tennis balls that had been attached to the hind legs to assist in making the movements of the walker easier. Carleen had not missed a beat in trying to improve her husband's quality of life. Carleen continued to dote over John as he made his way to the table. "Okay old lady, I can make it. I told you I would give you a ride in my rolling buggy, but I know you are scared I drive too fast!" Laughter found its way to the table and John's sister sat down so they could all say grace. John bowed his head and began. "Heavenly Father, we thank you for this day and for what you have done for us. We don't take life for granted for we know that it is a precious gift that only you can give. We ask you blessings over this food and the one who made it. Let it be as nourishing to our bodies as it is satisfying. And God bless this young couple that has come to visit us today and please Sir have mercy. You know their aches and pains God. The pains of the heart. Just bless them Lord and give them the ability to hear clearly from you. In Jesus' name, Amen." John wiped his eyes not embarrassed to show his tears. The episodes of his life and the reality of what was to come had softened and sensitized him. The foursome stared at him as if they were waiting for his cue. "Well, what y'all waiting on, Sarah can't cook that good so it's best to eat it when it's hot so you won't taste the flaws!" Another collective laugh was followed by the procession of food around the table to each of their plates.

⁓

"Well Ms. Sarah, I don't know what Mr. John is talking about! Sistah you can throw down! Everything was the bomb!" James sat back and patted his belly in satisfaction.

Sarah's wily grin received his compliment. "I hope you guys saved room. I made an apple pie and I have ice cream in the frig." They all looked at her as if she had lost her mind.

"Sarah you must be crazy! Do you want us to pass out at the table?" John never missed an opportunity to joke on his sister.

"What your darling brother is trying to say is maybe we will have some later in the den. Let's clean off the table and get the dishes squared away. James can you help John to the den?"

"Woman don't play with me. You know I'm not gonna let a young buck out do me!" John gave a reassuring smile to James.

"Okay then get your tail out of the way so we can clean up," said Carleen. Deanna rose and attempted to take some of the soiled dishes into the kitchen when Carleen caught her arm. "No honey, you go on in with the fellas and sit for awhile." Deanna looked puzzled for a moment and then she remembered why they had come in the first place.

"Okay Ms. Carleen, but you know my mama taught me better than to just get up from the table and leave my dirty dishes."

"Its okay this time, baby. Someone needs to share something with you." James and John had already found comfortable seats to reside in when Deanna found her way to the den. They had quickly jumped into a "man talk" conversation about sports and what not when Deanna emerged into the room.

John interrupted their conversation quickly when she entered. "Well, uh, I guess there is no need of stalling, I uh need to share something with the both of you." John sat up in his seat and then rocked back. He was a picture of his wife just a few short days ago when she couldn't seem to get her words out either. "Uh, well, I know you all don't know us that well, but my wife has taken a liking to the both of you and we have been praying for you for quite some time. We don't like to get in other people's business, but we couldn't seem to stop lifting you all up during our prayer time. Then one night we both woke up after having what we discovered was kind of the same dream. I don't want you guys to get scared or anything, but we know that God is trying to tell you something. Remember, anything that is ever prophesized over you should be a confirmation of what God has already told you, not something new and foreign. I think that is why so many Christians are messed up today because these so-called prophets are going around sharing what thus sayeth the Lord to God's children and He ain't bit more told them nothing of the kind. Prophecy should be a confirmation of what y'all already knows." John had a way of slipping back into his southern Arkansas dialect at times. He seemed to use it more for effect than as a crutch. "I want you guys to know that the Lord loves you both dearly and well . . ." Another pause filled the gap in John's monologue. James and Deanna automatically sat up and moved closer to one another on the couch. "Well, kids here it is. I know how hard it is to wait on God for something. I have believed God for healing for a while now and well, I've concluded that whether He heals me or not He is still God. But I'm reminded of the crippled man who waited at the pool of Bethesda for thirty-eight years for healing. I'm reminded of the 40 years that the Israelites wandered in the desert seeking the Promised Land. I also reflect on Elizabeth and Zacheus and how long they waited for God to bless them with a son and how he became so vital in the ministry of Jesus Christ. What I am trying to say is that any child that you all have would be a blessing from the Lord. My wife and I believe that God wants to use you both for His glory in bringing up a child who will grow in a loving, God-fearing environment. He wants him to help lead His people back to a place of righteousness. Now the devil knows that too, that's why I know God has spoken to you both about how He plans to be with you all the way. Don't be fearful or afraid. Be strong and know that the Lord is not planning to leave you on this journey. Sometimes the enemy knows the plans for our lives better than we know them ourselves. He can block and hinder God's plan for a time, but it is only for a season. God even uses that time of delay for His glory."

James was reminded quickly of the scripture found in Joshua that Deanna said she had studied when they began to talk about children. God was definitely not a forgetful God, slow at times, but not forgetful.

John went on, "Here it is in a nutshell. The devil seems to be hindering a child from coming forth because he knows that you all will bring him up right and teach him to serve the Lord in fear and trembling. The enemy does not work as hard against people who are not saved or people who are not rooted in His word. If they have a child he knows he can cause chaos and more confusion during the rearing of that child. He is not going to fight the unmarried teenager or the drug addict as hard. Unfortunately, children born under those conditions can make it, but they have a much harder time from the start. It is a shame how lightly and carelessly parenthood is entered into these days. God did not fashion family or childbirth to come about that way. It's not the natural order of things, you know." John paused to scratch his salt and pepper-flavored head. "I know that for black people, our healing is directly related to where we ascended from. We were raised on the fruit of the land and were healed by natural herbs and minerals. Again, I don't want you to take my word for it. Do your own biblical research in

Genesis and see how God prescribed for us to eat of the land for growth and healing. Our ancestors lived for many years that way and were healed of various diseases just from the fruit of the ground. The Chinese came up the same way. The difference is that when we were taken as hostages from our own country and brought here, we lost a lot of values, and more importantly, the keys to our health, our healing culture. You hear many people laughing at Grandma's old-fashioned remedies these days. They would much rather take medicines that have been synthetically derived to only treat symptoms and not treat the cause. But that is a whole different story. The Chinese, on the other hand, were able to bring their medicines with them because they came here with less of a struggle. Again, I don't want you to take my word for it. I definitely want you all to come together in prayer and see if this is what God would have you to look into. There is a Chinese herbal doctor who I have been going to for several months now. He can almost look into your eyes and tell you what's wrong with you. In regards to your barrenness, he may be able to shed some light on what is really going on. You do have to have faith, though and believe that God can use him to bring forth healing. Will you all do me a favor and go see him for me?" John did not pause. "I have already put the visit payment down with him in faith, believing that you would go see him soon. Just let him know that Elder Adams sent you. I believe God is using him for my restoration. I don't know how long I have left in my journey, but I do plan to make it the best while I am here."

James looked forward and then over at his wife who he suspected was in tears. She was a tough cookie, but could cry at the drop of a hat. Maybe she was truly strong because she had not learned to suppress her emotions like he had. Strength could be established on solid foundations, not faulty ones. Sure enough, James followed the tracks down her face to a small puddle forming on the hardwood floor. Deanna didn't mind exposing her weaknesses when she was in the presence of God. Her thoughts of preserving beauty and control flew out the window when she was in that special place. James thought she was more beautiful then than at any other time. Made up beauty had its place, but natural spiritual beauty was priceless. He knew that her tears were not just about what had been spoken over them, but also from the pain of the current state of their marriage, specifically for who he had allowed himself to become.

His disguised pain had overtaken him and made him into someone that he knew God did not want him to be. Breaking out would be so much harder than he could expect. He had never evaluated the possibility of exposing himself and the pain his life had experienced. He thought for all intensive purposes he had survived, so he didn't need to expose himself any further. Life had made him a survivor by default. He was beginning to feel like his past was sprinting ahead of him and it was getting harder and harder for him to catch up with it to suppress and attack it. James instinctively, but hesitantly grabbed his wife's hand, sort of expecting her to jerk away. She did not. He could feel fear and hope tied up together in her hand. Fear and faith could not reside in the same place he had been taught, but they sure could fight for lead position from time to time. James knew he needed to be the one to respond to what John had told them, but finding the words had become a difficult task. Carleen's entrance gave the room enough distraction so that James could figure out the best way to respond. Her careful smile instantly took away the anxious air that had built up in the room and instead of finding a response to what John said, a comfortable silence took over. The group hug that took place around John in his comfortable chair brought on a unanimous cry that no conventional dam could stop. The emotional overflow of joy and soundless pain took over and no one could speak.

John began to pray. God was in the place and He wanted to be talked to. "Heavenly Father, we thank you today that once again you have looked down beyond our faults and seen our needs. We pray Lord that you Lord would please Sir have mercy. You know us better than we know ourselves. You own the cattle on a thousand hills and there is no thing that you will withhold from those who walk upright. Lord, we come standing in the need of prayer today. We need thee Lord every hour, O God we need thee. Before we were conceived in our mother's womb you knew us and we are grateful this evening that you love us anyway. Lord, we come standing in this circle of prayer believing that you are God and God all by yourself. We are asking Lord, that you would look down on us and please Sir have mercy. We need you in a special way today. We come standing in the gap for my dear young sister and brother knowing Lord that you are able and that you are the giver of life. We know that the enemy lurks around like a roaring lion seeking whom he might devour. But we also know that when the enemy comes in like a flood you will raise a standard up against him. Lord, we're coming today asking that you would please Sir have mercy. The enemy is attempting to take this family in a chokehold and squeeze the life from their mortal bodies. We know he has tried to sift them like wheat, O Lord. He does not want this marriage, this family to survive. He will stop at nothing to destroy us, but your Word O God has full power. We know God, that nothing happens to us that you don't know about. In fact, that old rascal the devil has to get permission from You to even look our way. We are grateful that you are a loving God and that you will not allow us to be subjected to more than we can bear. We come believing Your word today. You told us O God to be fruitful and multiply. You told us that you make the barren woman the keeper of the house and the joyful mother of children. You said O God that you would love us and bless us and increase the fruit of our womb and our land, God and we believe you. I am reminded in Exodus how you told your children that if they blessed You that You would give them long life and protect them from miscarriages and barrenness. Lord, you are still God no matter what you do. You are the same God today, yesterday and forevermore. Just keep us in your will, God. But we come asking that you would bless this family, this God-fearing family with a child. We believe God that you keep your promises and if it be in Your will please sir have mercy. We trust you no matter what God because You do know us better than we know ourselves. And when this old life is over we want to be able to stand before you God and have you say, 'Well done my good and faithful servant.' We trust you God today and I decree just like Simeon in the Bible that I can die a peaceful man if you will allow this child to come forth in my lifetime, that I might see the prayers of the righteous avail. We love you God and it is in your name that we pray, Amen."

There was no dry eye in the place and Carleen went in search of tissue.

"Well Mr. John and Ms. Carleen, I think we are speechless. We know God is good and that He wants what's best for us. He certainly gave us an extra portion when He allowed us to meet you. Your words of encouragement and confirmation have been more than a blessing. Without even speaking to my wife I know that she feels the same joy that I feel in my heart, just knowing that God loves us enough to continue to give us signs that He hears our prayers. It does get difficult, even scary at times when you feel that God is not listening. Everything we go through is to make us better, not bitter and we know that, but reminders are always good. I am sure it will take us a while to ingest all of this. Just like we wanted to savor the good natural meal you gave us, we now in prayer need to ingest the spiritual one. I am sure through prayer and reflection we will make the best decision. Give us the information on the doctor you want us to see and we will let you know what happens. Really and truly we want to thank you so much for everything. We can't express enough how grateful we are." Deanna sat in silence nodding her head in agreement. The night had been a special one. Things for them had to be shaping up. God had assured them that night of His love through His people. Deanna and James said their final goodbyes and Sarah insisted that they take dessert home with them.

The car ride was a lot longer than it needed to be because of the distancing silence that stood between them. It was like they had never even been to the Adams' home. James toyed with the automatic child safety lock on the door panel, challenging himself to level it directly in the middle. Deanna followed her image in the side car door window as it metamorphosed with the changing backgrounds. The only common bond they shared at the moment was hearing James' favorite gospel rap group Cross Movement ferociously pound out "Cry No More." Like the song said, one day we would not have to cry or worry about world crises, famine, violence, pain or even infertility. One day the only thing that would matter was sitting before the King, singing praises to Him who reigned supreme over the enemy. At times like this, James wished those days would come quicker and faster so that he did not have to continue living the falsehood of his life before himself, his wife and most importantly, before God. How do you continually lie to yourself day in and day out and become consciously aware of the pain that you cause, but yet continue on?

James reared back in his seat and calmed his nerves enough to speak. "De, I know we just took in a lot and you may not even want to hear from me right now, but I do need to say this. I know you are anxious or maybe a better word would be excited about going to see the fertility specialist, but I really would like to pray about going to see this Chinese guy first. I mean what could it hurt, right?" James scratched his nose as a distraction to himself. He knew his wife would view this diversion from their original plan as a stall tactic, however, it truly wasn't. He did want a child as badly or maybe even more than his wife did. His fears did not allow him to move forward as aggressively as his wife would like him to. What if he was truly the problem? What if he was the reason that they could not bring forth life together? Had his past again crept into his future? He was not ready to deal with those realities just yet. He did not know how he could stand before his boys or more importantly, his earthly father and tell them that he was the one who was physically incompetent, that he was the one shooting blanks. Nah, not yet, not now. Too many other things in life had him by the collar. He watched Deanna squirm in her seat and he purposely focused on the neon blue lights on the dashboard. The hue sedated him, if only for the moment.

"James honestly, you know that I believe in holistic natural healing so I think it would be a good idea for us to go. Whatever you are ready to do

I am for it. I feel like we need to be doing something. We can't stand if we haven't done all there is to do."

He could tell she wanted to say more but the overwhelming events of the day had drained his wife of her energy to fight. "Well, let's pray this week every day about it and fast on Wednesday to get some clarity about what God would have us to do. Do you know what scriptures John was referring to in regards to the herbs and eating of the land?"

Deanna waited for a moment not to seem too eager. She had practically memorized the scriptures about eating and health in the Bible when she became a vegetarian. "I think it is somewhere in Genesis, but I will check it out tomorrow."

James could tell that his wife's short answers meant leave her alone, so he completed their ride home in silence. He made an executive decision to not even ask about the gym. The gym excursions had been something that they did together when they were at peace. He would take his frustrations out at home in his small workout room and then in a few games of *Madden 2004* before bed.

~

The Chinese herbal and nutrition store called Nam Nu Ling was their destination on the following Saturday morning. They parked on Cermak and made nervous jokes to one another about what they might experience on the journey. They walked by each storefront taking in the scenes and sounds of the area in Chicago that was labeled Chinatown, because of its rich Asian heritage. That was one thing that always amazed the Carringtons about Chicago. The city was a surplus of little towns, including Greektown, Little Italy and Chinatown. You could experience the richness of several cultures within a matter of blocks. Even though the division by culture led to segregation, it really added more to the diversity of the city.

They came upon the intended destination, a moderate size storefront with a yellow awning with an attached sign printed in red letters. The air in the store smelled earthy, bitter and a bit pungent to the Carringtons. James took a side look at his wife because he knew she had a nose like a bloodhound. He wanted to see her reaction. He often joked that she might have been one in another life. The store was in no means an unkempt place, but it had the feel of an old homey hut. Sounds of the choppy and swift Chinese language filled the air around the store as the Carringtons took in the nature of the conversations around them without having a clue what was being said. It was

RHONDA C. WHITE

amazing how laughter, sadness and serious discussion had the same tones in any language. The Carringtons stood out like a sore thumb in the store, in the midst of yellow-tinted people with bright smiles and almond-slanted eyes. They felt welcome though, even across the barrier of different cultures and immediately felt at peace. The petite unruffled lady behind the counter approached Deanna and James and in very broken English said, "May I help you?"

James attempted to shy back and allow Deanna to explain the rationale behind their plight, but he realized that her silence was electing him spokesperson and he took the reigns instead. "We want to see the doctor."

"Ah, okay, come wit me. What you problem?"

James nervously chuckled and explained how they had gotten to where they were and reported that they needed help with having a baby.

"Ah, I see." She turned quietly to an elderly gentleman who was reading with his head down while it rested on the top of a weathered and worn desk. She spoke to the doctor in their native tongue and James and Deanna continued to smile nervously at one another as if to say, "What did you get me into now!" The gentleman who they would later find out was "the doctor," motioned for James to sit down in front of him. He began a series of tests including taking his pulse, blood pressure, inspecting his tongue and looking into his eyes. The whole diagnostic battery seemed odd and quite different from traditional western medicine. Despite the language barrier, Deanna and James felt as comfortable with him as they did with their grandparents. He held a wisdom in his eyes that you not only wanted to respect but wanted to glean from. As James buttoned up his shirt, the "translator" began to say that the doctor felt that James was "hot, little bit, in the stomach." She asked him if he ate spicy and fried foods. James could do nothing but nod. Deanna had been on him for years to adjust his diet from fries, spicy dishes and junk food. The lady insisted that he stop the spicy foods and instructed James to wait for the doctor to mix him 3 bags of herbs. "$5.00 a bag, okay?"

Deanna slid hesitantly into the examining chair as if she was doing the grapevine in the swing dance she had learned a few years back. Immediately the doctor began writing down stuff in what looked like hieroglyphics to her. He then started an intense conversation with his assistant. She immediately said with haste, "Ah, he says you the problem. You system weak, you need system strong to hold baby. What you eat?"

Deanna remembered how a few people had warned her that her strict vegetarian diet was going to inhibit her from conceiving. She shared her non-meat eating habits with the doctor and was immediately reprimanded.

"You need to eat meat! Eat chicken, pork, fish and beef. Eat vegetables too! But more meat, you need to get strong!" She instructed Deanna to wait for her 6 bags of herbs to take daily. James and Deanna left the store and returned 30 minutes later when their herbs were prepared. They leisurely strolled throughout Chinatown toward their car as the brisk hawk whisked down their backs.

CHAPTER TWELVE

"Thou wert my guide, philosopher, and friend"

Alexander Pope

Deanna experienced a day that she was going to remember for a lifetime. It had been her bright idea to take her mother to the museum for the "Body Worlds" exhibit for her birthday. She thought the whole thing interesting from the start. A German anatomist invented through plastination, a way to preserve cadavers in order for the world to see what the inside of the human body looked like. She learned that plastination was a vacuum process in which a body's water and fat content are replaced by a plastic fluid that later hardens to retain all of the tissue structures. She had not fathomed the magnitude of going to see the exhibit. It had been more intense from the start than she expected. The exhibit displayed several graphic bodies exposing their muscles, vessels, organs and glands as God had created them. Deanna had seen this type of work first hand during graduate school. She had not understood at the time why psychology students had to be responsible for knowing the anatomy of the entire human body. They only had to be responsible for the brain. However the class, although it was tough for her, had been a rewarding challenge. Regardless, none of it had prepared her for what she would see midway through the exhibit. After learning about the circulatory, digestive and muscular systems, the exhibit proceeded to show the world about the reproductive system. Deanna's body stiffened as she shuffled with the crowd towards first, a placenta of fraternal, and then identical twins. She could do this, she thought. She could feel her blood pressure racing. Unfortunately, she and her mother had gotten separated back at the liver display. They had been astonished at how important the liver function is to the body. It is the main detoxification source. She thought it a shame that so many people abused it by an overdose of alcohol and fatty foods. Their amazement had obviously been enough to scatter them and now she moved forward knowing she had to do this on her own. She could do it, she had to. Even though her body stalled, her soul continued to push her forward. She knew what babies and embryos looked like, but she had not yet observed one since her own miscarriage.

The seven glass cylinders filled with a clear liquid seemed to echo her name over and over again. She could tell they were embryos frozen at different stages of life. She breezed by the embryo at the fourth week of life and was amazed at the rapid growth that took place from the beginning of that week until the end of it. As she moved to the fifth week a cool sweat broke out above her lip and under her arms. She only experienced that when she was nervous or cold. By the sixth week the embryo had its organs in place and had formed facial features. Then she saw it. She saw what her baby would have looked like. She didn't realize that she had moved forward and right next to it. She supposed she had gotten there like the characters in Spike Lee movies that just glided from one scene to the next on an invisible moving sidewalk. Her baby would have had a spinal cord, appendages and would have been the size of a marker top. She had not realized the magnitude of the life growing inside her until then. It truly had been a person, someone who should have gone to kindergarten, high school prom, married and watched his grandkids grow up. Until then she had not imagined that the baby was more than a few specks. How could anyone want to take a life away from the unborn? She was not a strict conservative pro-lifer who would go to great lengths to end abortions like advocating the murdering of doctors who performed such feats, but her eye's view of abortion had changed greatly on that day. In her mind she had justified abortion in extreme cases like rape and she still felt that all scenarios could not be judged in one setting. But what she viewed made her draw the conclusion that life was life no matter how it arrived.

The exhibit had been a bittersweet engagement for her. She loved spending time with her mother and even though seeing that baby, her baby trapped in an eternal glass jail had been hard, it had been healing for her. It healed a hurt inside that she did not know was still there. She dropped her mom off and arrived at her empty home. What was she going to do with herself for the three hours before James came home? They had been taking the Chinese herbs for five months and frankly she was tired of the smell, the headache and the hassle of taking them. James seemed content though, like they were a pacifier he used to plug up her mouth because at least now they were doing something. She was still ready to see what the fertility specialists had to say. She was confident that they might be able to help them. A combination of the two couldn't hurt, but James seemed to be content with the lack of success the Chinese herbs had rendered thus far. In her mind it was another way for him to stall. She sat depleted, frustrated and emotionally drained from the day. A sense of sadness draped over her as she thought about how she could not share all the emotions that sat pinned inside her with her husband. He had been so aloof lately. What was really going on with him? Deanna suspected some shady stuff was jumping off, but she did not have the emotional strength to confront him or the brick wall that was standing between them. The doorbell took her away from her thoughts momentarily.

~

That man had a way of making her smile upon contact. She could not believe he stood before her eyes wearing a grin as wide as a subway station is long. "Cairo Tanner what in the world are you doing on my porch?" She greeted her best friend with a hug the size of Texas. She was quickly reminded that she had not spoken to him in at least two months. He often took hiatuses away from her when he was not proud of what he was doing, but his grin indicated that there was some surprise in the air that he needed to share.

"Chicken head! I didn't expect you to be home. I thought I was going to have to break in the joint and sit and wait for you and my boy to get here before I could surprise you."

Cairo and Deanna walked towards the living room in a comfortable silence. She automatically tucked the pain she was feeling behind her eyes so that she could share in the bonanza that it seemed her friend wanted to drop. Overtaken with the joy of his presence, her grief was suffocated for a while.

"Deanna Carrington, my Negro. Wha's up with ya?"

"No my friend what's up with you? Why are you here and how did you get here?" Deanna sat silently rocking in her prized chair. Her grandmother had made sure it was left to her amongst other things when she passed. Somehow all the money in the world did not mean as much as her being able to sit in the spot where her grandmother had sent up many prayers for her and the rest of her family. She found more comfort in it during the many lonely days she shared recently with her cat alone in the house.

"Don't pop your pickle trying to ask me all those questions at once! Big C ain't going nowhere for a while. You have time to spend with your man. I mean, well you know, your real man." Cairo chuckled as he spoke. "Where is that no good husband of yours anyway?"

Deanna thought he must be reading her mind, but she decided to save the gripe session about James for later. "He should be home soon, but I want to know about you! Quit beating around the bush Negro. I know Chicago and the cold don't mix for you so something important has you here."

Cairo grabbed the *Men's Fitness* magazine from the coffee table and began casually flipping through the pages. "I am here for a conference for work. Our principal couldn't attend so she sent the next best thing in her place." Cairo's sly grin had a way of lightening up any mood. "I didn't give you a ring because I didn't know how long I was going to be here and I figured I would call once I arrived. But as it turns out, I don't have to be back at work until Tuesday so I decided to share myself with you all for the weekend."

"We don't have time for you this weekend," Deanna said jokingly. "You know you are too much drama for one weekend alone!"

"Well baby, you are just going to have to deal because when I am not in session I will be here in your face, white girl!"

Deanna laughed as she remembered that Cairo had given her that nickname in school when she was trying to be proper. Most black folks developed a "white voice" when they needed to be professional. They could easily change into comfortable Ebonics when they were in like company. It was sort of a language of their own. "Dude you need to quit with that. You are the one who can jump back and forth from professional to ghetto in two point five seconds." One of the couch throw pillows landed directly on top of Deanna's head before she could duck. There was nothing like having your best friend in your space. She loved being spoiled by the one friend in the whole world who she knew for sure didn't want more from her than she could give. Her husband had filled that comfortable spot in her life as well, but lately the demand was larger than the supply. "Well, I didn't cook anything yet. Let's go down to this new spot that opened up and grab a bite and some drinks. James is not due home for a while and we can call him to meet us there."

"Cool. You were reading my mind. You know a brother was hungry! I still need you to make me a pound cake and some lasagna before the weekend is over. So don't get comfortable with the dining out thing! I know James does not let you get away with that." They finished laughing as they entered the garage.

"Man I can't believe you are here! What's it been, two or three years since you've been to the Chi?" James leaned back in the high barstool at the table the trio found at the bar and grill called the Dovespot. Deanna sat in between two of her three favorite men, soaking up the atmosphere and the enjoyment of being the queen of the table.

"Yeah man, you know I have to make sure you are treating my girl right every now and then. I think I was up here for our fraternity conference two years ago." James knew Cairo was joking about how he was treating his wife, but the sting of the reality of his statement staggered his thoughts for a moment.

"Well you know we are always glad to have you up here, man. De misses her friend, no doubt. She probably didn't share that with you but when y'all don't talk on a regular she starts tripping man!" James shot his eyes towards Deanna to see if his comments had elicited some kind of smile. He hadn't been on her best side lately and he knew before Cairo's visit was over, Cairo would hear the low down on what had been going on in their relationship. James was going to ride the wave of contentment until he was given notice that the waters were too dangerous to wade in because he had been exposed.

The delicious smells of their meals brought their conversation to an immediate halt and after they said grace their plates saw no more mercy. They feasted on salmon, blackened chicken and prime rib and listened to the featured jazz band at what had become the new neighborhood hot spot.

Deanna could tell that her friend had something else on his mind but she couldn't figure out why he was continuing to stall with coming out with it. Finally her curiosity got the best of her. "Okay mister, I need to know what's up for real. You have been cheesing like a Cheshire cat since you got here. You can't tell me that something is not up." James had gone downstairs to start a fire in the family room where they would later go to watch movies and play pool.

"You think you know me, or something? I do have to tell you something but I know you are going to trip a little. I appreciate you keeping me true to my game, but sometimes I have to go on my gut feelings and do what my heart says. That's why I haven't said anything yet and why I've been ghost for the past few months. So don't trip even though this ain't like me at all!" Cairo shifted in his seat and averted his eyes for a moment. If anybody knew him like a book and would keep him accountable and above water in life decisions, he knew it would be her. His hesitancy was based on the unpredictability of his recent life choices. He could tell that Deanna was getting anxious and if he held out much longer he would hear her wrath, which could be relentless at times. "Okay dude, here's the deal. Let me finish before you jump on a brotha. I want you to know first that I am really happy and life is really good for me. Spiritually I've been doing well too. I've been going to my aunt's church . . . and don't give me those bug eyes! I've actually been enjoying myself and went forward the first Sunday I was there to rededicate myself to the Lord. Being in His presence again has been truly the bomb! I have been reading and praying every day. I don't know if I am going to join that church quite yet, but here is the funny thing that happened. You know how you always told me that when I was ready to turn my life over to the Lord that He was going to bless way above what I could imagine?" He watched Deanna shift her weight to her other hip and smile simultaneously. "Well, that word is found in Ephesians 3:20 and it has become my basis for life."

Deanna tried her best not to look surprised. She, however, was so proud of her friend she was almost ready to spill joy over onto the floor. She calmed herself long enough for Cairo to finish.

"I know He is able to do exceedingly and abundantly above all I could ever ask or think. But here is the tripped out part. While I was sitting in church getting my praise on the following week, out of the corner of my eye, I saw the finest sister, outside of you, of course, that I have ever seen in my life. She was not necessarily the type of lady that I am usually into, but something inside me was ignited when I laid my full vision on her!"

"Cairo you know something is always igniting in you with women. You sure you weren't just horny!" Deanna cracked herself up, but she quickly realized that Cairo was serious and that he was not as excited about her choice to be a comedian. "I'm sorry man, you know I'm just tripping, go on finish, finish!" Deanna exclaimed.

"You know I don't need to tell your tail another word, I told you to wait until I was finished! But . . . anyway, I went to talk to this lady after service and was at once not only attracted to her face, but more importantly to her spirit. She is the director over the Children's Ministry at the church. She was married before, but her husband was killed in a bad car accident four years ago. She took it pretty hard, but she's gone to grief counseling and seems pretty healthy. She and her husband were trying to get pregnant when he died, so one of her ways to give back in the area of children was to become a part of ministering to them. But here's the deal. To make a long story short, I asked Alesha to marry me last week and she said yes!"

Deanna could not contain her excitement any longer. She jumped from her perch by the kitchen counter and gave her comrade a huge hug. "Boy, why didn't you tell me before now! I can't stand you. You know you were supposed to tell me before now! As long as I have been waiting for my boy to tie the knot and here you let a week go by without letting me in on the news! Boy, I ought to whip you with a wet noodle! How did you ask her to marry you? What does she do for a living? Where does she live? What's her momma do?" Deanna was on him like white on rice.

"Girl, if you don't back up off me, why you sweating me! I'm gonna tell you all that in a minute. I didn't want to share it with you because so much was going on spiritually and emotionally I just wanted to make sure I was being true to myself and more importantly, to God. So many things were going through my mind and for the first time I was not interested in what this woman could do for me, but what I could do for this woman. I'm telling you Deanna, I am so into this woman that I feel like Orlando in that movie *Diary of a Mad Black Woman* when he told ol' girl, "All I want you to do is wake up in the morning and I'll take it from there." Cairo's eyes were lost in space for a moment as if he had found the smell and touch of her in the air.

"Whoa, man I think you are sprung for real! Earth to Cairo. I know this lady ain't got the playa playa from the Himalayas turned out! I'm for sure going to have to meet this lady."

Cairo smiled and went on with his story. "I was leery about what you would say since I know my relationship with God hadn't been all that in the past. But believe you me, living your life in front of me has been a great influence and I'm grateful to have you as my friend."

Deanna gave him a confident smile. "Okay enough of that mushy stuff, tell me about the girl, when do we get to meet her?"

"Well, like I said, she is the director of the Children's Ministry and she works in actuaries at Atlanta Life Insurance Company. She is this brainiac who loves to play the guitar and dominos. I know. What a combination! We have been spending any and every moment together since we met and believe it or not we have decided not to get busy until we get married."

"Oh, is that why y'all got engaged so fast?" Deanna's comment softened the seriousness that had flown into the room.

"No," Cairo replied. "Although we are engaged, we have decided to not get married for a year or so. We know the importance of getting to know each other better and more significantly, the importance of getting closer to

God. Oh yeah, I was told by my aunt I did pretty well on the ring. Alesha didn't suspect anything when I proposed. I took her measurement by her glove size and I asked her to marry me in the park after a carriage ride with a violinist serenading us. I gave her a two-carat clear princess cut diamond with a platinum band. Did I do alright?" Before Deanna could give her comments, James appeared in the room wondering what all of the commotion had been about.

"James, Cairo has done what we never thought he would do. He is engaged to a saved sister! Can you believe it?" After looking at both of them a couple of times to make sure they were serious, James met Cairo with a huge handshake and a man hug.

"Congratulations man, it sounds like your girl approves, so I'm happy for you too. I guess we will have to get to the ATL soon so we can meet the future Mrs. Tanner!"

CHAPTER THIRTEEN

"For of all sad words of tongue or pen,
The saddest are these: "It might have been."

John Greenleaf Whittier

The absence of Cairo showed up immediately after he left the Carrington home. They had put on a great show while Cairo was there, trying to be the couple they once were, but since he was gone the stage performance was over. James went right back to spending an extensive amount of time at work, the gym or any place that didn't include his wife. It was amazing how Christians who learned so much about hypocrisy could end up being the very ones who were best at the game. The ability to put on the "Church face" to save face was a class that most seasoned Christians had taken and mastered. You wouldn't dare let someone else know you were struggling. That might let God down or show that you have a lack of faith in His plan for your life. As absurd as it was, many Christians felt like they were saving face for Christ by lying to the world and pretending that the perils of life did not affect them. When in fact, the very reason Jesus came into the world was to be the problem fixer and a mind regulator.

~

On one of the rare occasions that the Carringtons were having dinner together with the third family member in their home, the television, they were interrupted by the doorbell. James didn't even look towards his wife for her to answer it. He was happy to escape from the silence that sat between them like a permanent fixture. James opened the front door to the weary face of Steven Cook. He had lost what seemed like fifteen pounds since they had seen him last. Steven would have been shocked to know that finding the couple at home together had not been the norm recently.

"Hey Steve, you look like you were just hit by a Mac truck, man! What's up?"

"Man, if I look that bad, I feel even worse." Steven pushed by James and proceeded to the den. "Hey De, what's going on with you?"

"I'm cool Steve, but what is going on with you? Can I get you something?"

"Yeah, I really could use a stiff drink right about now, but it probably wouldn't do me any good. Whatever you bring me to drink will be fine."

Deanna proceeded to the kitchen to refill their empty glasses with the sweetened tea she made and filled a new glass full for Steven.

"Okay man, so what has your face looking like someone beat it with a bat or something?" James had a way of being blunt and straight to the point. There were times when he said exactly what was on his mind no matter how it came out or sounded.

"Man, Theresa really up and did it for real this time." Steven's bronze-tinted skin appeared to turn ashen as he fixed his lips to share the rest of his horrid tale with his friends. "When I got back to our house today to be with the kids and cut the lawn and things, I rang the bell as I have been doing for the last few months. That irritates the hell out of me that I have to ring the bell at my own crib. But anyway, I kept ringing and no one comes to the door. Now that is strange on a Saturday morning for Lil' Stevie not to be racing to the door between cartoons. I gave it a few more minutes and then I went around to the back to see if T's car was there. I not only noticed that her car was gone, but the kids' bikes were gone and some of the lawn furniture was gone from the shed. It didn't look like someone had robbed us because the shed had been neatly closed and locked. I panicked though, thinking that someone really had just done a good job and had gotten us. I felt so guilty, man, not being there for my family. I couldn't figure out why T hadn't called me, though. Then I really got scared and figured that they might be hurt." Steven's tears disobeyed his will and began streaming down the sides of his face. It took a lot of hurt for a man to let go of his tears, even when he was in the company of those he loved. "Well, I forgot my new-found manners of waiting for my own family to open the door and I used my key. I rushed in calling to Lil' Stevie and Courtney. I was all the way into the kitchen before

I realized the echoing that my voice had been making throughout the other rooms. I turned around and finally noticed the emptiness that sat around me. Everything was gone. And when I say everything, I mean everything, except my things and the furniture that I bought before we got married. It finally sunk in that she was gone. I walked through the rest of the house knowing that this was a joke and that I was just imagining that my family had left me without notice, but it was all true. Outside of my things, the house looked like it did the day we closed on it. Every room had been cleaned like it was ready for sale. I was surprised that it didn't have a for sale sign out in the yard. But I guess she couldn't go that far without me knowing." Sorrow lingered in the air long after Steven had finished speaking. He broke his silence and Deanna and James waited patiently.

"So I closed up the house and went back to my sister's place. And just when I thought I had gotten my mind around the whole thing, her doorbell rings. For some reason I could tell that this was not going to be a guest that I wanted to invite in. I started praying on the way to the door. Sure enough, there was this Asian dude at the door who wanted to make sure I was Steven Cook. He handed me a large white envelope and jogged off. Well, I knew what it was before I even opened it. Theresa filed for divorce and wants full custody of the kids. She listed the grounds for divorce as irretrievable breakdown of marriage relationship. Now how is she going to list that as the reason for us separating when I have been trying to get us to go to counseling forever? And even though I have been gone for four months, I still have been going over there every night to help with the kids and I have been doing the yard work! Her part of the marriage may have been broken down but I am still here!" Steven's tears had dried by then and made tiny white racing lines down the sides of his face. His sadness had turned into rage. It was as if he had taken a taxi from the village of sadness to the land of anger right before them. The Carringtons let him go on without stopping him for clarity on anything. Good friends knew when their friend's faucets needed to flow. "And do you know the craziest part of it all? Me and T got busy, like two weeks ago. And when I say got busy, I mean got busy. It was no quickie and then get out kind of thing. She pulled out the negligee and a couple of tricks I had not seen before. I was thinking yeah, we are going to be alright. I guess I got my face cracked." Steven stood up and walked in front of Deanna and James like he was the lead prosecutor giving his closing arguments in front of a jury. "How did she get all of that stuff moved out? How did she pay for it all? And most importantly, what did she tell my kids? I cannot believe that Lil' Stevie let that go without telling me. That Courtney is more grown than we are and she stays mad at me all the time now, so I know she could have held it in. She must not have told Lil' Stevie until they left. De, you didn't know anything about this? Aren't you still picking the kids up on Tuesdays?"

Deanna heard a little accusation in Steven's voice, but she let it slide. She knew his emotions were getting the best of him. "No, actually I haven't been to pick the kids up in a month or so. T told me she had gotten them into some after-school program and that she could manage picking them up from there. I really haven't talked to her much in let's see . . . well, probably the last time I talked to her was about a month ago. She didn't say anything about leaving or moving." Deanna felt bad about not checking up on her friend, but she had detected in Theresa's voice a sort of disconnection the last time they spoke. She did not have much to say and her answers to the questions Deanna asked were short and simple. She had become leery of pushing Theresa when she was close to the deep end; most of the time that pushed her farther away. And even though she longed to speak with her friend, she had grown comfortable with the legroom that had developed between them. She guessed Theresa had obviously done the same. James stared off into space for most of the conversation. He looked like he was dazed by sleep and awe.

Steve chirped in, "Yeah, I guess I know how Theresa is. She does not want "right" to stand in the way of what she is doing. She doesn't want anything or anyone to stand in the way. Her mode of operation is to shut herself off from the world to make sure that she does not get steered off her plan. Yeah, that's my T, well, was my T. I can't believe she's really gone and gone without a trace. I bet she had it in her mind to do all of this when she put me out. She wasn't interested in working on us. I should have known that then. You know we had our ups and downs, but we always seemed to get back on track, I thought. I know she doesn't think she is going to keep my kids away from me, though. She couldn't have moved out of the state without me knowing. If she did, boy, I will have her arrested for kidnapping so fast, she won't know what hit her!"

James finally emerged out of his stupor, "You can have her arrested for taking her own kids?"

"Hell yeah, man and I would too. She has no right to take my children anywhere out of the state to live, without my full consent. I think I would have to sign some papers or something. And even though I would not want to put the kids though a whole bunch of fighting between us, I would. I will not let my kids grow up like I did, not knowing that they had a father who cared for them. They are my heart and soul. I can't live without them." Steven gasped as if his lungs had decreased their capacity to take in air. Hurt hung on his face like a distorted picture.

Deanna took her turn in the conversation. "I can't imagine T taking off somewhere without you knowing. That would be so cold, plus all of her family is right here in Chicago. She always keeps in touch with her family, even when times are bad for you two. I'm sure that she just moved out this weekend and will get you all of the information soon. Deanna's attempt at making the situation brighter did not seem to work. The dead silence that followed her statement made her quickly see the need in both men to have some time alone without a female's presence. She gathered herself and made a prompt, unannounced exit.

~

James' quandary flew in the room on the wings of change. The friends moved from Steven's unsolvable problems right into James' in an instant. "Man I know you're worried, but I need to share a little about what is going on in this house. It seems like trouble is on every side, man. I just don't know what to do about me and my wife's inability to have kids. I think it's driving both of us crazy. I feel like a day is like an eternity man, dealing with this infertility stuff. So far, they can't find a reason why we aren't getting pregnant and all this testing Deanna wants us to do is frustrating and expensive. She's ready to start these treatments and I don't feel good about it. The only reason I am thinking about going through with it is to get her off my back. I don't know if I'm scared to find out for real what's going on or if I feel like I am losing my faith if I don't sit and wait on God. Man this whole thing is a trip. Folks who don't want kids get pregnant everyday. What's up with us? I want to be strong for De, but this stuff is too much. I've been avoiding conversation with her like the plague because I don't have the answers for her. You know I'm supposed to be the man. I'm supposed to be the one who lets her know everything will be okay. But on this one dude, I am clueless. Each month we find ourselves childless, I feel like I'm attending a funeral of a close relative, the death of our baby who never came. I could swear sometimes when I come home during those times that Deanna is dressed in black, sitting on the front pew, mourning and crying. To be honest, sometimes I want to join her on that bench and cry with her."

The men sat in awe of their present circumstances, neither of them daring to give a response or reply to the other's questioning heart. They sat in silence for what seemed like hours, but only equated to a few moments. They had an unspoken conversation with each other's spirits, hoping to dispense life into one another without words. They oddly found comfort in the silence. They knew inherently that their answers did not depend on them, but on the One who made them. Would they let Him do what He needed to do in their lives to bring about the glory He deserved?

"Well man," Steven sat up on his bar stool with a new vote of confidence which came from somewhere in the depths of his soul. "I guess it's like Vince Lombardi says, it's not whether you get knocked down, it's whether you get up." The sound of the song *The Entertainer* disrupted their conversation, announcing an incoming call on Steven's phone. "This is Steven . . . . Hey Charlene what's up?" A long pause ended with Steven saying, "Yeah okay, I will be there in a minute." He grabbed his coat faster than a twinkling of an eye. "Looks like Theresa has finally decided to let the world know where she is. She called my sister a few minutes ago to let her know that she and the kids were okay. She left a number, but no address. Boy, if I could give her one good sock in the face I think I would be okay!" They laughed together for the first time since Steven had arrived on the Carringtons' doorstep. "Tell Deanna I had to run and thanks for listening, as always."

"No problem man, just keep your head up. God is going to see you through."

"You do the same, man. I know it will work out soon." They gave one another their customary handshake and Steven was out the door, headed for the new drama waiting to unfold in his life. James sat listless, waiting for some direction, some inkling of a vision about what he should do. He had been to this place in his life before, but this time he did not feel like he had the strength to fight the battle that lay ahead of him. The darkness that had overtaken his life was consuming and almost unbearable.

CHAPTER FOURTEEN

"Who, for the poor renown of being smart,
Would leave a sting within a brother's heart?"

Reverend Dr. Edward Young

The waters of the Carringtons' lives flowed in so many different directions. It was difficult for them to know themselves if they were coming or going. They once had danced life together like Fred Astaire and Ginger Rogers, but now their life performances were much like Milli Vanilli. They were lip-syncing through their days, which seemed to roll on at a donkey's pace. The strain of the fertility treatments had become laborsome. They decided reluctantly after the failed herbal treatments to finally go see the specialist referred by Dr. Banner to pursue intra-uterine insemination. They found out later that it was just a fancy term for using a syringe to squirt the sperm higher up into the uterus, giving them a better opportunity to meet with an egg to initiate life. Neither Deanna nor James said more than two words to one another unless they needed to swap information for the next fertility exam they had to take. Ultrasound after ultrasound, blood draw after semen analysis had proven to wear the couple thin. They no longer had a marriage, but they had become two strangers passing by one another hoping not to significantly disturb the other. They both knew in their hearts that it did not make sense to pursue having a child under those conditions, but their stubbornness and Deanna's unwillingness to quit, kept their raft afloat on infertility waters.

The inseminations required Deanna to shoot herself in the stomach with medication every evening and go into the office for ultrasounds and blood work every three days. James had to drop his sperm sample off one hour before the insemination for it to be cleaned and washed for the procedure. The night before that Deanna stuck herself with a longer needle containing hCG or human chorionic gonadotropin to ensure that her precious eggs, her gifts of life, were released at the appropriate time. The pricks that she took in her stomach were less painful than the blow they felt each time her period showed up like an unwelcome houseguest fourteen days exactly after the procedure. Every morning that James woke up after a failed treatment cycle, his soul felt like it had a hole in it big enough to fill the Texas stadium. He tried to fill the gaping wound the void created, but his attempts turned into repeated failures. He refused to go any further in the treatments after the third trial. The specialist had recommended the next step, which was in-vitro fertilization. The process was more detailed, involving the retrieval of Deanna's eggs, which were then placed in a Petri dish with his sperm to begin fertilization. After the standard three-day wait, any eggs that had successfully fertilized were placed back in the womb in hopes of starting a successful pregnancy. In-vitro fertilization was fine for some people, but he was not willing to go there. His wife wanted to try at least once, but his answer remained in the negative.

James' devotional time that he'd set aside for God had dwindled each month, each time he did not clearly see God's hand in his life. On one rare occasion, he gathered the nerve to ask God "Why are you so secretive about this baby thing?" To his surprise, God quickly whispered in his spirit, "Because I want you to listen to me even when I am quiet. A teacher does not talk while He is administering a test. You know exactly what you need to do." James did not want to hear that answer. He did not want to deal with himself. He wanted the pain to go away. He wanted his life and his marriage back the way it was before this lot in life began. He ran away again in his mind, faster and farther than he had ever dared to go. What was the point in staying around anyway? Why continue to feel lifeless and numb? If only for a moment, he needed to feel real again. He needed to feel wanted and desirable. He needed his ego to be stroked in a way that only one person he knew could do. As much as he hated himself for reaching out in the wrong direction, he could not put aside the draw that he felt in his heart to spring towards the forbidden fruit of someone he knew wanted him for more than what he could deposit in a cup. He supposed his wife loved him, but for all he could see at the moment, she just needed him for his chromosomes. That was her only mission it seemed. His thoughts flew back and forth like a ball in a tennis match. It was so true what his pastor said in a sermon many years before. Your soul and spirit were like two dogs fighting. The dog that had been trained and fed the most was sure to win. James knew his spirit was losing day by day as he fed his emotional frenzy with thoughts of a prohibited affiliation with the one he was not married to. It was only a matter of time until his moral limits would be reached and surpassed.

~

Deanna found work as a place of escape from her present day traumas. Her ability to dive into her work made life a little more rewarding. At least she could help someone else's child do better if she couldn't help the one that she did not have. It was funny how life could continue around her without anyone truly knowing what she and James were undergoing. She had not felt comfortable enough to share the ends and outs of her daily routine with anyone she knew well. In fact, she found herself being quite embarrassed about the whole thing. It was like she would have to explain why she thought God was punishing her and leaving all those people who didn't even want children to suffer no consequences. She still had faith in God, but maybe having children her way was not God's plan. She felt like she was in a plastic bubble where everyone could see her, but no one, including her husband, could get close enough to her to understand her true feelings. She prepared her office for the appointment she had later that day with the Johnsons.

~

Mr. & Mrs. Johnson set a meeting date with her over two weeks ago to discuss her opinions about their son's possible need for Ritalin. Jefferson Johnson had been prescribed Ritalin to deal with the symptoms associated with his new diagnosis of Attention Deficit Hyperactivity Disorder. As much as Deanna believed and loved her profession, she did believe that too often children, especially boys, had been diagnosed way too early with a disorder that could have them labeled as learning disabled for many years to come. She knew all too well of children whose behavior had changed drastically with structure and the proper diet. She was also willing to skirt the thin line of her profession to offer parents alternate solutions to having to use medication.

She believed medicine should be the last resort. Her beliefs were confirmed daily as she looked at her own life and what had come of it. She had felt all along that fertility treatments were great for others, but she had not wanted to ever rely on them herself. And now here she sat with a bruised arm as a remnant of all the blood work she'd undergone. She remembered the bloated stomach and swollen breasts from all the medication. Wow, she had taken a plunge that she never thought she would take.

~

Mr. and Mrs. Johnson were an interesting couple on sight. Mrs. Johnson sat across from Deanna in a two-piece red business suit, looking polished and well groomed, while Mr. Johnson sat at least five inches shorter than his wife, obviously coming straight from a work site with cement-stained pants and scruffy hands that would not come clean even after an attempted wash with *Goop*™. The couple spoke well of their son and seemed to be on one accord. They reported that there were some steps that they could take in adding some more structure to their son's life, especially in the area of his diet. Jefferson had been born premature and as a result was a very picky eater. They found themselves catering to his diet, just so he would eat something. Of course, his foods of choice included red punch, chips, cookies and anything else that was not nutritious. Mr. Johnson spoke up, "You know Mrs. Carrington, we appreciate you sharing this information with us. We are all for trying to make some changes to Junior's diet and lifestyle." He scooted up in his seat as if he needed to take a closer look into Deanna's eyes. "You know we did not expect Junior to live. He was born so early and to have him be in fourth grade now, well we know it's a miracle. We thank God everyday for him. That just goes to show you, when God wants life to occur, it will."

The note Mr. Johnson played with his comment struck a chord in Deanna's heart. The strange thing was that she felt like Mr. Johnson's comments were orchestrated specifically for that moment, and the three of them met where destinies cross and hearts intermingle. Deanna's tears began to descend like a fine falling mist. "Mr. Johnson that is so true. I know you all are here to get my advice, but I have to say that you have blessed me tremendously with your presence. You reminded me so much of God's power and how He is working in my life even though I don't feel it. My husband and I have been trying to have a baby of our own for a while now and, well I just thank you for helping me." Deanna excused herself to the bathroom off from her office to adjust the makeup that had become flawed from her tears. When she returned she felt like she was in a fairy tale, but she couldn't quite figure out why.

Mrs. Johnson spoke up for the first time. Her voice was soft and soothing like a nice cup of warm herbal tea. "Mrs. Carrington, I know this may be a little off kilter with us being here in a school and all, but we wanted to know if you wouldn't mind us praying for you and your husband. We believe so much in the power of prayer and we want to be a blessing in your life. You know children are a heritage from the Lord and His rich reward."

Deanna did not let time seep in between Mrs. Johnson's comments and her response. "You sure can. I would be honored to have you pray for us." The trio joined hands and the hum of silence danced between them for a moment. Deanna heard the faint rhythms of Mr. and Mrs. Johnson beginning to pray silently to themselves in an unknown tongue. Even though she did not understand their voices, she could feel in her soul that they were petitioning their Savior on her behalf.

Mr. Johnson chimed up after only a few moments. "Lord, we just want you to know that we believe in you and trust in you. We thank you and we praise you for being a God who looks beyond our faults and sees our needs. Lord, we thank you that you are a God who is willing and able. We thank you for this couple who desires to know your blessings through having children, thank you that it is in your plan God for us to be fruitful and multiply. We are believing you to remove any hindrances that might be stopping your blessing of children, God and we pray that you would bless them in a special way, Lord. Cause everything in their bodies to line up Father for your glory. We pray Father for a son and a daughter for this family in Jesus' name, Amen."

Deanna was on cloud nine for the rest of her work day. She felt like her burdens had been lifted and her thoughts were unclouded. Her belief about conceiving without medical assistance was revitalized. That was the way she wanted it anyway.

Unfortunately, the pleasant emotions she had managed to carry with her all day long were being exchanged at the door of her home with a thick emotional air that almost knocked her off her feet. She walked right in on James who looked ready for battle. "Deanna, do you think you could pick up your clothes from off the bedroom floor, the bathroom floor and the floor of the den?" James felt his anger beginning to bellow over his head. The fumes from his mental anguish caused sweat beads to form along the cusp of his balding head. "It just does not make sense for someone who is supposed to be so in control to be the biggest pig I have ever seen! The kitchen is a mess, the living room is a pig sty and when was the last time you cleaned your car?"

Deanna had managed to remain quiet and focused on the wonderful experience that she thought she was coming home to share with her husband, as she listened to him go on about nothing. It was not until he got to the car thing, that she lost it. "Oh no you didn't Negro! I can't believe you are going to get at me about the car. First of all, I washed the car last week, it just so happens that the car happens to be a magnet for bird poop! Every time I wash it, the birds find their way to it! And anyway, taking care of my car has always been your responsibility. When is the last time you put gas in it? I guess that's my job now, huh?" Silence hung in the air for a brief moment as the opponents reloaded with ammunition. They had once been fighting on the same team, but now they were destroying their own foxhole with lies, deceit, anger, defiance and insurgence. James was not sure why he had gotten his wife started. He was no verbal match for her, but he was determined to continue what he started. He was bored and he could not stand another moment in that house with her without any verbal or physical contact.

"You know what? I thought that was the way the game was being played around here these days. I mean, you don't cook anymore and I guess now the laundry is my full-time job. I thought you could at least do something and fill your own car up. You drive it don't ya?"

The gloves were on and neither fighter was retreating. James nor Deanna was using the rope a dope technique where a fighter tries to tire the other out by taking his opponent's blows as they laid collectively on the ropes awaiting the perfect time to explode. No, not this time, both of them were coming out of their corners like Mike Tyson and Evander Holyfield. The sad thing was the fight had been started over nothing and would not end with a winner holding his gloved hands up high as the champion. No, fighting in marriage did not yield a winner. One may hold the champion belt for a while, but the challenger was always waiting in the wings trying to catch the defender off guard and win with a love TKO. Their fights these days were seamless. The prayer that the Johnsons had rendered for their family fortunately would linger in the heavenlies.

RHONDA C. WHITE

CHAPTER FIFTEEN

"It is easier to suppress the first desire than to satisfy all that follow"

Franklin

An uncomfortable silence filled the days that passed after James and Deanna's fight. This made it much easier for James to escape to thoughts of Angie. He was in way too deep, but his need to feel complete and whole was stronger than his will to let go of his relationship with Angie. He was falling fast for her and if he did not let go of the emotional rope that she had around his neck, he was going to find himself lynched in more ways than one. It wasn't that he even cared that much for her. He allowed their relationship to develop again this time as a way of escape from his failure to become a father; from the disappointment he saw in his wife everyday. He needed to see confidence in the eyes of a woman who cared about him. He needed someone to see that he was a success, that he was all the man the world and the devil were telling him he wasn't.

~

"Angie I'll give you a ring later . . . peace." He ended his phone call with Angie prematurely. He was on his way home and he had to prepare his mind for the night that he would spend with his wife and with the members of their church. He truly did not want to go to the Married Couples Formal Affair, but his lack of attendance would prove to be more of an alarm that something was wrong than his going and being phony in front of the crowd once again.

~

Deanna finished her daily devotional reading from Proverbs chapter six sitting on the oversized beige leather couch in the den. She only had a few more moments before it would be time to get ready for their evening. *"But a man who commits adultery lacks judgment; whoever does so destroys himself. Blows and disgrace are his lot, and his shame will never be wiped away."* As Deanna closed her brown and gold African engraved Bible, the words she read resonated. She could see on her mental blackboard in bold print and all capitals the letters, **C-O-M-M-I-T-S A-D-U-L-T-E-R-Y L-A-C-K-S J-U-D-G-E-M-E-N-T.** She thought only for a moment and then used an eraser to remove the thoughts from her mind. At the same time, she heard the garage door opening. Its all too familiar hum announced the return of her husband. She hurried and put on the emotional mask that she would wear for the rest of the evening. She and James had been at a non-stop masquerade ball for the last few months and tonight in front of their many friends, it would be no different. Despite the subterfuge that she was ready to display, she was looking forward to seeing the Alexanders. They had not spent any genuine time with them since their trip. She was eager to share with someone what they had been dealing with regarding infertility. If any couple would understand, she felt like Cara and Rodney would.

Deanna began her regular routine of laying out their clothes for the evening. His black Armani tuxedo and light peach shirt would be a perfect match for her Vera Wang creamy orange blossom ruched tulle strapless dress. She was proud to be responsible for dressing him well. Not that he did not have taste of his own, but it was something about a female's eye for men's clothing and style. She often thought she should be the only woman included in the show *Queer Eye for the Straight Guy.* Many people came to her behind the scenes to give him compliments about how he dressed. She was responsible for his swagger, but she never let on to anyone about their secret. In their eyes, James was the man when it came to coordinating his attire.

After the clothing coordination was done she immersed herself in a long bath. She dried and lotioned herself and then began to apply her makeup. As she attempted to apply her false eyelashes for the third time, small clumps of glue formed into gray eraser shavings on her eyelids. She wiped and reapplied the spidery-like objects once again on her eyelid. In the still silence that the air made between the bathroom door and their bedroom, she overheard James trying his best to argue in a whispered tone. She nuzzled up against the door to hear a little better.

All she could make out was a hushed frustration and his last words. "Look we need to just chill for a while okay. This is just a little much for me right now, and you are cutting this too close. I told you not to call me anymore tonight!"

She waited to breathe. Her feelings raced to the bottom of her body and straight back up to the center of her forehead. She did not want to think the worse but, intuition flooded into her brain and its waters refused to recede. It felt like her heart skipped a few beats before time went on again. No, it could not be true, not again, not during this time in their lives. Not when so much of the success or failure of the fertility treatments depended on their emotional state and well-being. Not now, not at a time when all hell was already breaking loose. She did not want to believe that her husband had been inconsiderate enough to lay their very relationship on the line again. Her normal mode of operation would have been to go off and destroy the whole evening, but this time for some reason she found the strength not to accuse him of anything prematurely. Her heated emotions drained out of her like glue from a hot gun. She wanted to make sure she had all the facts straight before she ambushed James with her discovery. If her assumptions were correct, he was up to something wicked, something that would destroy their already sheared marriage. She hoped and prayed that he was not foolish enough to once again get hooked up with the same heifer who wreaked havoc on their marriage a few years ago. But before she could whisper the name in her spirit, she knew that Angie had resurfaced. She managed to affix a plastic smile on her face and she went on as if she had not heard her husband's incriminating comments.

~

The rented smoke gray stretch Chrysler 300M dashed toward Chicago Hilton and Towers. James made small talk with the driver in order to make the time pass away. Anything not to speak directly to his wife. She sat at peace with herself and her present circumstances. No need to worry just yet. It was strange for her to be so calm facing the ninth hour. She found solitude in the plans she was making to unveil the truth that was hiding behind her husband's lies. It all made so much sense. Clarity hit her on the top of the head like a ton of bricks. How could she not have suspected it? She had been so engrossed in her own mess that she failed to see what had been going on right before her very eyes. It was okay, though. After this event she was going to get to the bottom of this brewing pot of stew, but until then it was Showtime!

~

The evening was rich with excitement and laughter. Couples dancing and enjoying one another's company were everywhere. Six-foot ice sculptures, dimmed lights and the special effect fog that lingered along the floor made the room and the ambiance magical. The air was electric and everyone sparkled. They romped to the beats of the all-female jazz ensemble until most of the women had come out of their five-minute party shoes and were either barefoot or in the slippers they brought specifically for comfort after they stopped trying to be cute. It was funny that James and Deanna had managed to paint the illusion that all was well once again. How was it that no one could see through the lies that they had built around them? If anyone had looked closer, they would have been able to see that their dance was just one-step off beat, one stride behind the rest. On the other hand, maybe they all were just too off beat and too consumed in their own misfortune to notice.

While James pranced around throughout most of the evening trying to stay away from his wife, she sat with Cara and Rodney catching up on life. "So Kigeri is finally doing much better in school and we can take a break from having to stay right on top of every assignment and lesson he has to turn in. He has gained his own sense of responsibility." Cara sat back in her chair and turned toward the dance floor as the music changed from a fast upbeat number to a melodic slow song.

Deanna took advantage of her pause and chimed in. "Well, y'all I've been meaning to tell you that James and I are going through infertility treatments. We started three months ago with artificial insemination and they haven't gone so well as of yet. I really want to keep trying them, though." Deanna sighed as she waited for the response from her friends.

Rodney and Cara sat stonefaced for what seemed like an eternity. Rodney decided to be the brave one and share their united opinion. It was like they had rehearsed their collaborative tune long before they knew what the Carringtons had been up to. "Well De, how do you know with all that treatment stuff that it's even James' sperm they are using? I thought you all had decided to wait on God. I don't want to rain on your parade, but maybe it's not the right time for you all to have a baby. What if you are just trying to push the hand of God? Aren't you afraid that because of that treatment stuff that something might be wrong with the baby? I've heard of so many people having problems because of that stuff. I just don't know, it seems like that's a controversial thing isn't it? I mean, are they taking your eggs out or are they someone else's?" Rodney continued to shoot question after question out like a round of artillery. Deanna looked for relief in Cara's eyes, but found none. She couldn't believe that the two people who had been so supportive all along, now seemed to be telling her that it was not in the cards for her and James to have kids and that they should just hang up the towel. Deanna felt the sting of abandonment and the pain of the inability to share her emotions with the Alexanders all in one moment. The conversation ended without a final word. Another couple appeared at the table and started talking about Bid Whist. She realized that a door, if only for a moment, had been closed on her line of communication with the Alexanders and she had to be okay with it. She had too many other fish to fry. She smiled through the pain and let the rest of the night go on uneventful.

~

James immediately went to his office to escape from her and the evening. She figured he would squander most of the night away in front of the computer or the television. He had been spending many hours there before coming to bed on purpose to prevent having any encounters with his wife. If what she thought was about to jump off actually happened, he would have to come out of his "cave of an office" earlier than usual. She undressed, changed and went right to the cabinet where James kept the bills. It had always been strange to her that he kept the bills in a place away from the business office. She rarely looked at any of the bills, even though James had made sure that she knew exactly where everything important was. He took care of all of the bills and of all of their financial decisions. She preferred it that way. She found the Cingular Wireless bill at the bottom of the pile. A thin line of sweat formed above her lip. She knew already. She just needed proof to solve the mystery. As suspected, line after line of James' portion of the bill were calls to a cell phone in Dallas. She could never quite figure out why James insisted on being so blatant with his entanglement with her. Was he that cold or did he not think it through? She could easily look through the bills at any time. He had not tried to hide it or his dealings with Angie at all. She wanted to search for older bills to see when all the drama started again, but her soul was tired and her heart was fixed in a state of numbness. Moments drizzled by like rain gliding down a windowpane during a morning shower. But her shock turned to heat in a flash. She was seething with anger instantaneously. Thoughts of rage encapsulated her and thrust her forward like a bullet. If she allowed herself, she could pounce on James with the agility of a leopard. She wanted to punish him. To make him feel as bad as she hurt. How could he do this to her again? She quickly put out of her mind the Proverb that said that a wise woman builds her house up and an evil one tears her house down with her own hands. She was convinced his actions had torn down their house this time and she was going to be responsible for premeditating revenge. The emotional roller coaster ride began for her. Her nightmares had become a reality. She sat in the darkness and silence of the room while ghosts from her past whispered in her ear. Time had let go of its secret and the truth was ready to be told. She felt like she was bathing in an eternal darkness, her spirit blinded by the pain that was sure to come. Her soul had a way of pushing her into revealing corners without her permission, locking her into places she could not escape. Why did she have to pry so much? Every time she looked for something, she found it. Her anger melted into shame and the embarrassment she felt for herself and her marriage caused her to curl up in a ball on their bed. She allowed the weight of her blankets to soothe her bewildered soul.

—

The next morning and two more mornings after that, she found herself in the same place where she'd been since she had found the revealing bill. She was glad the evidence had been exposed over a long weekend and she was not expected to be at work until Tuesday. She could not have made it through one more day of facing someone with a lie written all over her face. Deep down inside she knew her true anger was really not at her husband. She wanted to understand how God could let her down again. Her cadaverous jowls were an indication of her sunken soul. She had not eaten in the past three days. It was amazing how the strains of life could drop off in days what the treadmill could not do thirty minutes a day. James had done his best to stay away from her. He knew something was up, but today he would have to answer for the mess he'd made. As she lay slowly returning from an unrestful night's sleep toward a coherent state, the whites of her eyes followed him intently as he paced to and fro. He walked quietly through their darkened bedroom getting dressed for the day. She hoped to bore a hole in his thinking cap so that she might understand what was really going on in his world.

Deanna cleared her throat and began her rehearsed speech. "James, I know. I know about Angie. I know about your call from her the other night. I know you all are dealing in some way with one another again. I've seen the phone bills and I know in my spirit. Do you have anything to say?" No sound emitted from the room except from the entrance of their cat Delilah who perched herself on the bench at the end of their bed. It was as if she wanted to be told the truth as well . . . .

CHAPTER SIXTEEN

"They can only set free men free . . .
And there is not need of that:
Free men set themselves free"

James Oppenheim

A single tear made its way down James' face as he sat on the bed and poised himself for what he thought would be a long, dreadful encounter. He could not be mad at anyone but himself and fate. His prepared lies for the moment at hand escaped him like runaway slaves. He knew that one day he would have to reveal what had his attention for the last few months and he had rehearsed his speech. But when he attempted to share the planned monologue, his words became an untrained dog off its leash. Deanna sat silently waiting for a response, some reprieve, some commentary that would make everything okay. Her silence was not helping him. He usually had time to escape mentally during her ranting and raving after she discovered or found him out. Not this time. Something was different and he could not tell if it was bad or good. As part of a stall tactic and a need for divine intervention, James grabbed Deanna's hand to pray. Deanna's eyes did not close. She kept them affixed on the space between his eyebrows. The space between his brows looked like a wide open street with no cars parked on it. She could almost see his thoughts racing back and forth on that street trying to find a place to turn off and escape. Despite the intrigue and pain that overwhelmed and twisted inside her like the red and white on a candy cane, she was determined not to get trapped in his plan. If this was a scheme to divert her line of questioning, she was not falling for it.

"Lord, we need you right now. We need your spirit and I need you to speak for me. I do not know what to say and I apologize to you. I am asking for your forgiveness and Deanna's forgiveness for trying to run away. Help me Lord to understand me . . . Help me . . . . Help me . . . James' voice trailed off into a sea of tears.

Deanna was not moved. She waited for the liquid show to end and she loosened her hand from his grip. Without an emotion escaping from her body, she replied to James' silent pleas. "Well James, why do you think you keep falling into the same trap with this woman? You've mentioned before the need to have female friends in your life, even before we were married."

His long pause was ended by a sigh and the clearing of his throat. "De, I just don't know. I just, well my brain has been fried lately. I've been so confused, so lost in my own world of uncertainty and puzzlement. I don't know why when I feel less than, or not where I should be in life that I turn to the easiest thing I know." James seemed to transcend into his thoughts and was taken back into another place and time. His recollections fit through a small doorway that no one else could or dared to enter. He felt like he was riding a wave runner without a life jacket on a storm-possessed sea.

"James, what is it that happened to you that makes you feel like you have to run to Angie to make you feel better? It has got to be something and if you aren't sleeping with her then what's the big deal?" Deanna threw her last comment in on the sly to see if she could calm her curiosity and anger. She held onto both emotions which were mixed up and twisted around in her like a rubber band ball.

"I don't know how to make you understand. I wanted to have sex with Angie and then I didn't, but it's not even about that, it really isn't. I think I just wanted to talk to a female who was not demanding something from me." James' word struck a nerve in Deanna's heart, but she dared not say anything while he was on a roll. "I guess I didn't mean that like it sounded. When Angie and I talk, it's not about what I'm not doing right; it's not about my failures. It's not even about me. It ends up being shallow conversations between her and this made up guy who I have inside of me. One who tries to hide all the pain, hurt and confusion that's inside. She doesn't even know about any of the infertility stuff we're dealing with. I guess I was too ashamed to share that with her, nor did I want her or anybody else to know that I might be the reason why we are childless. Really and truly she has this false impression of me and who I really am. I guess I do too, for that matter. I have never let her see the real me. And as weird or retarded as that sounds, in some ways I guess it builds my confidence or for a moment lets me be who I have always wanted to be . . . fearless."

While James' words were having some effect on her anger, Deanna still could not understand what the hidden ghosts were. It was as if she had always seen her husband through Plexiglas®. She could see him clearly so she thought, but her ability to touch, feel and taste his emotions remained unattainable. Every time she reached out to grab him, to really understand him, she hit her hand on a transparent emotional wall.

James interrupted her thoughts with a confession. "To be honest De, I realize now things were going a little too far with Angie. Before, I thought I could handle it, especially since she didn't even live here. We would talk, trip out and that would be about the end of it. But this time she made her mission quite clear and she was determined to get me to go farther than I wanted to go. She let me know that she was at my disposal no matter how far we lived from one another. I guess that's the tricky thing about the enemy, especially with men. He will have you believing that you are so under control and that you can do anything; that you will be strong enough and wise enough to stop your devilish games before you get in too deep. But all the while you are getting sucker punched in the head with silent, deadly blows."

Deanna did everything in her power to calm her nerves, which were spurting off in her like fireworks on the fourth of July. If she was going to get anywhere inside his brain, she had to remain calm. She knew the quickest way to get him to shut up would be to make him think she didn't understand. She unloaded her response in her mind before formulating it into words. She let her emotional tides roll in and out once more before she spoke. "Then James, don't you see that it was just a matter of time before you fell? If she was determined this time, why do you think you were going to be strong enough to withstand? The strongest-willed man in the world has trouble withstanding a determined woman. Especially if she makes a placemat out of her body and gives him the opportunity to dine on it whenever he feels like it."

James sat in silence letting Deanna's words marinate in his psyche. He knew she was right. "I guess I look for comfort in fake and unhealthy relationships because for some warped reason they make me feel whole. For only a moment, they make me feel fearless again. Every time I run, it's because I am scared or confused. I hate that part of me." James rung his hands together for the eighth time since he sat down. The resulting pain in his hands in some way was providing him comfort. "I know you probably don't understand all this or even have reason to believe me, but I guess when I should turn to you for reassurance, I turn the opposite way. I don't know if I have set up in my mind that I can't trust the women in my life who I truly love because of . . . because of . . ."

Because of what? Deanna wanted to shout! What was it that was damaging their marriage possibly beyond repair? What demon, what stronghold had her husband so bound that he was willing to threaten the very fabric of their marriage for it? Up until then she had always had a way of making her dreams come true. She had lived her life always setting up a second option. If God did not show up the way she thought He should, her plan B was ready to be put into effect. But what plan could she come up with now when she did not even know what or who the problem was. She was a problem solver and she was not in control when problems around her were left untouched and unresolved. She silently laughed at herself as she realized the fullness of her "control freak" attitude. She was one of the ones who tried to half clean her home before the housekeeper came, just so she could place her stamp of ownership on the new order and tidiness. And now, here in the midst of James' problem she was going to try to fight the invisible.

James stood and focused his attention on his neighbor's children playing in the yard. The crisp fall air made smoke-like trains transcend from their mouths as they laughed and played in the burnt orange and chimney red falling leaves. The fall of those leaves took him right back to the fall of his heart, to the spot where all the pain began. He stood straight and erect attempting to face the unveiling that was coming at him head on like a man. The collision was inevitable and unavoidable. It was amazing how, just one picture, one word, could dislodge a memory that had been jammed tightly and trapped in between the doors of one's mind. Those scenes from years gone past laid dormant in the thicket and in the alleys of his brain, in a place that he had sworn to himself he would not venture into again. He had vowed on his own life that nothing that terrible and unthinkable would ever happen again to him or to anyone he cared for. The thoughts from that past came seeping out of the attic of his mind, rushing forward like an electric current. They made cuts in his emotions as their jagged edges hit and bumped up against the walls of his brain. It was all so clear, so vivid, like it was yesterday. How long had he allowed it to go on? How long had he suppressed the awkward emotions that entangled and confused him as a young boy? Had he enjoyed the forbidden and been embarrassed by the betrayal of his body? His body had let him down. He had succumbed to what he knew in his heart was wrong, but yet he could not stop the flow of the scenario. Pain rushed forth and his emotions went numb. He had buried his guilt and shame for years and it was not until then that he realized he truly could not have been responsible for what happened to him. He was the child. He was the one who had his innocence snatched away at the hands of someone else's pleasure. He saw his god sister's face, then he saw what she had insisted on him doing, over and over again until she did not want it or him anymore. In an instant he remembered all the lies she told in order to keep him captive to her. She had been successful in making him believe that what she made them do together was okay. She was years older, so she had to know, right? It was like someone was using a jack knife to pry open his thoughts, and no matter how hard he tried he could not stuff them back from whence they came. They ballooned all over his mind and stopping them would have been like trying to stuff a down feather-filled comforter back in the bag it was originally purchased in. His attempts were unsuccessful and futile. James awoke from the misery of his thoughts with his wife holding his hands and wiping his tears. He realized that he must have been processing his pain verbally and Deanna had been right there. The one he kept running from, the one who truly had his best interest at heart. She was right there when he needed her most.

~

For the first time since they had discussed anything about James and Angie, Deanna saw her husband without his blinders on; the blinders he had worn for the world and for her. He had placed a smoke-colored windshield over his life with good reason. How could he face his family back then? He was supposed to be the man of the family. His father had been absent from his life as a young child. He couldn't disappoint his mom, little brother and sister. In his eyes, he could not show them the weak spots in the fence around his heart that the abuse caused. He had been misused by a close family friend. Someone whom he trusted and looked up to. And someone he would never be able to confront or question. His god sister, his perpetrator died on her nineteenth birthday in a tragic car accident. A piece of James died that same day. He admired and looked up to his god sister and for her to violate him and forsake his trust, delivered a devastating blow from which James had not returned from some thirty years later. And for her to die without having to admit her guilt made the pain all the worse. Who knows what evils had betrayed her and caused her to forsake her innocence so early in life? There were very few, if any, sexual perpetrators who had not been violated themselves in some form or fashion. Had she ever confronted her assailants? The vile web that was weaved with the silence, the lies and the deceit of molestation and abuse, entangled the hearts of many and ensured that each victim was probably only divided by six degrees of separation. If the victims did not know each other personally, they did know one another emotionally.

RHONDA C. WHITE

"James, it sounds like you have never shared this with anyone. How do you feel now?" Deanna said.

"I feel like I am waiting to be reborn. I feel confused and this is weird but I feel sort of empty. That space in me was filled for a long time. I don't know what to feel or think. I guess I just need time to figure this all out."

Deanna's job training fought her like a pit bull to voice her opinion about him going to see someone regarding the ordeal or even share it with his family. As mean as the fight was, she knew that her advice would be pointless, so she stood her ground and did not say a word about it. She was learning slowly but surely to not only be a good listener, but be one that could identify when others were looking for an answer from her. She heard her inner voice . . . "Be still and know that I am God." Deanna finally moved away from the bed to strip herself of her three-day old mourning clothes. Yes, she had been hurt and yes, she still felt betrayed, but for once she understood James, she really understood him.

~

The rest of the day went on as if it had not been bothered by the morning's events. Life went on as usual, unaffected and uninterrupted. The El train announced its arrival and interrupted James' thoughts and scattered his ideas. Its rumble along the tracks behind his office caused his imagination to jumble into pint-sized detonations, throwing him into more confusion than he had been in on his own. His source of pain had been revealed, but now what was he supposed to do with it? Where was he supposed to put it now? How was he supposed to integrate back into the world with his sore thumb exposed? He had become a champ of making excuses and telling untruths to protect himself. Could he get help? Did he even want it?

CHAPTER SEVENTEEN

"He gives strength to the weary and increases the power of the weak."

Isaiah 40:29

What seemed like months rolled by before she and James had some semblance of peace. Deanna for the first time felt truly trapped in the covenant she made with God regarding her marriage. She had promised on their wedding day that she would be there for James, to help propel him into being all that God wanted him to be. She had not realized at the time the size of the price tag on that item. She questioned if she was a big enough girl to pay for it now. James had insisted on he and Deanna having a phone conversation with Angie. James tactfully explained to Angie that he had been wrong once again and that their relationship could not be. He apologized again for dragging her into his drama. Angie played the macho bad girl role and dismissed their association as if it had not been important. Deanna could hear the pain behind the sassiness, but she could not feel sorry for someone who insisted on hunting down a married man. Her full anger had been directed at James. He was the one married, but nevertheless, she could not totally let go of the string of resentment she held for Angie. If she had done what she wanted to do she would have tied the two of them together, tarred and feathered them and punched them in their faces until the night turned into day; until she felt her emotional revenge subside. No, but now she was supposed to be responsible. She was supposed to be so spiritual! She supposedly had grown from the girl she was in college. The one who would have gone through with her initial plans without a second thought about the repercussions. The one who had slashed her boyfriend's tires and broke his side view mirror when she found out he was cheating on her.

The funny thing about that whole scenario was that she was the other woman too. The guy had professed his love to his baby's momma who lived in Tennessee. However, since that woman was not there, she was pulling first lady rank. Wow, had times changed for her. Instead, now she sought comfort in the Holy Spirit and ran into the arms of her God fearing, prayer warrior friend, Carleen. Almost daily, she thought about what could have happened if she had not exposed James' lies about Angie. Would he have truly gone too far this time and slept with her? Had he really done it this time and covered up the act like a professional? Her full trust in him died the day she accepted what he'd done. Yes, she loved him, but love and trust were two different things. James had to be willing this time to rebuild the loyalty in their marriage brick by brick. He would have to add the mortar as often as need be, to help her to even consider trusting him again. She knew that God was able, but she had roped off certain boundaries in her heart and she refused to let James undo those ropes this time without struggle. Ultimately, she knew that her marriage would take a blow for the shallow assurance that it would be rebuilt on, but she was not willing to take a chance with her heart any longer. Carleen had shared with her the need to forgive all the way, if she truly was going to stay a part of the marriage. She wanted Deanna to understand that if she did not forgive all the way, all the way back to the way she felt about James when they stood at the altar, then she would never be able to move forward and grow. As long as she held onto a little bit of the pain, even one ounce, she would continue to make him repay for what he did. If she was going to move forward, she had to take her finger off the rewind button and quit looking at what he did on the fifty-inch screen in her mind. She had to move forward and judge his character "post insult." James was working overtime to prove he was sorry and that he did want better for them. As much as Deanna wanted to, as much as she needed to let go, she could not. Her lack of commitment to him had become a safety valve that she refused to open.

It was Deanna this time who refused to go to any counseling. As hard as James tried, she would not budge. She felt much like her friend Theresa did right before she put Steven out. Why should they continue to go to counseling and hear the truth over and over again and then do nothing with it? How many more times could they sit in front of church folk and lie? She'd decided that she was not going anywhere, that she was not leaving her marriage but she did not need anybody telling her that not leaving, wasn't enough.

Maybe if she focused her energy on something else it would give her heart time to mend. Maybe she would start a new project. Heck, maybe she'd write a book. Who knew? She had to do something to extinguish the pain. She had to push the anguish she felt about her marriage into some closet. A closet that she could hang her grief in and go to at her leisure. At those times when she wanted to have a private pity party James was doing everything but bending over backwards to prove his love to her, but Deanna was not impressed.

As the chirp of the telephone interrupted the silence of her morning, she realized that even though life was the one who asked her to dance, other people did not mind if they cut in and became his partner without her permission. They always seemed to put their insignificant details before her comfort. Yes, it was nine o'clock on Saturday, a truly legitimate time to call someone, but she just didn't want to be bothered. She concluded that consideration for an individual's private time had flown out of the window and that this was just another somebody either trying to take from or help her add to the chaos of her world. "Mrs. Carrington? This is Diane with American Airlines Travel Tours. I was calling today to confirm your trip for two to Galveston Island for the twenty-fourth of this month. Deanna sat up in the bed slightly bewildered and astonished. "I am sorry I'm not aware of any trip on the twenty-fourth. Are you sure you have the right Carringtons?"

"Yes ma'am, a Mr. James Carrington made reservations for four days and three nights to Galveston, Texas, leaving from O'Hare Airport on the twenty-fourth at 7:18 pm returning on the twenty-eighth. I can give you the hotel confirmation number if you like." Deanna thought for a moment. Was James trying to plan a trip for them as a make-up gift? She had always wanted to visit the tiny island off the border of Texas. "You will be staying at the Normandy Inn Bed and Breakfast." Deanna quickly jotted down the information that the young lady repeated twice. She, of course, was not sleepy any longer. No, she was not moved by her husband's generosity, but he was trying. She thought selfishly for a moment. Shoot! She deserved, no, she earned this trip! She knew a lot of sisters who would have been gone by now but no, she was standing. She, for whatever reason, was staying. She was a survivor. She could not help but think though in the same breath that she would be going to the same state that bore the home of her adversary. Angie lived in Dallas and true, Galveston was closer to Houston; nonetheless, she was not impressed that James had so conveniently planned a trip to her home state. Yeah, she did want to go to Galveston, but being in the same state with Angie put a bitter taste in her mouth.

Deanna eased out of bed and slipped into the office where she knew she would find James. "So James what's up with this trip to Galveston? What, you weren't going to tell me about it? Or was it for you and someone else?" Deanna was excited inside, but she did not want James to see her emotion. She wanted him to see a hard tough exterior, a Teflon® coating that no deception or lie of his could penetrate. She was not interested in pushing him completely away, but she did not see anything wrong with making life just a little bit rougher for him.

James' unpredictable eyes darted from the computer screen where he was working to Deanna's silhouette. She was even more beautiful when she was angry, or at least trying to be. He knew she was mad but, that she really did love him too. And even through all his mess, he could count on her to still want their marriage to make it. He just hoped he hadn't gone too far this time. But at least he did understand himself a little better. He had taken her as a casualty of war in the battle against himself. He hoped that the waving of his surrender flag would be enough to heal her wounds. "No De, I'm not trying to take anyone else anywhere. I can't believe they called and talked to you. I specifically told them I was trying to surprise you. Well, I know it's short notice, but are you down with traveling with me for a few days?" James' face displayed a crooked boyish grin; the one that Deanna had never been able to refuse. James stood and his commanding figure hovered over Deanna. For a moment, she was taken back by the essence of his body. No, she was not going to get caught up just yet, but she did decide at that moment that there was no way she was going to miss out on this trip. She could put on her mask one more day. She could fake it for the sake of fun. The cologne he had worn the day before lingered in her nostrils. He had that strange ability to hold aromas on him longer than the manufacturers anticipated. The sweet smell intoxicated her but before she was taken completely in, the reality of her marital situation brought her sharply back to earth.

~

The plane ride was uneventful. They landed twenty minutes earlier than their expected arrival time. It was amazing to Deanna that pilots seemed to have the crafty ability to make up time in the sky. They left O'Hare forty minutes later than they should have because of some back up with the air traffic controllers. The mystery of flying never ceased to amaze her.

Their room at the bed and breakfast was breathtaking. The bay windows provided a picturesque view of the crystal clear blue waters and the rugged coastlines that had been carved out by the hands of the ocean. The weather was perfect, not too hot, not too breezy, with hardly any humidity. The trip was perfect for those who were madly in love or ones attempting to rekindle the fire that was burning only dimly in their lives. Yeah, old James knew what to do. He prided himself on being a playa back in the day. A man who could woo his female exploits with his charm and knack for developing creative and exciting outings. Since they had been married his creativity had died. The challenge was over. He had gotten his prize when she said "I do." But now he knew he needed to start all over again if he thought Deanna would ever truly come back to him. He pulled out all of the stops during their mini vacation. They visited Schlitterbahn Water Park during the day and played all evening at Club twenty-one. They enjoyed the best seafood either of them had ever tasted at Palms M&M restaurant. James had the maitre'd seat them in a quiet private dining area where a harpist serenaded them throughout the evening. Dessert came before they could order. "Hey, I didn't order any dessert." Deanna exclaimed. "I couldn't eat another bite. I feel like I'm about to explode right now."

"Madam, I believe it would be in your best interest to check out this dessert that was chosen especially for you." The long, slender, Italian waiter's eyes glistened as he stood waiting for her to remove the silver dome that covered her treat.

"Okay, if you say so." Deanna's eyes immediately filled with tears when she noticed that the dessert was none other than an aqua box with a white bow affixed around it. The black letters on top read "Tiffany & Co." She looked up at James to find his lips fixed in a broad smile. She silently opened the box, trying her best to keep her composure. The silver 18-inch chain with the large diamond-filled circle sparkled even in the dim light. Her eyes brightened and she sat fascinated at the lengths James had gone to this time. He had pre-ordered their meals and as always had chosen exactly what she would have ordered on her own. She reached across the table to lightly caress James' chin with her fingertips. He did know how to throw the mama jamma on a girl. *Keep it together Deanna. Don't let go, this whole deal is nice, but you've got to stay cool* she thought.

They walked barefoot in the moonlight on East Beach and danced at the end of the pier to the sounds of the jazz band that was performing. Deanna had dreamed this very moment sometime before in life. She was in another world. And as much as she wanted to hold onto her pain like a security blanket, tonight she could not. They ended their last evening there with a horse carriage ride through historic downtown neighborhoods of Galveston.

Yeah, she could retire and live the rest of her life right there. They returned to the bed and breakfast and James had somehow gotten the maids to prepare and drape their room with loose yellow and orange rose petals. The petals covered the floor, the bed and the waters in the large Jacuzzi tub. The flowers blanketed the room like a soft multi-colored quilt. The soft music of Dave Koz played in the background. A massage table had been delivered along with special oils and fragrances. It sat in the middle of the room tempting her to mount it. James had thought of everything. Their matching robe and evening wear lay across the king-size bed as if someone had just slipped out of them. The red and gray satin looked inviting, sultry and cozy. The mood was perfect. The night was theirs. Deanna had managed to keep herself from her husband throughout the whole trip, but tonight, she felt like he had earned it. She could not take it anymore. She was his for the taking and she hoped that her mind would not get in the way of the pleasure that she knew they both wanted to give to each other.

After their flesh pleased one another the first time, their bed became their cruise ship and took them to places with lilies in the field and continuous sunshine. Her legs remained pretzeled around his waist and there she was able to monitor his respirations by the constant billowing of his stomach. The trip had been flawless. It made Deanna all the more confused. She was stuck between anger and love. Her nose was open again, but this time it hurt, it truly hurt to be under a spell of someone who you weren't sure was going to hurt you again. They returned home and back to their lives, as if nothing had gone on.

She could not think straight and things in her life, especially in her marriage were totally confusing. She did not know if she wanted to put back together their serrated lives. Maybe a baby might make things right. Maybe she had been going about the whole thing the wrong way. She was tired of riding on the interstate of her life, not being able to exit. It was like her pursuit of being a mother was a life science project that she had tweaked and redesigned repeatedly, never accomplishing the goal of winning the first place prize. She had to ask herself what she truly wanted in life. Was her goal to parent a child or to obtain genetic continuity through bearing her own child? The lines had never been so unclear before. She did not look at adoption as she once did. It was no longer a road of defeat, but now a possible path to fulfilling what she hoped was her destiny. She and James were slowly patching things up, or least seeming too. That was her answer. She would pursue adoption. She hoped James was game enough to jump in the adoption car and take the ride with her. She did not know what to expect from him, but he had been so agreeable to everything she wanted since the discovery she had made. Surely her pleas for a try at adoption would go over just as well. Yes, she would stretch out her hand of faith again and seek a partnership with her husband about adoption. Her mind was made up and she was ready to pursue a new goal, one that she hoped would fully mend them back together again. Even though she had that quiet before the storm feeling, she knew that God was still in control despite her wavering faith regarding what was coming up next in her life.

CHAPTER EIGHTEEN

"Men are wise in proportion, not to their experience,
but to their capacity for experience."

George Bernard Shaw

After the trip, Deanna and James made it a point to share breakfast time together to reflect on their marriage in attempts to keep the peace flowing. Prior to their trip, they could not remember the last time they had actually sat down to eat with one another. That particular morning, scrambled eggs, hash browns, fried green tomatoes, shrimp and grits and wheat toast sat in between them. The steam from the piping hot food rose up in the middle of the table as Deanna's thoughts rose in her head about what she needed to say next. Finally, she got up the nerve to share her heart with James. "Honey, I'm tired of feeling like my life is sitting in a stalled car, just waiting for someone to come along to give me a jump. I mean, we are either in this together or we aren't." James sat waiting patiently for an explanation about what she had just delved into. Deanna was a master at sharing half of her thought with someone, expecting the person to whom she was talking to automatically understand where her mind had already been. Taking his silence as a clue that she needed to go forward, she proceeded. "I guess what I'm trying to say is this: the fertility treatments did not work and I, or I mean we still want to have a child, right?" James sat still and assumed that she had issued a rhetorical question. She went on. "Well I was just wondering if you would consider pursuing adoption? I mean, I know it wasn't what we planned, but we have always talked about it and I don't see any reason why we shouldn't go forward with it now."

James perked up after his wife finished her soapbox statement. Even though he did not feel that he had the right to even ask what was on her mind, he went forward with his question. "De have you prayed about this?"

That was all she needed to hear. That was his staple statement, one he used primarily when he did not want her to do something and he knew the Holy Spirit was the only one who could redirect her path. "Well, James I can't say that God didn't say don't go forward with it. He has not said one way or the other if we should. So I believe that we are to move forward with it until He shuts the door." Deanna knew that she had not totally committed her works to the Lord, but she prayed and hoped that this time He would bless her situation without her full faith attached to it.

After a long silence, James responded. "You know what, I don't know if I am one hundred percent sure that I'm with this, but if this is what you really want to do I guess, or rather I know I'm in."

She left his comments to linger in the air alone. She did not want to have to explain or deal any further with questions she could not answer. The next time she was at work she would find out all the necessary information and begin pursuing obtaining their child through adoption.

~

As she left for work her excitement ran two paces ahead of her. She was on pins and needles about contacting the agency that her co-worker had gone through to adopt both of her sons. She had to do something with the ball of energy that was being volleyed back and forth in her stomach. She picked up the receiver of her work phone and dialed Theresa's number. T had been so distant from her since she'd left and moved from her home. Deanna had only seen her godchildren once in the last few months and that was at church. Most of her phone calls were not taken and T would only respond to them on her cell phone's voice mail in the wee hours of the night when she knew Deanna was asleep. Despite the space between them, she knew that T would be excited for her and she wanted to share what her next moves were with someone who cared. She called T at work and blocked her number, hoping to catch her on the sly. It was an unsuccessful attempt. She had gotten excellent at leaving her messages. "Hey T, this is me. Just wanted to see how you and the kids were. I wish you would answer the phone sometimes. I really miss ya and I wanted to share with you that James and I have decided to adopt. I was kind of nervous about making the call to the agency and I thought we could talk for a moment. You know, so you could boost my confidence. But, well I guess you are busy. Give me a call when you get a chance. And quit making a sistah sweat you. I'm feeling like a nerdy guy standing on the wall at a club trying to get some time with a chick he knows is out of his league!"

Deanna couldn't help but laugh at herself. It hurt to be shunned by her friend, but it was not anything she was new to. It wasn't the first time it had happened and she was sure it wouldn't be the last. Heck, she was guilty of running from those who put a mirror up to her face and made her see her true reflection too. She held down the flash button and prepared to call the agency. Her fingers, however, had another plan. They dialed Cairo at work in Atlanta. Her boy would not let her down in the time of confusion.

"Chicken head what you doing calling this time of day?"

"Hey, how did you know it was me?"

"Now you know my job has moved up in the world, we do have something called caller ID. Just because you work at that broke down school in the slums don't mean everybody is rolling like that!"

"Shut up boy. You always got something to say!" She welcomed his banter. Anything to get her mind off making the call. "Well, I know you are at work, but I just wanted to get your advice on something right quick!"

"You know I always have time for my Chi-town queen."

Deanna stood and flipped the phone cord over between her fingers a couple of time before she began. "James and I are looking to adopt. We have finally decided to go forth with it and I guess I'm not scared, and well . . . , I'm about to call the agency and I'm just a little nervous."

"What are you nervous about kid? You know you and my boy are going to be perfect parents. Hell, if I could, I would go back in time and let you adopt me! Nah seriously though, you'll be straight. Any mom would love to have you all as parents for her kid. For real! So what you trippin about?"

She had neglected to share all the drama that she and James had been through in the last months. Since he really didn't know about any of that, he would think that it was okay to move forward. After all, their marriage looked spotless from the outside. She had done her best to hide it all from Cairo. She did not want to mess up his admiration for James by letting him know how deceptive he had been. Her friend and her parents could hold grudges towards James longer than she stayed mad at him. She'd learned that the hard way. That was why she did not share most of their trials with anyone. Why was she always protecting him? He certainly had not earned that right recently.

"I guess you are right." Deanna agreed. "I'm probably just scared because of all the horror stories you hear about regarding the whole process."

Cairo abruptly interrupted. He needed to take another call. "De hold on one moment." The pause gave her time to think about the decision she was going to make. Was her home a place that she would even want to bring a child into? Was it stable? Could their marriage survive another alteration? Well, she could not think about that now. She wanted to fulfill her dreams of becoming a mother and that is just what she was going to do. Cairo quietly slid back into their conversation, suspending her thoughts. "Yeah dude, I am with ya on the whole possibility of a failed adoption happening. You do hear about all these cases where the birth parents are ready to sign the surrender papers and then an inkling of doubt seeps in and changes the whole program. I know it's got to be tough to give up your child, but do you think that they ever consider the devastation that the adoptive couple feels?"

Deanna's spirit agreed with him wholeheartedly, but somewhere down deep inside she found compassion for a woman who struggled through nine months of life living in her, only to give that life up to someone who she was not sure had her baby's best interest at heart. It would have been tough for her too. "Cairo, my friend you are so right, but I guess I will have to put that part in God's hands. If He wants it to come to pass, so shall it be."

"Amen to that my sistah, now go make your phone call. A brother like me has to go make my money, make some more money!"

"You know you're a fool, right?" Deanna's giggles were enough to encourage her to do what she had set out to do.

~

The Carringtons made the long drive back from Downer's Grove after they attended an initial meeting at Hannah's Christian Services. Deanna gazed into the street intently as if she was staring into another world. She and James proceeded home in total silence. The street lights appeared consecutively like lighted orange candy canes all in a row. Their illumination exposed more than the pavement and the cracks it held. Her soul was being exposed. She was seeing for herself all the pain and frustration that her marriage and infertility woes were causing. She was excited about finally being proactive about fulfilling their dreams to be parents, but fear revolved in her mind like people on a Ferris wheel. The light snow caused the car that preceded them down the road to make two continuous lowercase Ls in the street. The headlights of the car behind them gave James what appeared to be an eye mask from the glare caused by the rearview mirror. They sat in silence, wondering what the other was thinking. James had his mind on whether he was making a mistake or not with following his wife, while Deanna thought about what their adopted daughter or son would look like.

~

A few weeks passed and Deanna and James attended all of the required pre-adoptive classes. They ranged from parenting 101 to how to handle the tough questions that all adoptive parents have to face like . . . "why didn't my biological parents keep me?" The classes had been intense and thought provoking. Much more went into adoption than they ever knew. After being fingerprinted they obtained the necessary information to proceed with the home study and their adoption license. Once their home was inspected and deemed a safe environment for a child they could apply for their adoption license. The process had made them somewhat anxious, but they had made it through and now they just needed to wait to be chosen by a family in need. The high Deanna was on the day they got notification of the approval for the home study and license made her feel like her body, soul and spirit connected with every molecule in nature. They were even more surprised when their match counselor called them only a week after they had submitted their portfolio that birth mothers searched through to determine who they would give their child to. A mother was interested in them. She and James had included pictures of themselves on their trips to Mexico, London and Brazil. She also had one of herself parasailing for the first time and James on his motorcycle. They had enjoyed going through the pictures together to determine which ones to submit. Somehow, their ability to reminisce eased the tension of what they were actually going through.

~

Before Deanna and James could digest what they had gotten into a teenager dropped into their agency and made a request to view some perspective African-American adoptive parents. Their minority status had been a blessing for a change. They had been the only family available for the young girl and her family to select from. The girl specifically requested a young heterosexual, African-American Christian couple. Deanna and James fit that bill to a tee. They were ready to roll. They would continue their meetings with the birth mom and prepare in two months to bring home the baby girl or boy that she delivered. The whole process had been simple, almost too simple. They had been childless for almost five years, and now in only a couple of months, they would be walking out of a hospital with their own child. Why had they not done this whole thing earlier? They got some more surprising information from their attorney, Monica Harris. They would even be able to receive a $10,000 tax write-off for the adoption. That eased their minds considerably since they did not have all types of liquid cash just sitting around to pay for the adoption. Wow, the process had been quick, efficient and effective.

Deanna was glad to be living in an era where life could be as easy as rose petals falling to the ground in a light wind. For the most part she was happy. There was only one void in her life and if you did not look closely, you would not see the absence. And now, that void was going to be filled with a child. Someone she could love completely, effortlessly and faultlessly.

~

In the sermon on Sunday, Reverend Marshall said something key as always and it seemed so applicable to their plight. "You have got to realize in the depths of your soul that your pain is profitable. In fact, God says, your pain is a gift from Him. Cherish your pain, no matter how much it hurts, look at it through His eyes. Your pain will prosper in due season and develop into the beautiful prize that He destined it to be. You must trust that your labor period will bring forth the gift of life all in perfect timing." What more needed to be said?

CHAPTER NINETEEN

"Hope deferred makes the heart sick, but a longing fulfilled is a tree of life"

Proverbs 13:12

Deanna rolled over in her king-size bed enjoying the feel of the brown polka dot 300-thread count sheets she purchased the week before. Simple pleasures were such a luxury these days. She imagined God covering her and comforting her like the linens she was wrapped in. If only life and facing this day could be so easy. It had come down to the wire now. The mother of her child to be was due to have a Caesarean today. The young girl's pelvis had been too narrow to even consider a vaginal birth. If only she could fast forward a few hours and know the hand that fate held for her. "Lord help me to recognize that my trials are really only relevant to my humanity. How I appear in heaven is where the true victory lies." She knew that she had not been the best Christian these days. God's love was real, but she had shied away from Him again because she was afraid that He was not going to give her what she wanted. All of her praying and fasting had come down to this very moment. It was sink or swim. Sure, they could start the process over again if this for some reason did not work out, but she just did not know if she had the strength to even pursue the process again. She was even more convinced that James would not be up for a second round. He had been supportive and externally vested, but she could tell that his heart wasn't truly in adopting a child. Maybe after he held the baby in his arms for the first time. Maybe then he would finally connect and know down on the inside that this child was his whether it came from his own chromosomes or if he paid for it. She wanted to be there for him emotionally, but she was having enough trouble staying afloat herself. It was crazy that Deanna thought she was big and bad enough to handle all the emotions that were tied to this process by herself. How could she even believe it was healthy for the child for her to go into being his mother without being whole herself?

Panic came over her like an evening shadow. What if the baby could sense her insecurities? What if he could smell her fear and instinctively know that she was not all she was trying to be on the outside. She knew from working with children for so long that they had a fifth sense about them and for whatever reason were able to see right through to the true character of an adult. She envisioned the baby eating her alive. What in the heck was she doing anyway! She was not ready. She was not prepared. No, she could not do this, not now. Not while she had a bundle of confusion sitting on the apex of her soul. But what choice did she have? She supposed she could always forfeit and back out of the adoption. She could turn away from her dreams of being a mother and accept failure. But was that her? Right or wrong, she had never been one to back down from a fight, even if it was against her own emotions. In her mind it was too late to turn back. She could not live with herself if she blew possibly the one and only opportunity she had to be a mother. No, she would not back down this time. She had gone too far to turn back. She was in the middle of the road and going back would have been a more agonizing journey than completing her mission. As much as she wished she was at a point with James where she could share her innermost thoughts with him, she could not. She felt something like cold steel between them. Yes, overall they were better but the freedom they once shared in their marriage disappeared into the timeless rhythms of everyday life. She just wanted to breathe normally again. She wanted her real life back. She did not want to live in this delusion filled with the ups and downs that she was experiencing. She hadn't had that dream anymore of getting rid of her baby, but the turmoil that kept running rampant in her head made her feel just as insane as she figured anyone would feel who would throw their baby away.

Wow, all this and she hadn't gotten out of bed yet. She was supposed to be excited right? She reached over to grab some comfort from her husband but instead her hand fell on a cold, uncomforting surface. James must have been up hours before her and silently slipped out of bed. He had gotten that task down to a science. There were many mornings that he got up to work out, read or just watch television and he had found it best to not disrupt his wife's rest if he did not want to deal with crabby abbey the full day. It was so funny that she was the king of the night and he was the master of the morning. It was a wonder that they ever met up in the middle. She considered the next best thing to snuggling up next to her husband for a few moments. Yes, a bath would have to do.

Deanna let the bubbles flip flop on top of the water as she filled it for the second time with warm water. She had fallen in love with bubble baths. They were able to keep her wrapped in a robe of suds for hours. The warm water enveloped her skin and moistened it on the outside, then beneath on the layers that nobody could see. She wished she could immerse her brain in a bath and wash it of its loose particles and debris. As good as the bath in the rolling waters felt, she could not shake the unsettling nervousness that set up camp in the pit of her belly. Prayer was the only thing that could numb the burn that her emotional reflux was causing. Even though she had been trying to handle all of it on her own, her Father was still only a prayer away and she reached out for His comfort.

~

She and James received instructions from their match counselor to wait by the phone for a call from her to alert them of when to go to the hospital. Deanna was elated that the girl and her family had decided to let them be ready to go in to see the baby immediately after its birth. Every time the phone rang, both Carringtons got giddy in the stomach. The butterflies that soared in between them felt more like bats. False alarm after false alarm came in until they received a call about 3:30 pm that Tia had gone to the hospital to be prepped for the Caesarean. James and Deanna figured it would only be a few hours more before they got the call to come to the hospital. They busied themselves cleaning the house, playing board games and catching up on work they had each brought home. The purchased items for the baby sat quietly and neatly arranged in the room that had been prepared especially for the new addition. When two hours turned into four, they both got nervous. James' face was a shadow of agony. They both knew that either something had gone wrong with the birth or something had gone wrong with them becoming parents that day. They both unbeknownst to the other began to put on their emotional funeral garments. Their dream seemed to have nine lives, but unfortunately it had died again. They did not have the strength to revive it. Not this time. They sat together on the couch exactly two feet from one another. They took turns flipping the channel back and forth from the HGTV to TLC to the ESPN channels. TLC was knocked out of the rotation when they began to show a marathon of *The Baby Story*. By 10:30 pm the phone rang a bizarre and startling ring. Usually their voicemail picked up on the fourth ring, but this phone call seemed to penetrate the laws of the answering system and continued to ring several times until Deanna finally got up to answer it. The last ring had a long drag to it that seemed to scratch the back of Deanna's ears. The walls inhaled and the air in their home stood still. Even the creaks in the floorboards paused. Everything, including the furniture leaned in to hear a little better. She silenced her soul and took in a deep breath. She looked into James' eyes; her voice cracked and reverberated in at a much higher pitch than her normal tone. "Hello . . . ."

~

Life drained out of her just like the water had drained out of her tub earlier that day as she received the dreaded news from the match counselor. Had she heard correctly? Did she just say that the family had decided to keep her baby? The baby that was going to restore and revive her life and marriage. No, she didn't say that! She stood stiff as a board as she let the counselor's words resound inside her ears. She and her husband's heartbeats were the only sound in the room. They played an off beat, out of rhythm number, speeding up and slowing down at the same time. Their counselor made it clear that they should not go to the hospital. The family had a change of heart and would not be signing the surrender papers. Her conversation with Cairo shot back and forth in her head. No, this could not be happening. What was this all about? If they were not going to be able to have this child, why had things run so smoothly? She thought about the prayer she had always stood on. "Lord let your will be done, I am moving forward in this thing that I believe you have called me to do, but if it is not from you, I know in the ninth hour you are big enough to close the door." That prayer rang true in her ears right then, but she did not want to hear it. She wanted to turn the truth off. It was not comforting her at the moment. The gap that was sandwiched between her and James before the phone call closed. They sat entwined in each other's arms, crying, weeping, praying and sobbing. Their tears mixed together and created a river of salty pain.

The process had been bittersweet. As upset as Deanna was, if she was truly honest with herself, she knew that the adoption was going to fail from the very beginning. She could almost see it in the young girl's eyes. Tia was being forced to make a decision that she was not old enough or brave enough to make. It was a shame that a child so young had to make such a life altering decision anyway. Deanna could perceive the doubt and the question in Tia's eyes. Those dark liquid eyes, ones she would never forget. She was sure that the child that was supposed to be hers had those eyes. She would remember them for a lifetime. She did not even know if Tia had a boy or girl, but it didn't matter anyhow. She would see that child's face every time she looked into another baby's face. Every time she smelled a baby's sweet aroma and breath. She would see exactly what she lost and the pain she was trying to bury would resurface every time she was in an infant's presence. She had to think about the sacrifice that the birth parents were making in even thinking about giving up their child. She never wanted to say never, but she thought she never would have been able to fill the shoes of a mother who needed to give up her child. It seemed too hard. Her feelings were hurt. Her emotions were damaged, but deep down inside she understood. Even though she and James had gone to three match meetings with the young girl who was going to give them the gift of life; even though it seemed on the outside that their dream was going to finally come true, she could not be mad. She would have to experience the five stages of grief just like everybody else.

They had met the young girl at Gino's East for pizza and then once at the Loews movie theatre. That was when they decided to pay for her maternity costs. They wanted to take Tia and her baby into their custody. Her mother had almost put her out when she heard about Tia's unexpected pregnancy. She suffered through her mom wanting to press charges against the married man who had spoiled her daughter. The quixotic thing was that the young girl and the man truly had a relationship and wanted to be together. It seemed to be the grandmother all along who was interested in the adoption. Their match counselor had been hopeful, upbeat and thought that the adoption was quite possible. The counselor knew that she shouldn't bet on things like this, but she felt really good about this one. The counselor seemed more hurt than she and James were. It must have been a blow to her track record. She was new to the job. Unfortunately, she would have to suffer through many more times of failures and successes before she became a seasoned veteran in the field. But through it all, this time, it seemed that it just wasn't meant to be. Deanna went to bed that night hearing the song *Que Sera Sera* sung by Doris Day playing in the background of her mind.

CHAPTER TWENTY

"Happiness is a butterfly, which when pursued, is always beyond our grasp, but which, if you will sit down quietly, may alight upon you."

Nathaniel Hawthorne

Spring moved upon her like a thief in the night. Deanna's ups and downs were causing her life to sound like an old car with a faulty ignition. Each time she tried to jumpstart it, it turned over and over, never successfully completing its task. She was tired of losing, tired of failing, tired of smelling the sour air that her misery emitted. She couldn't hold onto the strength that she needed any longer. She had to get back to the only thing that would keep her above the waters of pain that wanted to take over her respirations and cause her to suffocate on life. She felt like a plastic bag had been placed over her face. Her response until then had been to take small breaths in hopes to maintain her air reserve. She was failing miserably as she jerked from denial straight into anger as if someone had driven her there in a stick shift. She was mad and she was mad as hell. Mad at herself for even starting the whole adoption process, mad at Tia and her family for getting them twisted in their wicked web of deceit and finally when she got truly naked with herself, she was mad at God once again. Huh! Her Christian walk was getting tougher and tougher for her to handle. She needed to throw out a life jacket. It was her only chance for emotional survival.

"Carleen, I just can't seem to take it anymore! This is too much! God said He wouldn't put more on us than we can bear, but I think He might have gotten me mixed up with the girl in the line before me!" Deanna sat back in the chair her grandmother had given her before she died. She circled the top of her steaming teacup with her index finger. She held the phone tightly in her other hand hoping the sweat from her palm did not cause the headset to slip. The steaming vapors from the cup seemed to open up the pores of her soul. She thought to herself, even if Carleen could say something to get her on track, she still did not know what she was going to do.

"Baby I know that it doesn't seem like it will end. I know you feel like you are at the end of your faith, but . . . . well . . . I don't want to sound like one of those prudish Christians who have all the right clichés to say at the right time but baby, what else do you have left, if you give up on your faith?"

Deanna did not let Carleen's words completely fall from her lips before she broke in. "That's just it Carleen, I know all of the right scriptures for a time such as this, but just knowing them is not doing me any good; and the faith to put them into action is nowhere to be found. I mean how could this happen? Failed fertility treatments and now a failed adoption attempt! Carleen, I could have strangled that girl's family when I was told that we could not see the baby, especially when we paid out heavily for the birth of the child! We thought surely it was a cruel joke, but after no one called back and we got a follow up call the next day from our counselor to tell us that Tia and her family were preparing to go home, I literally wanted to jump through the phone and shake her for setting me up for all this mess! She might as well have stabbed a hole straight through to my heart! She had the nerve to tell us about the counseling services they offered for failed adoptions for perspective parents. I wish I would. I would not be caught dead in that place. I know, I know already what you are going to say. It's not the counselor's fault, and yeah you're right, but I just want to blame somebody." Deanna gulped in a deep breath as her tears flowed. Carleen let her continue to vent her full anger. "I could not even stand up straight. I felt like someone had come along and sucked the air right out of my lungs. My heart seemed to crumble in pieces and drop inside my body straight to my feet. It was probably best that I did not see the family because I am sure I would have paired up with the devil and kicked all of them back into the hole they crawled out of! All of them, the fourteen year-old girl, her twenty-seven year-old man and the silly thirty-two year-old grandmamma! Imagine that . . . a grandmamma before I can even be somebody's momma!"

Deanna's pain turned to anger. She did not want to be calm. She was mad as hell and she wanted someone to pay for it!

"Deanna please try to keep your head on straight! Can you hang in there until I get there? And where is James? What does he have to say about all of this?"

"Carleen don't even go there! You know he wasn't completely down for this in the first place. We cried together and then just a few hours later, he acted as if what we had been told was something as trivial as the Bulls losing or something. This morning he walked out of here on his way to work as if nothing happened! Don't let me get started in on him. He is my last worry right now! I could care less how he's feeling. He put up that front after we had that big falling out and paid for that trip and all, but really all of that was just surface stuff. Stuff he did just to make sure I didn't get any ideas of leaving. He doesn't seem to want to be here for real and I'm tired of trying on my own. Maybe that's why God prevented us from getting that baby. He could see the mess that we were walking into and spared him the trouble."

Deanna was up pacing now. Her abrupt stance almost knocked her cup to the floor. She saved the spill and allowed seepage from the liquid to drip from her fingertips. She wanted to throw something, anything, but nothing truly would satisfy the burning pain in her head and in her heart. She did not want to talk to God and she definitely didn't want to talk to Carleen. "Carleen, I don't mean to be rude, but I gotta go. I'm sorry I called. I need some time to think!"

She was two seconds from dropping the phone onto its receiver when Carleen spoke. "No baby, I am not taking no for an answer. I'm already on the expressway and I will be getting off at your exit in a few moments. Don't run from me right now. I know it hurts and it is easy to just drown, but I can't let you. You may not want to talk and that's okay too, but I am coming even if it's just to listen to you say nothing." When the line went dead, Deanna realized her spirit felt the same way.

~

"*Holiness, holiness is what I long for; holiness is what I need . . .*" Carleen hummed the popular gospel song by Micah Stampley. She tightened her hold on Deanna as they lay in the middle of her king-size bed. Carleen had come and fixed another cup of tea for Deanna while she waded through all of her tears. Deanna cried until her eyes gave into exhaustion. She finally fell into a light sleep with Carleen holding her as tightly as her mother had when she

RHONDA C. WHITE

was a child. Carleen's spirit was comforted by the consistency of Deanna's light snore. This child, her spiritually adopted child needed to rest. She did not need another sermon or scripture. She just needed someone to care enough to be still with her. Carleen knew that Deanna's biological mother would come and take over in the morning. She only lived a few hours away. That was one thing that Deanna had, a wonderful support team. Anybody could make it with God on their side, but the people He put in place to help them make it were priceless. Deanna slept for three hours straight and Carleen did not budge. She knew Deanna needed to feel God's love in the form of physical arms. She watched the bedroom's fireplace flames sputter and flicker as the afternoon light seeped into the evening hours.

Deanna rustled. She opened her eyes and quickly closed them. It was as if she wanted to stay wrapped in her dreams versus facing the cold reality of her life. She managed to form a slight curl with her lips while her eyes remained closed. "Carleen thank you so much for being here. I know you have a lot to deal with of your own . . ."

"Deanna don't even go there with me. I don't want to hear it. Just hush about me okay?" Carleen said.

"Okay, but I do just want to say thank you. I think this is the first time I've rested for real since all of this adoption garbage started. Once I finally wrapped my soul's arms around it, I thought sure that this was how God was gonna bless us. But I guess He had other plans." Deanna pulled gently away from Carleen's arms and gave her body a much needed stretch. They both sat up in the bed and rested their backs on the down-filled king-size pillows.

"Deanna, when you are ready I need to share something with you, but only when you are ready, okay?"

Deanna knew what Carleen had to say was important. She just wanted to not think about anything right now. "Carleen right now I just want to eat something . . . . what is that I smell downstairs?" Deanna's mouth watered in anticipation of what she thought might be in store for her stomach.

"I had John's sister bring us dinner. Who knows what she has brewing down there, but I am with you, let's go!"

The food filled more than Deanna's belly. The meal had been satisfying to her soul as well. Comfort food had a way of doing that. As she filled up physically, her spirit man felt slightly nourished. She was tired of feeling like a Christian schizophrenic, but unfortunately, that was the best way to describe her emotions. She was up one minute and down the next. They cleared the dishes and Carleen took an incoming call for Deanna. James would be home soon. Even the thought of her husband burned the inside of her throat. How could someone she loved so much cause her so much pain? Although she really could not be shocked at his reaction to the demise. James had never handled rejection or disappointment well. His answer had always been to run, so why should she expect more now?

~

She guessed now was as good of a time as any to hear what Carleen had to say. She was sure she was not big enough to hear it, but she knew it would be good for her. "Carleen, you said you wanted to say something to me earlier. What's on your mind?"

Carleen cautiously looked into Deanna's intense eyes. She did not want to cause her to relapse into isolation this early. "Deanna, are you sure you want to talk now? Believe me I understand. It can wait."

Deanna stood and propped herself up against the dining room table. "No Carleen, it's cool. I know I lost it earlier and I am sorry. I guess I just had to get it out."

"Please don't apologize for that. Come sit here next to me." Carleen poised herself for what she needed to say and grabbed Deanna's hand. "God has told you many things during this journey. He told you first not to be afraid and that He would be with you. He also told you that you were blessed because you believed and that there would be a performance of those things told to you by the Lord. You never heard Him say that your blessing was not going to be through natural conception. Don't you think it is strange that you put off adoption until now? You could have done that long ago. Now adoption is not a bad thing, but guess what baby, when God wants you to know something He has always spoken directly to you either through your spirit, through someone or through His word. Every word in the Bible is just for you so when He says that He will make the barren woman the keeper of the house and the joyful mother of children, He meant that for you. When He said that He would love you and bless you and multiply you and the fruit of thy womb, He meant that for you. When He said that you would not be barren and not miscarry, He meant you. You have got to understand the depth of God's love for you, baby. You cannot waver on that fact. In every situation, you have to know no matter what, that His love for you is endless. It is easy to waver when you look directly at the circumstances, but when you look at them through Him, you see it through a completely different perspective. Stop reneging on your faith, baby! Remember Abraham in Romans: *And being not weak in faith, he considered his own body not dead when he was about an hundred years old, neither yet the deadness of Sarah's womb. He staggered not at the promise of God through unbelief; but was strong in faith, giving glory to God; and being fully persuaded that, what He had promised, He was able to also perform.*

Sometimes, God has to deal with women in a special way. See, our pride or self-worth, truly comes from us being able to birth something or bring forth life. That's what God created us for; to be the mothers of this earth. Some of us are solely mothers of children; others are mothers of invention and creativity. But every woman on this earth is not complete unless she has generated life in some form or fashion. Sometimes the best way God can humble us is to take away that ability. Look at all the women in the Bible who could conceive easily. Hagar taunted Sarah, Leah taunted Rachel, Peninnah taunted Hannah. We can become full of pride at times when we think we are solely responsible for bringing forth life. When we omit God from our plans, that's when things get messy. See, man cannot start or stop anything that God intends to happen. What God says will happen, will come to pass. So think about it, all along you have shared that pride was your downfall, your stronghold. God used your miscarriage, your unsuccessful infertility treatments and now this failed adoption to pull the humility out of you that you have been craving all along. Don't look at this as another setback, baby. God is still in control. I know it is hard to see, but He does have a plan for you and if He promised, He will supply. You have got to get yourself right with Him. You know one of my favorite teachers, Joyce Meyer's statement is, if you don't do what you can do, God won't do what you can't do." Carleen grabbed Deanna and tried to hug all the frustration, hopelessness and pain out of her. She believed that the Lord would contact with Deanna's soul and that He was going to heal her in due time. She had full confidence in His power and authority. She would lend her faith to her fallen comrade and trust God completely for the plans for her life. She had been there herself several times and she knew the internal struggle that she was fighting. She prayed over Deanna and anointed her head with oil. The oil was a balm in Gilead for Deanna. Carleen left shortly after James arrived. She figured even if they did not talk directly to one another that they needed to be alone. Before she left, she joined hands with both of them and they prayed collectively just like they did some months earlier.

Lying completely awake in her bed, staring at the ceiling, Deanna realized that her change of heart would be a choice that only she could make. Yes, she would pull herself up by her internal bootstraps. She would need all the strength she could fathom to make it through. She was willing and she knew God was able. She confessed her sins of unforgiveness, revenge and doubt. She accepted Christ's atonement for her faults. Her bed became her altar. She felt renewed and free for the first time in a while. She decided that she would have to stand on the backs of what she had coined "her great cloud of witnesses": Sarah, Rebecca, Hannah, Ruth, Harriet, Sojourner Truth, Mary McLeod Bethune, Mamie Till Mobley, Fannie Lou Hamer, Rosa Parks, Wilma Rudolph, Dorothy Height, Katherine Dunham, Gwendolyn Brooks, and others. Yes, she could do this. Life had been a crap game for her, but she refused to roll a seven without putting up a fight.

CHAPTER TWENTY-ONE

"And we know that in all things God works for the good of those who love
Him,
who have been called according to His purpose."

Romans 8:28

Deanna always found peace in running. Running during the fall season was the best. The air was crisp and hygienic and it invigorated her lungs. She hadn't felt that good in a long while. No great changes had occurred in her marriage, but she was feeling better about who she was in Christ. She felt like she had experienced more peaks and valleys in the last year than many had experienced in a lifetime.

She dressed in the same attire she had worn in high school during track seasons. It was amazing to her that she was still able to wear the black nylon tights with the stirrup heel-loops that she and her teammates had been issued their junior year when they won the Illinois Class A Track Championship. Her eyes sparkled with the memory of her yesterdays. Putting those tights on again on a regular basis was an instant reminder of a time when the important things in life had nothing to do with bills, conception, death or reality. It was a time of secret crushes, passing origami-shaped notes in the school's hallways to friends, going to track and basketball practice after going to detention, riding the 95th street bus to Evergreen Plaza to window shop, eating cheese and carmel popcorn from Garrett's after sneaking downtown on the El and standing in Senior Square to get the tidbits of the latest gossip that occurred between third and fourth periods. Man, youth was definitely wasted on the young!

She didn't consider herself a senior citizen, but she realized that she had taken her childhood and adolescence for granted. She thought of Stevie Wonder's song, "I wish those days would come back once more!" She remembered how she had created a wedding book for her home economics class. The book was created out of one of those extra large photo albums. It had a burgundy cover with gold trim around the edges. Their class assignment had been to plan their future wedding in full detail including the bridal party, reception, honeymoon and marital plans. Of course, unbeknownst to James at the time, she had created their wedding together so many years ago. Besides the church, the minister and the date, their actual wedding played out almost according to the high school assignment. Her bridesmaids even wore similar peach dresses like the ones she picked out so long ago. And who would have thought to have them wear short dresses? Only Deanna would attempt to pull off something rare and out of the norm.

Wow, the seasons of her life had flown by like the birds passing over her head as she ran. She was sure she had seen those same birds somewhere before flying over some other time in her life. Their constant presence over her head reminded her of God's consistency in her life despite its ups and downs. His promise was true and He had not left her even when she did not quite see or feel Him. Her chest rose and fell, forming the imprint of a loaf of fresh-baked bread through her warm-up top as she ran. The adrenaline rush she got from running could not be compared to anything else.

She was not sure why she had chosen to go down Kismet Avenue that day. She often changed her running route just for a scenic change as well as to distract anyone from becoming familiar with her pattern. Kismet had proven to be a picturesque street with manicured lawns and fall flower-accented landscapes. Flora oranges and burgundies darted out at her like lightening bolts. She was intoxicated by their faint aromas and awe—struck at the beauty they provided. The falling leaves floated like butterflies gently to the ground and were swept up in the tiny cyclones that the mild but brisk winds dispelled. She gave kudos to her distant neighbors for taking the time out to care for their property even as the fall ensued. Some people just did not seem to care anymore. She couldn't figure out if the world had gotten too busy or if it was that people did not care about nature, God's gift to the earth, anymore. Gardening had proven to be a tedious and laborsome hobby, but one that she could cherish and take pleasure in. Gardening taught her a valuable lesson: serenity was not found in a completed work, but found in the sanctuary of doing the work. It made her enjoy the process of everything she did versus rushing through to the end, only to begin to look for another project to complete.

Her thoughts tumbled together like clothes in a dryer, but she was at peace with herself and at one with God's workmanship. It was difficult to believe that she and James had been through so much in such a short time; possibly an affair, unsuccessful fertility treatments, a failed adoption, and now maybe a shattered marriage. Wow, life was rough, but she was quickly reminded that things could always be worse. There were people out there who were homeless, ill and had lost loved ones. Her problems did not amount to the tragedies that were being experienced in the world even at that very moment. Her iPod blasted in her ears a hodge podge of upbeat, fast-paced music ranging from contemporary gospel, old school rap to deep house. Busta Rhymes seemed to always pump her up during the middle of her run when he teamed up with A Tribe Called Quest to push out the *Scenario*. "Here we go yo, here we go yo, so what's so what's the scenario!" Deanna's pace quickened as she made her routine visual spin to check her surroundings. Her mother had cautioned her about running alone with her earpieces in, but she felt serene with her music and nature.

It was strange, if you surveyed people who had been through a misfortune they would almost always tell you that they smelled the aroma of danger right before it appeared. It was usually too close when they noticed to do anything about it but brace themselves for the worse. She smelled their scent of malevolence and vile before she noticed their images. One grabbed her from behind and the other threw her legs in the air and grabbed them like they were pick-up sticks. All she remembered about her location was that she had only made it half way up the block. She wrestled in the air without success. Her lower lip stung from the blow it had endured as a result of her attempts to free herself from their plan. The metal liquid taste that flowed into her mouth was that of her own blood. Somewhere in the distance she could hear Busta Rhymes ending the *Scenario*. Her ears ached as she was reminded of how cruelly her iPod had been ripped out of her ears when she was thrown to the ground. Her hands clenched the intruder's shirt as he hovered over her. Her grip was so tight that her fingers vowed to remember their position long after she unclenched them. She had hoped to use them as jackhammers, to bore holes through his back into his soul. She wanted both of her perpetrators to remember what they had ripped from her long after the thrill of demoralizing her was over. A rag of some sort had been stuffed into her mouth so her muffled yelps were pointless. She gagged on a mixture of her own spit and blood. The liquid trickled down the back of her throat and used her esophagus like a moving sidewalk toward the depths of her stomach. There they mixed with her gastric juices and soon she was nauseous from the stench of the men's hate and the shock response from her own body. Hot breath from both men loitered over her head as they seemingly decided what they should do next.

They were obviously neophytes. She figured professionals would have had their way with her by now and been long gone, onto their next evil. The blood boiled behind her weeping bloodied eyes as they dragged her by her feet along the concrete floor of the abandoned garage. Surely she had left half of her skin behind. Maybe someone would be able to identify her by the DNA that seeped from her wounds as it left a new ground covering. How had this house managed to be abandoned in the midst of all the well-kept manicured homes? At midday there was no one home to hear the sounds of her demise. How had she gotten herself in this mess? Her black tights had survived years of use, but were now easily ripped from her body. All she could think about was James. If she survived this horror how could he look at her again in the same way? It had only taken minutes to strip away the purity and honor that she and her husband had built together. She had only been with him since they were married. She had made a promise of purity to him on their wedding day, a vow that she had now been forced to break.

She could not tell her pursuants' nationalities. All she knew was that they had come up from the same pit of hell that her enemy had allowed them to be released from. That made them blood brothers from the same God-forsaken family. Her anger at the moment was directed at her enemy, the devil and not the victims that he had used to complete his task. She knew he wanted to kill, steal and destroy her and the dream of life that dwelled in her. These men were just pawns in his game. Hadn't she prayed enough to protect herself from dangers seen and unseen? It seemed at the moment God's angels were not enough, even though in her heart of hearts she still knew better. It was eerie that even though her body and her soul were being ripped and torn away from one another, she still had a peace that she couldn't quite understand. God was whispering to her in her soul and somehow she knew it would still be okay.

She was raped by both men. The leaves rustling under the garage service door became her center of attention. The leaves kept her focused on the gleam of light that was transmitting through the door. If she could just focus on the light, things would truly be okay, if they let her live. She had not expected to respond like this. Calm would not have been in her vocabulary set if you had asked her about being raped before then. When the men got tired of ruining her sexually they continued to pleasure themselves by using her as a latrine. A toilet that would never be flushed. She could not believe that she was still coherent. She wished for unconsciousness, but it would not come. She cried until there were no tears left. All of her wells were dry. For a moment she was left alone and the air stilled. She thought she heard the walls screaming, "help" for her but it was to no avail. In the distance she could hear a muffled argument ensuing. They could agree to rape and brutalize her, but they could not decide on what to do with her next. Her life hung like a trapeze between two loathsome strangers who now could not decide if she was worth breathing. Her reproductive system had been good enough to torture, but whether she lived more on this earth could not be determined easily. She began to wail as a plea for her life. She did not have the will to live anymore for herself, but she felt like she owed it to her husband and her family to survive so that they would not have to seek justice from her murderers. Heaven's bells were ringing in her ears and she could easily be mesmerized and taken over by them, but she refused. The smell of things both living and dead was in the air. She could have easily chosen either one, however, something else kept her wanting to breathe. Life was cruel, mean and unpredictable, but she wanted it more than she wanted her mother to mourn over her death. In an instant, life was all she wanted now and that was the last thought she had as a fist connected with her face. Finally, through the fierce blow Deanna received some peace.

~

She awoke on the other end of Kismet Avenue wrapped in a torn paint tarp. Her feat of going down a new block in her neighborhood had been completed. What a rocky run it had been. Leaves and weeds crackled under her body as she struggled to gain her bearings. Her thoughts of the prior events and the days to come lay scattered in her brain like garbage and debris lying on the streets of an impoverished neighborhood. Broken glass lay like broken dreams; empty wrappers lay like ideas that were unjustly stolen; half-eaten food lay like uncompleted tasks. She couldn't have been there long; surely someone would have detected her strange placement by now. She began to move again and her body felt like it had been stung all over by one giant bee.

Her ribs racked with pain, bruises appearing by the minute. It was amazing that she could even attempt to stand, but her trial did not last long. The pain overtook her courage and her busted knee took the weight of her whole body as it rested back down on the ground.

She never knew that her savior would come in the form of little children playing in the street: one riding a skateboard, the other on a bike. They approached hesitantly, unsure of why a grown woman was slumped over on the corner of their street. The scene was not an average everyday occurrence. The more curious of the two approached with eyes bigger than waffles and a hand shaky and unsure. "Lady, what's wrong with you?" As soon as the other child saw the blood running down her face he took off towards home, leaving behind his prized skateboard possession. He was a big boy, but Momma needed to handle this one. Deanna did not want to scare the courage out of the little boy who stayed, only nine or ten in age, but he was a man too and she could not dismiss what had been done to her only a few moments earlier. She jumped slightly as he attempted to pull back the tarp that enveloped her distorted frame. She attempted to speak, but tears took over and saliva and blood lodged in her throat. All she could manage to say was "help me!" The young boy snapped from his trance long enough to realize that his friend had taken off towards home. They lived right next to each other. He was sure that he had gone home to get one of their moms. They sat there in silence as they listened to the ambulance sirens getting louder and louder. The little boy did not realize that his presence had done more for Deanna in those moments than any medicine or treatment could. She needed a friendly life source in her presence. Life that was non-threatening and nonviolent. She silently thanked the young boy with her eyes as she was lifted into the ambulance. He had been determined not to leave her side until he knew that she was safe. His mother attempted to persuade him to go home but was unsuccessful. The lady he found had reminded him of his third grade teacher, Mrs. Bateman. He cherished her too much to just leave her in anyone's care.

CHAPTER TWENTY-TWO

"I'd rather go blind than to watch you leave me"

Etta James

Physical wounds heal much faster than emotional scars. Deanna's physical health climbed up the smooth side of the mountain while her emotional health climbed up the rough side. Her doctors were amazed that in just a few weeks she was up and mobile and back to light duty at work. She had been able to share the gory details of her experience with the city police and investigators from all the outlying suburbs. The case had taken on the interest of many because it was the first rape and assault that had occurred there in a long time. And for an African-American woman who was a minority in the area to be singled out made the entire community flinch at once. The fact that she had been rushed to the hospital helped the investigators obtain the samples they needed to prosecute her offenders once they were captured. Juan Garcia and Alan Striker had been arrested expediently and were awaiting trial. The twosome had been on a drug binge the day of the rape and were also being held for petty larceny and auto theft. They were virgins at their game as Deanna had suspected. Two young teens molested in their minds by a mixture of drugs, alcohol and peer pressure. The neighborhood fortunately went back to some semblance of peace once they had been captured. The two nineteen-year old high school dropouts had been brainless enough to return to the scene of their crime to party and binge out on drugs and alcohol the following weekend. Stupidity and violence had a way of dancing the waltz together, but to a song that was off beat and out of key.

Her rape counselors thought it would be best for her to take some more time off but Deanna just could not bear being alone. One of the things that they were most impressed with was the fact that she had almost immediately accepted that the rape had not been her fault. She recognized that it didn't happen because she had chosen that block to run down, it hadn't been the time of day or even the clothes she'd worn that evoked her predators. She also accepted that the rape was not about sex, but more about power and control.

One of the biggest things that she still struggled with was the powerlessness that she felt as the victim. How could someone so in control, so organized and well defined allow something as horrible as a rape happen to her? Her counselors were more suspicious about the true recovery of women who were successful and assertive because most of the time their rapes were one of the only things that they could not manipulate. As Deanna probed more into her own feelings and emotions, her inability to conceive a child and her powerlessness to defend herself against rape had been parallel blows to her psyche. The warning had been shared with the Carringtons about the percentage of couples that divorced after a devastating blow like rape and assault. They admonished she and James to seek even more counseling and support since their marriage had already been under the pressure of infertility.

At the time James had appeared to be the best support a victim could have. He attended all of her sessions and cared for her every need. No one would have suspected the trauma that he as a husband felt as a result of feeling powerless and guilty. When a man cannot protect his kingdom, his very manhood is placed in jeopardy. "Better to flee than be a failure," had apparently become his silent motto. Their counseling sessions were designed to bring forth healing to them individually and collectively. It only required the vision to see through a sheer curtain to realize that their collective healing was nowhere in sight. Another factor that had been discussed with the Carringtons was regarding the debris from the wreckage that rape caused for the extended family, community and friends of the victim. What do you say? How do you offer hope? Most of the moments spent with the victim were filled with awkward silences and pregnant pauses. The Carrington's family was torn up by the storm the assault caused. They had been rendered defenseless by the enormity of the tragedy. Their grief could be compared on many levels to grief of the displaced citizens after a devastating hurricane. Those winds had a way of blowing in and out wreaking havoc in no particular pattern, but causing pain in very distinct and finite ways.

Because the incident had occurred so close to home, James hired a caretaker to keep the house and be "paid company" for Deanna. This move had proven to be positive, but one that still could not replace the presence of someone who truly loved and cared for Deanna. Paid attention was different from attention given out of adoration. Deanna was more than elated about the capture of her assailants. She was ready and prepared to testify against the two who had swiped the life out of her as she knew it. She was not afraid. Her ability to stand up and against violence empowered her in an eerie sort of way. And even though she felt like she sat alone in the place that God forgot, she knew she would have to do something proactive about her state of being in order to feel better. She rehearsed her pastor's famous saying in her mind, "You better be getting ready to live or you are getting ready to die!"

She was a woman who liked to attack her weaknesses. She could not breathe properly knowing that there was something out there that was attempting to conquer her. She had to do something else to keep her mind off the emptiness that engulfed her life and marriage. It was as if the whole ordeal had made Luther Vandross's song, *A House is Not a Home,* a reality. If her life had not been a roller coaster up until then, it surely was one now. She once thought that the whole infertility thing had been like a simple coaster with peaks and valleys only. The rape and the devastation it caused was more like a monstrous roller coaster; one that spun her around and around and shook her head so much that she was sure she was suffering from an emotional brain injury. As she had studied in school, brain injuries in many ways served a more critical blow than something like a spinal cord injury. In most cases those victims had full brain function, but a body that would not work for them. However, when a brain's function was destroyed it could no longer will its body to function as it should. Deanna wanted to believe that her fate had not cheated her of everything that she had worked so hard for. The despair she felt hovered like a putrid fragrance above her head. As she moved it followed her. She chuckled weakly as she was reminded of the old Peanuts cartoon that showed the rain cloud hanging over Charlie Brown's head from scene to scene. Her laughter ended before it could take any effect on her.

~

The rape had done more damage to James than to Deanna, it seemed. He had been devastated when he was contacted at work by the neighbor who reported the dismal news. His stomach balled up in a knot and he couldn't swallow without telling himself to. Guilt ridden for being self engrossed and distant, his emotions had blown so far away that he could not make them return on his own. He couldn't feel at that moment. His psyche was numb. The only thing that reminded him that he was alive was the beat of his heart. He did love Deanna, but he knew his actions over the past months had not indicated love at all. He could not take her eyes watching him anymore or looking to him for comfort that he did not have to give. How could he take looking into those dark liquid eyes without an answer? Without the key to unlock the doors of pain that had been sealed and dead bolted by the circumstances of life. He knew her strength would outweigh his any day. He could not face that anymore. He made up his mind that once he got his wife back home and up on her feet he would have to take a leave of absence from their lives.

One month after Deanna's rape, James made his departure from her life. It was unsophisticated and anticlimactic. He guessed his wife had taken so many blows at once that one more did not seem to impact her. She sat affixed on the daybed in the guest room surrounded by piles of catch-up work. That room had been more accessible to the things she needed during recovery and she had remained there long after she could have returned to their own bed. Even that made the transition he was going to make easier. It seemed to him that the walls tightened in on him. The air was instantly sucked out of the space and he choked briefly on his inability to breathe. His eyes met hers for only a moment. As much as he tried to hide, he had those eyes that confessed the secrets of the heart. For the rest of his departure monologue he would divert his vision to other parts of the room. He did not want to visually connect with the cut his words would make on their lives. He wanted to believe that they could be mended together again one day, but just not now. He couldn't take it anymore. Not his failure, not her pain, not the humiliation that he felt God had allowed them to suffer through. James simply said that he needed some time to think and that he had to be on his own for a while. He wanted to pull it together, he wanted their marriage to work, but he had to focus on him right now. He planned to still take care of the house bills and he would send her money on a monthly basis for her to take care of her other expenses. He explained again where all the important documents were and then with that final statement, politely turned and walked out her life and their home with tears streaming down his face.

The dance that life offered had Deanna tripping over her own feet. She sat silent and still hoping that soon someone would wake her from the restlessness of the nightmare she was enduring. She willed her legs to move, but they refused. The ache in her neck that had been threatening to explode hours before made good on its promise and let go like a fireworks display.

Briefly paralyzed by her circumstances, she launched out in a direction of certainty in her thoughts. "Well God what am I supposed to do now? Everything has been taken from me. My dignity, my life and now my husband! What else do I have to give? How else can life crack me up side the head and expect me to recover?" Deanna spoke out into the air not expecting to be heard. She had always built her faith on the fact that God was able to do anything, but that He was still God and He did not have to if it was not in His plans. She realized now that she had kept that mantra as a safeguard for herself. If He didn't do what she wanted then she allowed herself room to be let down lightly. She did not understand until that moment that it meant that she was not trusting in God at all. That her faith had been based on faith itself and in her own abilities to will God to do what she wanted. It wasn't until then that she recognized that everything had to be stripped from her for her to realize that she really did not have any control at all. That revelation, however, did not stop the anger, malice and rage from engulfing her. Deep down inside she heard a familiar, small, still voice . . . .

"Are you mad?"

Deanna shook her head in disbelief at the words that had just formulated in her consciousness. "Am I mad? Uh, of course I'm mad God! What an understatement! What a blow to the psyche, at such a time as this. Do I really need this now? Why do my dreams continue to splatter in my face like a deployed air bag? Yes, I am upset at myself for believing the "okee-doke" once again. But honestly, God, I'm upset at you, because sometimes your set-ups seem so cruel. Just when I believed you again, reality hits! It's like a building caving in brick by brick, month by month. I know you are in control and I guess that is why I feel so out of control. I want to scream, but it would do no good! Who would hear me anyway! I want to lash out, but it would only feel good for a moment. I want to take this mixture of emotions and do something with it but nothing I can think of seems to satisfy the dull ache that hurt brings. What do you want from me! WHAT DO YOU WANT FROM ME! WHAT GOD, WHAT!!!!"

Deanna beat the air with her fists. She threw things up towards the ceiling expecting them to reach God and help deliver her message of pain and abandonment to Him. She went to their bedroom and destroyed everything that ever meant anything to them. The pictures from their last cruise together, the trophy from last year's couple's golf tournament, the covenant agreement they had signed jointly to stay together forever. She pulled down clothes, shoes and paintings off the wall just hoping to let someone or something else in on the torture she felt as her soul burned with sorrow. The price she paid for all the chaos she created only brought her one thing, fatigue. Hours crept away and she cried again and again, each time starting over from the top of her grief as if she hit the replay button on a bad movie. She rolled on the floor in agony as she realized the devastation that her life had brought to her. Only the strong survived, but where did that put her? The realization of her lack of faith had been a bigger blow than anything else she had experienced recently. She felt alone, scared and ashamed.

Suddenly, in the stillness of her monodrama she heard that all too familiar voice, the one that felt as comfortable as a pair of old working boots saying, "But will you trust me?" Entrenched in the depths of her loins she felt a glimmer of power, a ray of hope. That same assurance she had felt a month ago when her attackers were attacking more than just her physical body. Through it all she was a heroine. She was a survivor! Her tears of sorrow dried in an instant and she began to flow tears of conviction and joy.

"God I am sorry, for trusting me more than You. I have asked you many times to show me myself and now I see. The blinders are off. I have been tricking myself for so long, believing that I had faith in you when really I only had faith in myself. I am limited, but you are limitless and You can do anything. I am determined Lord to surrender. I know that surrender is the truest form of obedience. Please give me the will to press towards having true faith in you and not in myself or man. I want to succeed in moving closer to who you want me to be, God. Lord help me! Help me!" She lay in the nest of the mess she made until late in the midnight hour. The cherry oak walls in the Carrington home let go of a loud sigh. They wanted so much to breathe normally again.

~

The shock of her husband leaving her was similar to the one your body felt when it was adjusting to jumping into a pool of cold water. The immediate chill could be overwhelming, but the longer you stayed in it the more adjusted to it you became. The temperature of the water did not change, but your body adapted naturally. Deanna's emotional body was slowly adjusting as

RHONDA C. WHITE

she learned to cope, despite the constant cold chill that she felt from her separation. She never imagined life this way. But she knew God had a plan. She no longer wanted to figure it out; she wanted to faith it out! She realized that what she did from that point on no longer depended on what she did, but on how much true faith, the unwavering kind of faith, the mustard seed faith that she put behind what God had already invested in her.

CHAPTER TWENTY-THREE

"Preach to the storm, and reason with despair, but tell not misery's son that life is fair."

H. K. White

She lifted her bubble-soaked arm out of the tub and reached for her glass of Riesling that sparkled in her Riedel white wine glass. She enjoyed the taste of the sweetened white wine. Taking a soak in her Jacuzzi tub with the novel that she started days before had been a welcomed retreat. God had been faithful to meet her emotional needs as long as when she felt herself falling she ran directly to Him instead of one of her own coping mechanisms. It was hard for her to believe that her life's profession was to help others think clearly and effectively. She had been her worst client to date. She knew where her strength came from, but it had been so easy for her to turn inward for sustenance.

~

She allowed herself to drift off into the lives of the book's fictitious characters, which enabled her safe escape from the real world. She had plenty of time to ponder her problems and push them towards the Lord, but now was just not the time. As the propelled bubbles surrounded Deanna, they soothed her physical and mental pains. She wished her life would flicker only half as much as the candles that sat perfectly in the corners of the tub. She remembered James fussing all throughout Bed, Bath and Beyond about her wanting to purchase the perfect gold, burgundy and peach candles for the bathroom's corner display. That day, she won the verbal fight about having her sanctuary coordinated.

She wished that her marital victories mattered now. She would do anything to change the current state of her marriage. Never in a million years could she have imagined facing life without her husband. She was reminded of a quote by Herb Brooks, the 1980 USA Olympic Hockey coach. In an interview after they'd won the title he said, "You have to make sacrifices for the unknown." The statement had intrigued her when she heard the interview after watching the movie, *Miracle*. She was ready to make the sacrifices even though the unknowns in her life were trying to scare the hell out of her.

She lay back on the peach terry cloth bath pillow and pleaded silently in her spirit for God to give her some answers. The retreat with her novel was short lived. "God what do you want from me? This time her question was not asked in anger but in desperation. "I did not sign up for all of this: a miscarriage, possibly an affair, a failed adoption, a rape and now a desolate marriage. I know plenty of women who would have lost their minds by now, but here I am Lord, what next? I finally understand what my Grandma meant when she said that I was born after the biblical hero Job. The man who had suffered greatly in his body and at the loss of his family and fortunes." Deanna just hoped to have half of his strength. "I don't think I am going to be able to say like him, *"naked I came from my mother's womb, and naked I will depart. The Lord gave and the Lord has taken away; and may the name of the Lord be praised."*

It was funny how she found herself frequently having open verbal communication with her Father, the one whom she had never seen. Deanna addressed the cooling tub waters by turning the hot faucet on full blast. She was quickly lost in her thoughts again. "I think I could have handled this up until my husband left . . . . My husband left me! I mean what in the world is his problem? I'm the one who has had to endure. That Negro just sat on the sidelines as a spectator! I was beaten and traumatized! I healed from the busted knee and fractured rib! I wonder if that was the same rib that God took from James to create me?" Deanna said snidely. "So much for the theory about being bone of his bone. He shouldn't be able to live without his bone! What did he do but sit there and look stupid and helpless. My soul hurts everyday God, because of what happened to me, but you don't see me running off, escaping from my misery. I know I have to face my destiny. I know I have to use this for my good and as much as I don't want to admit it Father, I know that even this, even this is working out for my good." She couldn't take it anymore. The tears blasted from her eyes like a jet taking off into space. She cried long and hard. It was as if her tears mixed with her bath water and caused the levels to rise higher than the flood drain.

As Deanna's spirit quieted and the tears dried up, God finally spoke and closed the seeping wound that had been draining the life out of her. Once again, He had been her Savior. Her spirit calmed as he spoke. "Daughter I am trying to get you to understand that your pride prevents you from enjoying the blessing of the journey. You are trying to get to the end of the race too fast. You are trying to report how good we were together and I am trying to get you to enjoy how good we are now. I am trying to be intimate with you now. I am trying to talk about how we are together now while all you want to do is talk about how we were and what I've already done. I know your trials have been long and you have endured. You have suffered, but it has not been to no avail. Just like I pulled greatness out of many whom I loved before you, so now I will bless you. If the enemy meant it for your demise, I mean it for your good, so you might continue to bring glory to my name. Lift up your head daughter! I have not forsaken you! Remember the words I spoke to you long ago: *Have I not commanded thee? Be strong and of good courage. Do not be terrified; do not be discouraged for the Lord your God will be with you wherever you go.* I will restore you, child. What is to come is better than what has been."

She remembered almost instantly what one of her girlfriends shared with her only a few months earlier. It had only been profound then, but now it was both profound and truly applicable. "God," she said, "wants you to know that when you placed your order He took it. But it is taking longer than you think because you thought you ordered from one of those fast-food places where your order was ready in less than five minutes. But you placed your order at a five-star establishment where the chef could not use any old ingredients. You ordered a specific gourmet entrée that required Him to have His gophers to go out and look for the ingredients since they were specialty items. Therefore, it takes a little longer for finer orders to be created. And another thing that happens when you order at a five-star establishment is that the chef comes out to your table to make sure your meal is prepared properly. God is waiting to come out to greet you so that you can thank Him."

Deanna abruptly opened her eyes. She felt for a moment that she had been taken from the room and placed somewhere else. She got her bearings together and realized that even though she was alone she was not alone.

She dried her water-wrinkled body, still allowing the comfort of God's words to soothe her aching soul. She looked haphazardly for her favorite warm-up suit. Just behind the head of her bed she saw something peeping out like a scared rodent. She grabbed it quickly and inhaled. As she expected, the strong sweat smell mixed with James' favorite cologne lingered in the workout sweatshirt that he had left behind. It was just like him to leave a memory behind for her to ponder over. The smell caused her to reminisce about hugging her husband tightly after one of his morning workouts. Where had those days gone? Deanna braced herself and slid down the wall she had been leaning on as her intense thoughts made her lightheaded and woozy. A small sweat broke out above her brow. "Deanna get yourself together! You can handle this. Its just a funky sweatshirt!" But just as the words left her mouth, her tears betrayed her and formed a small puddle in her lap. Her spiritual and emotional healing had begun, but how could her husband up and leave her after all she had been through? She had been violated. She had been betrayed by humanity. Why was he the one taking the easy way out! Deanna cussed for the first time in a long time. Just when she needed him most, he decided to check out. He had violated their sacred trust to always be there for one another. Sometimes she thought James was just stupid. But her anger lost the competition to the deep pain she felt in her heart. She knew God would fix it. He had reassured her of that, but the healing process still hurt no matter how much assurance she had.

~

She began to rise again only to feel the same dizziness that had plagued her minutes before. What was going on? Deanna thought. Maybe I just need to lie down and rest. I can't believe I allowed that man's shirt to throw me into a tizzy! Deanna let out a small laugh, gathered her clothes in a large pile and fell out on the bed where she remained until the next day.

~

A graveyard silence and then a robust churning in her stomach caused Deanna to awake forcefully from her restful sleep. A watery sensation in her mouth overwhelmed her and she immediately ran to relieve her abdomen in the bathroom. What was that all about? Deanna recounted what she had eaten the night before to determine what had been the culprit responsible for her demise. Besides the glass of wine she had and the oriental salad without meat, she couldn't even remember the last time she had eaten. In fact, her appetite really hadn't returned since her life had derailed from its tracks. She gathered herself and continued to prepare for work. She threw a sleeve of saltines and a can of Seven-Up® in the truck since her stomach still had not settled. Work did not agree with her and she took off after lunch and headed for home. She stopped off at her favorite restaurant, Soul Vegetarian, to pick up a veggie wrap before returning home. She had to force herself to eat something, but even the smell of one of her favorite meals did not appeal to her.

~

Delilah met her at the door and curled her tail around Deanna's leg for only a brief moment. The feline made a quick but grand entrance, however her exit was even faster. Deanna realized that cats were not the best pets to help improve an owner's ego. She thought for the first time maybe having a dog wouldn't be such a bad idea. Deanna peeled off her work clothes and popped the wrap in the microwave for forty-five seconds. The hum of the appliance made her think of how a swarm of killer bees might sound. She sure was having some crazy thoughts these days. Maybe she had been watching too much television. "Channel zero" as Cairo called any line of TV programming that showed ignorant, low-class people fighting about baby daddies, mistresses and gastric bypass surgeries. That unfortunately had become her consistent company. Almost every station had its portion of channel zero shows and Deanna had allowed herself to get enveloped in most of them. The non-informative, uninspiring programs had done nothing for her spiritual life. There was not a day or night that didn't go by that Jerry Springer's fans weren't screaming, "Jer-ry, Jer-ry," or Maury Povich was saying "And Romeo, you are *not* the father!"

Deanna dragged her feet and her meal to the den and flicked on her friend. She picked at her wrap and realized she was having a difficult time just swallowing. She felt like a large rock was lodged in her throat and no amount of Seven-Up®, cranberry juice or water would get it down. She dropped her food and picked up the remote to turn from Maury who was into his regular routine . . . "So Jancinta how many times have you been pregnant?" "Well, Maury, I been pregnant five times, but my first two kids are by my other baby daddy. He locked up now tho'. He doin' seven to ten, but anyway after that I had two miscarriages. But, now this is my youngest son, Macshon. He is eight months old and looks just like his daddy, Dementri. I can't believe he got me on this show because he don't think he my baby daddy. He know he got me pppp-rrrrr-eeee-gggg-n-a-n-t . . . ." As the word rolled off of the ghetto fabulous girl's lips, horror struck a cord way down in the depths of Deanna's soul. She snapped off the television and ran to the calendar on the refrigerator. "Oh hell to the nawl!" She could not be two weeks late. When had she had her last period? She had totally lost count with all the drama going on. She willed herself not to believe what might be true. Those thoughts were quickly followed by her running to the bathroom to relieve her stomach of its contents once again.

~

She sat in Dr. Banner's office after her exam and blood tests waiting for him to return with her results. She had never been asked to wait in his office before. The two other times she had seen him, he would just speak with her in one of the exam rooms. He had not seen her since her last checkup after the rape. Her throat became dry and rough and she willed some saliva to come from somewhere to relieve it of its drought. She popped a peppermint in her mouth and waited as calmly as she could to hear what she had been dying to hear for so long, but now was petrified to know. She realized that she had idolized the thought of motherhood and now with it piercing over at her, she was plummeting into shock, disbelief and dread at what should have been joyous. The doctors and rape counselors had discussed with her the right she had to take the abortion pill RU-486 after the rape, but she had refused. At the time, she could not bear even considering an abortion. She had not gotten pregnant in four years and had no reason to believe that she would be then. She squirmed in her seat as her thoughts squirmed in her mind. Perspiration met her upper lip again as she threw her head back to rest on the chair's back while letting out a large sigh. It sounded like she was letting air out of a helium balloon. She concentrated on everything else in the room, the drug advertisements and the several medical books stashed haphazardly on the shelves. She even tried to listen through the walls at what the other patients, nurses and doctors might be saying. She just needed to keep her head clear. The whole possibility of pregnancy was just a fluke. She had not gotten her period because of stress. It was bound to come as soon as she found out she was not pregnant. "Come on Lord, not again!" Deanna screamed inside herself, not knowing whether to panic or rejoice. She did want to be a mother, but not like this. And, O Lord what would Mr. James do with this news? He was already trying to take the easy way out. Could he even take the thought of her possibly being the mother of someone else's child? "Okay Deanna regroup, it is not going down like that!" She spoke out loud to herself willing her confidence to match what she had just said.

Dr. Banner slipped into his office and into his chair with the precision of a sleek leopard. His footsteps had been the only sound that brought her back to mental consciousness. His face was like an open book. In his line of work, it had not proven to be the best when being the bearer of critical information. "Well Deanna, I think you already suspected it, but you are about seven weeks pregnant. Everything looks good and you seem to be doing quite well physically." Dr. Banner went on and on talking about the precautions they would need to take because of her age and that he would be watching her closely. His voice faded in and out as she sat in astonishment.

She was caught in an emotional current and her eyes held a high voltage stare.

"Deanna are you okay? Can I get you some water? You look a little uneasy."

Dr. Banner's feeble attempts to comfort her snapped her back into his office. She wished she could go off on him, just because. Why hadn't he been able to deliver the news about her being pregnant before now, at a time when there had been no concern in her mind about her marriage, her future and who the father of her baby was? She wanted just for a moment to get him good but she knew it wasn't his fault. Why did she have to be so alone at such a time as this? She had isolated herself from everyone who had not submerged themselves in their own problems. The Alexanders and the Adams had done their part in consoling her up until then, but she honestly didn't feel comfortable with them. She wasn't part of a couple anymore and because of that she did not think that they could relate to her. They weren't living as a married single. And what did they know about being separated? They had never experienced the pain associated with a split in the marriage covenant they had made. They could not feel the sting made by a marital meat cleaver when it severed her life in two by throwing down its deadly blow. And Theresa Cook had been missing in action for months. She had only sent a card when she heard about the rape. T was only keeping her head above her own trials at the time Deanna guessed. Cairo had tried to make contact after he heard, but out of her own embarrassment she had refused to talk to him, until now. She had to let this out somewhere. She had decisions to make now. What was she going to do? Could she even keep this baby? A baby . . .

CHAPTER TWENTY-FOUR

The Mother
"Abortions will not let you forget.
You remember the children you got that you did not get, The damp small
pulps
with a little or with no hair, The singers and workers that never handled
air.
You will never neglect or beat Them, or silence or buy with a sweet. You
will never wind up the sucking-thumb Or scuttle off ghosts that come. You
will never leave them, controlling your luscious sigh, Return for a snack of
them, with gobbling mother-eye.
I have heard in the voices of the wind the voices of my dim killed
children . . ."

Gwendolyn Brooks

"Ladies and gentlemen, we at Delta Airlines would like to thank you for flying with us today. We hope your service to Atlanta has been great. If you are returning home, we wish you all the best in your future endeavors and if you are vacationing here in Atlanta, we wish you the best of times. The weather at Atlanta Hartsfield International is a sunny 79 degrees. We hope you always consider Delta Airlines when flying the friendly skies. Thank you and have a great day." The sassy airline stewardess made her way to the exit and began to let her passengers disembark. Deanna grabbed her carryon bag and waited as patiently as she could for the young man in front of her to gather himself and his three-year-old's belongings before they left the plane.

She had a sudden flash forward of how this might be the last time that she traveled so lightly.

~

As always, the routine was for Cairo to circle around the terminal drop-off area while she waited for him in front of the perspective airline entrance. She and Cairo had devised that plan long ago in college when they realized that neither of them would ever be on time when it came to picking the other up. The airport "Nazi police" as they had named them, were always more lenient on those being dropped off versus those being picked up. Even though Deanna hadn't spoken to him in weeks, Cairo was right there ready to be the friend to her that he had always been. That was something about true friends, no matter how much space grew between them, nothing could truly pull them apart. Time, distance nor circumstances could disconnect devoted comrades. Cairo's gray CLK-Class Coupe' Mercedes Benz made a sloshing sound as it sped through the puddle in front of where Deanna stood.

Cairo yelled out the window, "Chicken head!" He had not cared about traffic laws on the way to get his girl. He sped through every light and ignored every speed limit sign. He was determined not to have her waiting too long. He heard the stress in her voice before she got on the plane and knew he needed to be ready for whatever Deanna had to share. Somewhere down deep, he knew that this one had to be a doozey. She had not spoken to him since the rape and James' departure. He knew she just needed a little time.

"Boy, you are going to tear up this car before you get to drive it good."

"Dude, it ain't nothing but a car. There are plenty more where it came from. I'm getting a little tired of it anyway."

Deanna smiled at her friend's lack of humility. Cairo threw Deanna's bag in the trunk and gave her a warm hug.

"Girl you look like you're getting some hips on you. Who did you pay for those?" Cairo chuckled as he walked back to his side of the car.

"Negro please! I've always had hips, they were just hidden." The duo's banter continued as they made their way up I-85 toward Stone Mountain, Georgia. They stopped to get Chinese food and crashed in front of Cairo's 60-inch plasma TV that perfectly fit in his comfortable, ultra-modern living room. They ate until it felt like their sides would split open. Deanna hadn't had much of an appetite in the last week and her morning sickness hadn't allowed the little food she did enjoy to reside in her stomach long. She had made up in her mind though, that no matter what, from then on she was going to eat and enjoy her food. Sick or not, she was eating for two.

"So where is the soon to be Mrs. Tanner? I thought sure I would get to meet her at the airport."

Cairo readjusted his position on the floor. "Well sis, to be honest with you, I did not know what to expect when you got here. I just knew you had tried your best to stay away from me and I wasn't sure how up to company you would be. I had already made up in my mind that if I hadn't gotten to speak with you for real in the next week or so I was coming up there to do a drive by. Alesha and I decided that it would be best to hold off on the intros until we found out what was really going on with you. We both have been diligently praying for you and James. I cannot believe that you two aren't . . ."

Deanna interrupted what she thought was going to be a long sad line. "Cairo, don't even go there about James. I got so much more going on than him right now. And as peeved as I am at him for leaving me, I still know deep down inside that the brother is struggling with some demons bigger than I could ever care to deal with. I know God is whupping his butt right now. So as much as I really want to be the best sistah girl I can be and go up to his job and clown like I'm at the *Barnum and Bailey Circus*, I am just going to chill. In fact, I need him gone right now so I can clear my head." Deanna gave herself a silent high-five for being a big girl in the midst of her mess.

"Well, I am glad you said that. You know a brother thought you were coming down here to get me to witness you signing your divorce papers!" Cairo looked relieved, but still hesitant.

Deanna went on, "Shoot, as much as that would be the easiest answer for me, for real, I can't let the brother off that easy. I've done too much fasting and praying for that Negro to just let him go and give him up to some other woman. Look, every woman got to do her own time for her own man. When the rubber hits the road, I made a promise to stick with this come rain or shine. I know I probably haven't dealt the best with what's happened to me. I did shut everybody out, especially him, so I have to take some of the responsibility for our split. However, I am not ready to close the door, nail it shut and throw away the key on my marriage." Deanna felt her joker face emerging. "Plus the brother couldn't pay me enough in alimony to keep me quiet! I'm one of those sistahs who would fight for more than HALF!" Deanna laughed heartily at her own joke. She hadn't felt a sense of relief like this one since way before . . .

Instantly she was right back at why she was in Atlanta in the first place. Cairo leaned in as if he inherently knew that what she really came to talk about was about to erupt out of her mouth. "Well C, I guess I can't hang on to this any longer. I just needed someone who has been through it all with me to give me some direction. I need someone to tell me something to do other than to continue to sit and go crazy. The long and short of it is . . . I'm pregnant. I am about eight weeks along and because of the rape I don't know who the father is. I am stuck between being excited about finally having my dream come true and not knowing if I am giving birth to a mass murderer. I-I-I'm really afraid. I don't know what to think. My head keeps spinning around and around like a merry-go round operator put it on continuous motion. I don't know how I can raise a child that is not my husband's but I can't even think about an abortion. I assume that one of my rapists is the father since James and I hadn't been able to conceive before now, but I can't say for sure. The doctors never really found a reason why James and I could not conceive. Maybe our chemistry together just wasn't right, who knows. And my marriage is, I don't know. I mean, how do I ever put the rape behind me when I might possibly be looking in the eyes of my perpetrators for the rest of my life? And then what if I have to raise this kid on my own? You know that was never in my plans. If I know anything, I know a child has a right to grow up with a father and a mother. Children did not ask to be here. My life is just a mess, FOR REAL! It's like while in the midst of doing God's will, He allows something tragic to come forth that challenges your worth, value and efforts for Him. You know I love the Lord, but I have truly felt alone through all of this."

Cairo sat motionless as he allowed all that Deanna had just revealed to sink into his psyche. He tried to veil the hurt he held for his friend with a placid smile. He would have never thought that his girl, his pillar of strength, his spiritual hero would ever have to deal with something as heavy as this, something that would rock her spiritual foundation. What could he tell her? How was he supposed to respond? Could it be possible that the baby was James' after all? He took a moment to silently ask the Lord for guidance and the right words to say. It was odd for him to be on the other end of the spiritual stick. Usually Deanna was the one with the great advice and wisdom. She looked at him as if he had the ability to part the Rea Sea of her life with his words.

"Dang De, this is way too deep. I am sorry dude that I did not make it my business to be there when this all went down, but when you wouldn't

RHONDA C. WHITE

accept my calls I thought you wanted me to stay away for awhile. I should have done what I thought was best from the beginning."

Deanna's pondering eyes gave him the assurance that he needed to go ahead and tell her what God had just shared with him. "De baby, you already know the answer to your questions. Even if you never know for sure who the father is, you know you cannot destroy this child. I know I don't always understand God and most of the time I find myself questioning if He even knows what He is doing. I guess that is that control thing we have in common. But, the one thing I do know is that I have held onto the scripture that you sent to me long ago when my brother first got sick. *For we know that all things work together for the good to them that love the Lord.* He did not bring you this far to leave you. You know that whatever or however God wants to bless you, you will be satisfied. He is a good God even when we don't understand. Now about James, I don't know what to say. Honestly, the brother has disappointed me to no end lately. I thought so much more of him, but I do know that sometimes your past has a way of catching up with you and kicking you in the behind! Will he be strong enough to first work on your marriage and then accept a child that is possibly a product of rape? I just don't know. I want to believe with all my heart that he will do the right thing, but the protective brother inside of me does not want to give him another chance. Despite how I feel though, he is your husband and you have to be woman enough to deal with him if that is what you decide. No one else but God himself can help you determine that one. We can stand on the sidelines all day long and shout out plays to you, but when the clock starts you are the quarterback of that play." Deanna smiled inside as she thought about how much Cairo had grown. There would have been a time when he would have been like, bump that baby and that man! She could hear the old Cairo saying there are too many players out there to fall for the same game twice. He was her true friend and his assurance in what God's plan was for her life added confidence to what she knew already in her spirit. The rest of Deanna's Atlanta stay was spent with Cairo and Alesha going over plans for their wedding, which was scheduled for the following year. She thought it was the coolest thing in the world that Cairo had asked her to be his "best woman." They had always joked about that in the past, but finally they could put a period behind their open-ended joke.

Her trip ended with Alesha and Cairo waving bye to her at the airport's security checkpoint. She was headed home to start her new life as a mommy-to-be. At the same time her thoughts wound back to almost two years ago when she had the miscarriage. She needed not to focus on that possibility, but the four years of infertility on top of the miscarriage had proven to shatter her full excitement about her dream come true.

~

As Deanna glanced toward the stainless steel china cabinet that she had begged James to buy for them, it caused a slight laugh to come from her belly of pain. She was seeking renewal of her restless spirit and she now knew that the journey began with her. She watched her wedding picture intently and thought of how she had insisted that they go a month after their wedding and retake their wedding photos. She had not been pleased with her hair on her wedding day and did not want to go the next twenty years regretting not having a good wedding picture. How pointless did all of that seem now? James had decided to walk out of the photo of their lives just as easy as it had been to develop the film that had taken their picture years before. The funny thing was she wasn't sure how she felt about the whole marriage thing now. Did she want to be married to someone who obviously didn't want to be with her or at least had a horrible way of showing it? She had so much to think about, but now was not the time. Her dream was only months away from coming true. Even if it wasn't her husband's child, she knew she had to be its mother. She wanted to believe that James would understand and accept this child no matter what, but for now she had to think about the life that was within her; the precious gift that had been given to her through possibly drastic and devastating measures. She couldn't even hate her perpetrators. Her and James' intimate life had been close to null and void before the rape so she was almost sure that the seed within her could not be his, but she did not care to know. She had peace in a way that only a mother-to-be could understand. She dreamed only for a moment of the smile that would flicker on her baby's lips one day. She was unsure of her future, but she was sure of who was and who had always been her guide. He, her Holy Father had not left her. She ended her evening quiet and alone.

~

The days of her second trimester melted away like snowflakes as she flew successfully through her pregnancy. It had been rough mentally getting through the first three months. She wanted to be fully happy, but the strain of having to wait so long for her dream to come true had made her nerves wacky. She had heard other women who finally received their dream come

RHONDA C. WHITE

true after years of failed fertility treatments and miscarriages report that they were happy, but cautious, delighted but reserved. The struggle with infertility made even the excitement of the dream seem slightly deflated. Other people had been happier than she was about being pregnant. Most people cried or shouted right in front of her while she cautiously smiled and allowed the joy to seep through her insides. Even though her faith had been strengthened, she did not let go of that reserve until God finally spoke into her that she had to live above her natural instincts and stop begging Him about preserving her pregnancy and just believe Him.

That was all she needed. She headed into her seventh month like a champ. Despite her increased fatigue, Deanna could not remember one bad side effect after the initial nausea and acid reflux symptoms. Maybe God had decided to be good to her since the child's conception had been so devastating. It not only had been brutal to her body and emotions, but it had appeared to fatally wound her marriage. The one thing she had prayed would never happen. James was gone. He had walked out just as easy as he had walked in. He had made himself more visible since he found out she was pregnant. She had not wanted to share the information with him initially, but word traveled fast in her family so she thought it best to be the one to share the news with him.

~

James' thoughts flickered in and out of existence like fireflies while he listened to his wife tell him the words he so longed to hear years before, the words that said that he would be a father. The possibility of someone else giving life to his wife's child had crossed his mind a thousand times after the rape, before she ever gave the confirming announcement to him of her pregnancy. He made up in his mind that if she would let him, he planned to be a part of the child's life. Yes, he had messed up and he knew they would have a long way to go if they ever got back together, but regardless of how the child got here, it hadn't been his fault. He wanted to be a part of his life and his wife's life, if she'd let him.

~

The stillness of night was disturbed by the ringing of her telephone. Deanna was awakened sharply from a deep sleep. She glanced at the clock and realized immediately that this was no regular call. It was 2:30 in the morning! Deanna hoped that this was not a prank call, some child calling an ex-boyfriend in response to a broken heart. But no, this call had a serious ring to it. Deanna held her bladder long enough to say "hello." After she found out who it was, she could determine if she could use the bathroom in their ear.

"Hey, wha's up?" The guarded sound of her husband's voice caused her relief and pain all in the same moment. Was he okay? He sounded terrible.

"Hey are you alright?" She wanted to go to the bathroom badly. The baby had taken up so much space in her abdomen that she could not take a sip without having to expel it.

"Yeah, I am okay, I just need to talk."

As much as she wanted to do what she always did and use the bathroom while talking to him, somehow the comfort and commonality that their relationship had once shared was gone. "James can you hold on for one moment please?" She could hear a silent frustration in his voice, but he conceded to her request. She noticed she had started waddling as she made her way back to the bed. She settled herself and took a deep energizing breath. "Okay James, what's going on?"

"Well, I know it's late and I probably shouldn't have called, but I just need to say what I have to say and uh, I didn't want to talk myself out of saying it."

She glanced at the picture of them on her nightstand through her water glass, but specifically she focused on him. The glass emitted a blurred image of her husband and she realized that she had been seeing him like that all along. Her vision of him had been blurred not by his doing, but by the plans of the enemy to take him out way before then. Way before they had ever gotten together. She sat silently making sure that she did not interrupt his speech.

"Deanna I really don't know how to begin, but well, I've been doing a lot of praying, a lot of fasting and a lot of thinking. I've been thinking about us, about my life without you, about my past and now this whole baby thing."

Deanna sighed as she was reminded of the way they used to get over the sadness of their infertility by calling it the "baby thing." Only now, that phrase was not so comforting.

"I've realized that I let so much get in the way of who I really am and more importantly, who God wants me to be. These months I've spent alone have been so eye opening. I see now how the enemy wanted me dead way before now. His plans truly were to steal my life, kill my life and destroy my life. I did not understand the true meaning of that scripture until now. I guess I had to come to the end of myself before I could lay down my manly pride and see me for me. The abuse I suffered as a child had me fooling myself. I built a shell around me and I got so good with falsifying the truth to the world that it could not see my imperfections, my damage, and I ended up hiding from myself. And then you came into my life. You were so free and ready to tackle your problems, fears and phobias head on. I was intrigued and intimidated by you all at the same time. I craved the ability to stare my demons in the eye like you did yours, but instead I found myself running even faster from them. I lied to myself as a coping mechanism. I lied so much that I believed my lies were truths. I figured if I became successful in my career, had the perfect wife and home that the demons would get scared and leave. Unfortunately, they just got bigger with my success. The more I hid from them, the more they reared their ugly heads. The whole Angie thing was never about her. It was about how I thought her presence in my life filled the void that my childhood abuse caused. I truly never meant to hurt you or her. I used her and I abused our trust and I am sorry. And for what it is worth, I never became intimate with Angie. I recognize now that the deceit attached to that relationship is equal to truly having an adulterous affair. I didn't see that before now. I guess I saw everything in my life through smoke-stained glasses. I am so grateful that I see more clearly now. I know now I realized it way too late."

Deanna attempted unsuccessfully to hold back the tears that were stored up behind the lump she had in her throat. Tears had a way of always making her feel like a lion had just roared way too loudly inside of her. She was grateful that her husband had come to an understanding about himself, but she was not sure if she was the one he should be telling. Was she really ready to hear all of this? She wasn't sure that her trust in what he said could ever truly be restored. Too much time and too many lies had flown in between them like birds going south. She did not know. She quieted her spirit and continued to listen.

"De are you still there?"

"Yes, James I'm listening." She felt like he was reading her thoughts just like he always had. How could he know her so well and not know himself? Who was this man for real?

"Deanna I know you have been through a lot and the guilt and shame that I feel everyday for not being there for you, I mean truly there for you, almost suffocates me. I'm so disappointed in myself for not having the guts to stand with you through it all. I have questioned my faith and even my integrity as a man too many times to count. I don't know if I will ever truly get over the fact that I let you down."

She imagined his tears softly running down around the sides of his face, making their acquaintance at the bottom of his goatee.

"I guess I want you to understand that I am really and truly sorry for the pain that I've caused you and our marriage."

Deanna continued to let him ramble on. She couldn't remember a time when James had been able to genuinely pour his soul out to her. For the first time she felt that the dark cloud of mystery that hung over her husband's head had been lifted. She knew his past had so much to do with who he was as a man. But it was not until he saw it for himself that a true metamorphosis could take place.

"I guess one of the last things I need to say is that it's not Josh . . . . I mean the baby's fault that he was conceived the way he was. He is still our child. I am still married to you. I love you. And I don't have all the answers. I am just as confused about how to be a husband to you as when I left, but I want you to know that I want to work this out. I want another chance at our lives together."

Time proceeded at a donkey's pace between his last words and her response. Finally she spoke. "James, being there for someone doesn't mean you have to have all the answers. Sometimes a silent presence is enough. Awkward words and proverbial clichés often have the reverse effect. Just your spirit being in the midst during my trials would have added the comfort I needed to make it through." Tears clogged her voice and even though she had not wanted him to hear her cry, she broke down. "James I never wanted us to end up like this. No one could have ever bet me that we would not have survived anything together. I will always love you and you must know that. But, I am just plain scared of even thinking about letting my heart go again. Here I have spent almost seven months on my own, making it through this pregnancy the best I could. I just don't know if I have the strength to even consider us again." Her voice trailed off into the depths of the night.

"Deanna I'm going to let you go. I've said too much. I will continue to pray for you and do whatever you need me to do. I just pray that you will allow me to be a part of this child's life and . . . and your life too. I love you. Goodnight sweetheart."

RHONDA C. WHITE

CHAPTER TWENTY-FIVE

"Grow old with me; the best is yet to be"

Robert Browning

She watched herself stack the clean dishes over and around the dish rack like pieces in a Jenga game. Her thoughts were soaring. Surely the dishes would fall over and need to be washed and restacked, but her mind could not organize enough to perform the task correctly. She had recently read an article about hypnotism. Had James' new findings about his life hypnotized him and her into believing that they could possibly make it together again? Hypnotism was a type of suggestive behavior. She hoped that her mind had not suggested to itself that marriage again with James was ever possible. If that happened, more than her mind would have to be responsible. She wanted to hope, but she was not ready to let go of the security that not trusting him brought just yet. She could not believe that her life had taken so many tosses and turns in such a short time. In the beginning stages of the baby thing it had seemed like an eternity, now it was a whirlwind passing before her eyes faster than she could digest it. "Lord, I pray for my flesh to be weak and for strength in my spirit." Deanna prayed privately over and over again these days. If nothing else, her relationship with the Lord had changed for the best. She was stronger and wiser as a result of her storm. No one would have been able to tell her that she would still be standing after all of this. God was awesome. Instead of her just saying she was relying on Him, but really standing in her own power, she was completely standing on His power not trusting herself at all. Instead of being that sure, self-confident, self reliant woman, she was confident in God alone and solely reliant on His power. For once she felt that she was working with His power instead of fighting against it.

~

She had refused to find out the sex of her child during her routine ultrasounds, but she knew in her spirit that the baby was Joshua. She thought of him each day as he blossomed in her womb and wondered what his walking music would be. Would people know that he was entering the room when in their souls they heard the jazz of Jerald Dameyon or the melodious tunes of Fred Hammond? Would he be a preacher or a senator? A physician or an activist? How would he affect the world and what would its impression of him be? Deanna knew in her heart that her child already had a story to tell. His stark beginnings were concocted for his demise. The enemy had plans for his destruction before time began for him, but she knew as the keeper of his gate, the one given responsibility over his soul while he was on earth, that she would never allow his start to predict his outcome. She would bathe her son in prayer everyday of his life and like Hannah, she would be careful to give her son back to the Lord for His glory.

~

Deanna awoke excited to start her day. She and James had decided to go to counseling today for the first time. They recognized that they still needed to deal with the human side of their problems even though the Spirit who had never left them was there to lead them through. That was a fault that many reconciling couples made. They stopped being mad and got back together before any of their old problems were resolved. Those old problems quickly became new evils when the novelty of the relationship wore off again. In order to get through today the way she knew God wanted her to, she had to be totally in sync with Him. Her trials had made her recognize that when she was not in sync naturally with the Lord she had to make herself get in sync with him on purpose.

After an hour of praise, worship and Bible reading her soul was ready to go. She felt invigorated and satisfied. She dressed in the new multi-colored empire waist maternity top and jeans that she bought the day before. Her brown pointed low-heeled boots covered her slightly swollen feet to a tee. Her hair was fixed in tightly knit curls, James' favorite hairstyle on her. She was a package waiting to be unwrapped. She had not seen James since her last appointment with Dr. Banner and thought she should be dressed to impress because of it. Would this whole scenario determine the measure of her man? She did not know and she did not know what God had in store for their marriage, but she figured she would do her part. That's all she could be responsible for. James and the Lord had to do the rest.

~

She found herself waiting in a similar room to the one she had gone into so many months before for her first official counseling session regarding infertility. Wow, time had flown on the wings of eagles. She felt blessed to be a part of the journey she was on. It was funny how nervous she got instantly as she anticipated James coming through the door. She felt giddy like a school girl and her baby's kicks were not helping her any. Before she had more time to process her feelings the door swung open and fresh air flew in with the steps of her husband. He was dressed in brown cords, an oxford shirt and a coordinated track jacket. His smell intoxicated her. She could not deny the passion she had for this man. She had been in love with him almost all of her life. Her love for him was being made complete through this trial. Whether they stayed married or not, her love could not be denied.

~

One of the most important things that the counselor said to them that day was that when people look at each other as adults they are just seeing the residue of what they've been through. Residue could cloud one's view of the world and make a person respond in a whole different way. Adults have to recognize what the residue is and grow from what they learn. That statement was the essence of their marriage and their lives. It would have to be what they stood on if they were to be together.

James walked Deanna to her car. He told her that even her waddle was cute. They shot the breeze for a few moments and talked about how the birth would go in just over a month, and then all of a sudden James got serious. He grabbed her hand, "De, our relationship is like a universe and you are my sun. There is no light without you in my life. God gave you to me so that His rays could shine brightly through you to energize and soften me into the person I am supposed to be. Without you there is darkness. I know I've been wrong. I know I shouldn't have left you. I should have never left your side. I couldn't take seeing you, you who are my strength, just melt away. I felt helpless and

JOSHUA'S COMING

205

ashamed that I had not been there for you. I know none of this really matters now. You have every right to never want to be with me again, but I pray that you can see that I did not have any control over how I thought."

The petals of Deanna's heart began to unfold as she listened to her husband explain his indefensible actions. She had a lot of thinking to do.

~

Believing God for conception for Deanna had been a true example of Terri McMillan's book, *Waiting to Exhale*, but instead of waiting to breathe when the right man came along, Deanna had been waiting to breathe when she gave birth. She did not realize until that last push that she had been waiting to breathe. She had been holding back her true self until she could grasp hold of the dream that had seemed to slip from her fingertips for so many years. Breathing after Joshua's birth had felt funny to Deanna. She imagined it to be like breathing on another planet. She had been cut off from true breathing for so long, it felt intimidating and hazardous all at the same time. She could not have anticipated a more perfect birth and delivery. The pain that she endured was miniscule compared to the joy that she felt in her heart. She finally understood all the women who had told her that they forgot the pain of childbirth after it was over. She lay there waiting for Joshua to come from the nursery so she could feed him. She thought to herself, was she really ready to be a mother? After all the tears, after all the pain, after all the many lost battles to the enemy, after riding the seesaw of faith to faithless; what if after all this she let God down? What if after all the tough feminine macho tripping she had been doing before his birth was just for show? Deanna frightfully remembered the dream that haunted her many months before. She thought to herself, "Wait a minute. Stop tripping. I am not that person anymore. I can do all things through Christ who strengthens me. Nope, devil not this time. I have gone too far to turn back now." As if God had been right in the midst of her thoughts, Carleen walked into her hospital room. Deanna was happy to see her friend and proud to be able to show off the gift that God had blessed her with. Joshua was a prince. His dark curly hair and smooth carmel-colored skin was as comforting as the morning sun.

~

"Carleen it is so good to see you. How are things?" Deanna sat up in her bed and adjusted her sheets.

RHONDA C. WHITE

Carleen refused to respond to her questions. "Girl, I want to know about you. You finally did it, huh? You joined the mommy sorority. You look like you are in one piece. I am proud of you. And look at this beautiful child." Joshua squirmed slightly in her arms and kept his eyes tightly shut. He was peaceful and pleasant.

"Carleen I am fine. I was just sitting here getting a little overwhelmed with everything, until I quickly remembered who my Rock was." Deanna shifted in the hospital bed. She would sure be happy when she and Joshua could get home. With all of her family coming to help, she was sure this would probably be the last time that she would see him.

"Sweetie, you know I know. This whole deal with John has been more than a notion. But you are so right, our Savior is the only Rock that we can place our feet solidly on and expect to keep standing. I've realized now in my years of living that trials are compliments, not curses." Carleen rocked the baby one more time before handing him over to his mother for his feeding.

"Yeah but Carleen, I know I am so much better than I was a few months ago, but how do I completely let my guard down about my marriage and now my family? I want it all to work and I am ready to let it all go, but my flesh still gets in the way."

"Baby, your ability at this point to forget is way more important than your ability to remember. And when I say forget I don't mean that you are supposed to forget what happened to you. Never forget that. You went through all of that so you could help somebody else through. What I mean is you have to allow your body to forget the pain that was attached to the tragedy. You have forgiven James and yourself for all that has gone on. Stop thinking about it and do it reflexively. Your anxiety of going back into your relationship is based more on being scared about what other people think versus your true insecurities. Don't let nobody stop you from having the joy you know that God wants you to have in your marriage. People are gonna talk. And you will never satisfy them. But are you gonna let their nosiness and opinions stop the flow of God in your life? God wants to be able to say James looks more like Him because he was married to you. Marriage is not to make you happy, but holy. You have learned that at a young age. If you both can go back into it with that in mind, everything will work out fine."

Deanna was glad that Carleen had given it to her straight. She did not need that around-the-way version. The truth was the truth and it had set her free.

In the midst of all the movement that was going on in Deanna's home, she felt more blessed than ever. Her mother, Carleen and Cara were fussing over her and the baby. She had not washed one dish, changed one diaper or answered the phone one time. She was getting too used to this. They would be gone soon and what was she going to do with Joshua by herself? She was surprised when she got to the door that they had not yelled at her for getting the mail. She shuffled through bills and junk mail before she came upon a business-sized manila envelope from James. She quickly slipped into the bathroom and opened the letter. Her heart raced, her fingers twitched. What was this boy up to now? He had been over everyday since she and Joshua had come home. He spent as much time with Joshua as the hens would allow. The letter began, "You know our lives, our story, each day is a page and each year a new chapter. Since our separation, my heartbeat has been irregular. And I don't know if the rhythm that it had when I was with you will ever return unless we start turning our pages together again. I need you in my life. I know God put you on this earth for me. I cannot take back the wrong I've done. Nothing I can say or do will cancel that out. But I want you to know that I am sorry and the best way I can make it up to you is to spend the rest of my life showing you how much being in your life's novel means to me. Baby, please take me back into your heart, Love, James."

Wow, James was trying to work a mojo on her and it was working. She was ready to get her life and her marriage back on track. They started moving James' things back home the following weekend.

⁓

Again, the time on the clock flew and seasons changed without a glitch. Deanna and James were elated that the day had come to dedicate six-month old Joshua officially to the Lord. Deanna dressed in her light blue two-piece Tahari suit and 3-½ inch Via Spiga pumps. She had difficulty being humble that day. Not because of anything she had done but because of what God had done. He had mended her marriage and delivered her baby safe and sound. She could see James dressing in his tailor-fitted Italian suit with a light blue pin-striped shirt and blue pastel abstract tie. Wow, she had missed just watching him dress. She let go completely and rejoiced because of the awesome power of God. Things were not all just right yet, but they were working on it, and God was continuing to work on them.

"De, come on honey! Let's not be late today. We have people waiting on us." James yelled from the bottom of the stairs. Deanna looked down at her cooing son. He seemed to always have a peaceful expression, even during the few times that he cried. She was grateful that he had her eyes. As much as she loved him she did not want to be reminded of the horror in how he had gotten here by possibly piercing into the eyes of her perpetrator every time she looked at her son. Joshua looked so much like Deanna's father, but some of his features were unfamiliar and again she was grateful that they decided not to even consider DNA testing to determine his paternity. Joshua was theirs and there was no doubt about it. They did not need any test to stand in the way of their parenthood.

"How is mama's baby? Do you hear your father down there fussing?" Deanna's aunt made Joshua the cutest dedication outfit. It had been difficult to find a unique white outfit for him. It was made of an African embroidered print with a matching hat. The outfit was outlined in pearls and lace and was simply gorgeous. They had been blessed like that since Joshua had been born. People that they did not even know had graced them with baby furniture, clothes, diapers and other necessities. They would be set with things for him until he was two. Gosh, the boy had been spoiled before he could even talk or walk. Deanna grabbed the rest of her things and the baby and pranced down the steps to her knight in shining armor.

The service and ceremony were wonderful. Reverend Marshall made a big deal about every baby that came his way, but when he picked up Joshua he stared in his eyes and then up towards the heavens. Without saying a word Reverend Marshall shared the same moment of praise with the Carringtons and their loved ones. Carleen and John Adams stood proud as the godparents. John had walked up to the front of the church on his own with only a cane. He stood proud not only for Joshua but for his own life. A single tear fell from his eye as he was reminded of the request he had made of the Lord to allow him to stay alive until he saw the Carrington's baby born. Well, God had not only done that but John had been improving day by day. He was still considered to be a very sick man, but he was enjoying life and taking each day as it came. Carleen could not have been happier about her husband and her godchild. She was sure she would have to fight to continue to spoil

Joshua, but she was willing to take her chances amongst all the other people that the baby had in his life.

~

After the service, Deanna and James were standing on the steps saying their last good-byes to their friends and loved ones. Cairo and Alesha had flown in for the event. Steven and the kids, the Alexanders and the rest of the family were all heading to the designated restaurant to do the traditional baby dedication meal. Suddenly a sight for sore eyes walked into Deanna's line of vision. James inherently took Joshua and his things and descended the steps toward the car. He gave a friendly, but cautious nod to Theresa and turned to leave the women alone. They hugged and went back into the empty church. The janitors had just begun to clean so they would have time to have an unrushed conversation if need be.

"Well lady, I guess you have done it. You sure are a sharp mommy too! I don't think I knew how to be fly with a young baby to care for. I want to be like you when I grow up!"

Deanna chuckled slightly. It was wonderful to hear her friend joke around again. She had missed her, but she had been ready to move on if they never became good friends again.

"De, I am just going to get straight to the point. Your faith has strengthened my character. I am sure I read this somewhere and now I have lived it. God only gives you enough strength for today on purpose. If we had a supply for tomorrow, our worries would be greater and our anxiety higher. The strength we have today is a building block for the strength we will need for tomorrow. It follows the ideal supply and demand theory; you use what you have and that's enough. My voyage has matured my wisdom and refined my beliefs. Life stripped me down to the bone so that I could finally realize that God was enough. People, relationships and things in my life are only temporary. The only constant has been Christ. When I didn't have Him, I didn't have anything."

Deanna sat back on the pew as she listened. Without knowing the full story she was proud already of Theresa's growth.

Theresa went on with her thoughts. "In times past I ignored or discounted what you were saying. Not because you are ignorant or unwise, but because a lot of the times I did not want to hear the truth. The truth hurts, but I've learned through my own struggles and now my failed marriage that in the long run the truth is necessary for growth. God will not allow His word to stand with lies. I've realized in retrospect that I'd lied to myself, Steve, my children and most importantly, to God for way too long. He ultimately is my answer no matter how far I run. Even though my divorce is final, I realize that my relationship with Christ can and still must grow." Deanna continued to sit silently. "De, I need to share something with you." Theresa's pause was pregnant for one moment. "There are so many things I need to say not only to you but to so many who have tried to steer me in the right direction. I guess I need to apologize first for never being the type of friend to you that you are to me. My life had been based on lies and I guess I had a warped picture of what friendship truly is. It is not someone who stands by your side through thick and thin, but then will not tell you the truth when you need to hear it. I guess I have always resented you a bit because I thought you were just mean or never really supported me. You are the type of person who will share information and your life stories to help. You want to see people grow and I now understand that. But sometimes people don't want your advice. They just want you to listen. You can always know how people want you to respond. If they ask you a question about the situation then that's when they want your opinion, but if they are just sharing or venting then all they want you to be is a soft place for them to fall on. If they are to change, God will do the changing. See, all the stuff you were telling me was right, but I was not ready to hear that from you or God. But when He changed me, it happened. You can't be a change agent for everybody. However, I realize that the truth you always shared, no matter how crude it was, was the support that I needed most. I did not need people telling me, yeah, girl go on and leave that Negro. He ain't never been no good anyway. Although that may still be true . . ." A small smile graced Theresa's face. "I needed someone to help me to see me. It isn't all Steve's fault that we aren't together, but at the time I did not want to focus on that. I really just wanted to get out and I felt that if I ran away, that pain and disappointment would go away. Well, it didn't and I know that the pain of a divorce will plague me and my children for a long time. I don't even really know the impact that it will have on generations to come. But that is too deep for me to think about now. I just know that I need to get back on track with the Lord and seek some type of emotional support for me and my children. So I said all of that to say I am sorry for being too consumed with me to see your love and concern. I also want to apologize for not being there for you. You have been through so much De and I can only imagine how devastating it has been. You always were the strong one so sometimes I felt purposeless in our relationship. But I know that is foolish. God put us together for a reason and I just pray that we can rebuild some type of relationship again. You have had so many things to sort through alone and

I just commend you for being so resilient even in the midst of." De reached for her friend and they locked in a hug that was long overdue.

~

Deanna put Joshua down in his room that had been decorated in light greens and yellows so many years before. James' friends had likened him unto Noah who built the ark way before anyone had ever even heard of rain. Joshua's room had been finished and ready for his arrival long before his parents had been ready. They truly had come full circle as a couple. She remembered the dream that Rodney Alexander had interpreted for them so many months before. They certainly had been forced to deal with their sins head on. James' sin had been to conceal the pain from his childhood. That alone had almost ruined him and their marriage. Deanna's were the sins of pride and witchcraft. Yes, she was guilty of being too proud of what she thought were her own accomplishments. She had tried to move God in her own power and by her own will to bring forth their child. Every time she tried on her own to bring forth a child, it failed. It was not until God was ready did that blessing truly come to pass. Her new joy erased all the sorrow and all the pain she once had. The scars were there. She would never forget the circumstances, but she had grown and she had learned who was truly in control.

~

Deanna could hear James snoring as she ascended the steps to bed. As tired as she was she knew she had to write down a few thoughts in her journal before she retired for the evening. She climbed in their king-size bed and turned on the lamp on her night stand. James stirred only for a moment. She had always been amazed how he could sleep through anything. Time and their circumstances had not changed that. She thought of how pleased she was because that feeling of comforting trust had returned. She knew that they still had a long way to go, but God was right there with them, pulling, tugging and encouraging them along the way. They would make it this time for sure. The cord between them had been strengthened; their boat was no longer rocking. It was all good.

~

The last pages of Deanna's journal entry read like this: "I've spent so much time living life that I neglected to see the greatest gifts that God put right

RHONDA C. WHITE

in front of me. Discovery and revelation come after a storm; that which you wish you knew, so that the rain drops would not have felt so wet and so hard. Thank you Lord for my passage, for my voyage. Thank you for my marriage and thank you for Joshua's coming. I can truly say that I would not have changed a thing. Good night." Her journal fell from her hands and gently landed on the ground, just like they had.

~

The walls in the Carrington home returned to their normal breathing pattern. Now nothing was congesting the even flow of respirations that brought in new air and new life on a continual basis. They relaxed, excited that another dream had been fulfilled. Their confidence was restored. They could rest up for their next encounter.

EPILOGUE

Jesus looked at them and said, "With man this is impossible,
but with God all things are possible."

Matthew 19:26

"De, I can't find my protein drinks. Have you seen them?" Deanna tossed Joshua in the air as she proceeded to the kitchen to help her husband.

"I think you put the extra ones in the bottom cabinet." James was locating his drinks simultaneously with Deanna's profession.

They shared a similar smile that comforted and reassured the both of them. "Let me see my man!" James said proudly handed their son to him and watched James beam in the presence of the new life that was in their midst. James lifted Joshua to the heavens and imitated Kunte Kente in *Roots* when he lifted his daughter to proclaim the next generation of his family. "God, we are giving back to you what you have given us. Not our will but your will be done!"

Deanna's laugh quickly became tears of joy as she realized that James was not being his regular comedic self, but that he was truly praising God for what He had done. No, Joshua had not come to them in a way that they had expected, but his life was a true testament to what God could do with His children when they have willing hearts. She was reminded of the meaning of Joshua's name, the Lord saves. He truly had been a savior for their family in more ways than one. They owed their all to Him and Deanna planned to do her best to show her gratitude.

A NOTE FROM THE AUTHOR AND FRIENDS . . . .

God is so good and He does truly want to bless us. I pray that this story has inspired you to seek His will for your lives and to trust Him even during the hard times. God never told us that this road called life would be easy but, He did say that He would be with us every step of the way. The biggest lesson that I learned through writing this book was the lesson of obedience. A friend of mine, Pamela Johnson told me when I first started writing something that proved to be so true. She told me that God might be waiting on me to finish this book so that He could bless me. And do you know that almost to the very moment that I pushed save to complete the last chapter of this book, I found out that I was pregnant. God is so good and His love language is obedience. My experience is a true testament to what has been said: that you go through trials not for yourself, but for someone else.

God sends His encouragement and support to us often through the lives of others. In the next few pages, you will find letters that were written by ladies who had at one time in their lives been very much like Deanna and struggled with infertility. These letters are rich with wisdom, courage and hope. God is able, friends, and the same thing He has done for others He can do for you. Some ladies received their blessing in the way they expected and others received via an alternate route. Miracles come in different sizes and types. The biggest packages most of the time don't have the best gifts. It's those little tiny packages that sometimes are hidden that can bring us the most joy. Each letter has happiness at the end of its rainbow. God is in the blessing business and as soon as we take our minds off what we want and how we want it, He is able to bless us well above what we could have ever imagined.

*No matter what you are believing God for, know that He does hear and answer prayers. Infertility might not be your struggle, but I have realized that most of the problems we face in life are due to a lack of faith. I realize now that faith is simply this: **Fixing Attitudes Impacts Things Happening.** You cannot expect to receive anything from God, even salvation, if you do not first believe. Life has a way of ripping faith from you, but you must be strong, hold onto the sails of your faith even in storms. Your endurance can impact God's plans and His timing. Let your faith negotiate with God. Don't let go of your dreams, they can come true!*

Dear Friend, Oh do I know:

Marc and I had been married for almost four years before I decided I was ready for children. Just as you read in this fictional story loosely based on my life, my husband was ready long before children became a thought to me. Then all of a sudden I got this inkling that it was time. If I was ready, surely God was. I got off the pill, which I had taken on and off since I was nineteen years old and waited the prescribed three months before we started 'trying'.

Little did we know that trying would turn into an almost two-year struggle with infertility. My doctor was quite laid back about the whole process and only ordered preliminary testing after we made it to a year with no success. Our tests showed that my tubes were clear and that my husband supposedly had a low sperm count. I contributed his test findings more to the difficulty we had in obtaining the test sample rather than a truly low count. After our tests found nothing, approximately two months later we conceived. Unfortunately, I miscarried at only seven weeks gestation. We were devastated, but because of God's love that was shown through family and friends, we made it through. I became frustrated when we were still babyless after almost another year of trying.

Then almost two years to the date of the miscarriage we conceived again. This time we had some help through intrauterine insemination. It took me a while to decide if the procedure was truly for me. I had to accept that my way was not always a stop on God's highway. Doctors cannot stop or start anything that the Lord does not ordain. We suffered through one unsuccessful insemination to finally conceive on the very next trial. Despite the fear that I had in my heart, which had to be cast down through much prayer, we gave birth to a beautiful healthy girl on December 10, 2006 named Aerin.

I've had so many angels of light along my journey. I would not have made it without them. I know my suffering now was only so that the Lord could help others along the way through my story. He truly does use our trials to strengthen others. One of my favorite lines from the book is that trials are compliments, not curses. God is so good even when we don't have the faith to fully trust His timing.

Sincerely Knowing,
Rhonda

JOSHUA'S COMING

Dear Friend:

I remember like it was yesterday. We were married for three years when we decided, "let's have kids." I had been on the pill for four years and on Depo Provera shots for maybe five years. Yes, that was a long time to have hormones running through my body, to prevent me from having kids. We tried and tried. It seems like every month I thought I was pregnant and I wasn't! We were praying for God to bless us with a child. Our first child! I couldn't wait to carry a child. Having sex became a chore and not a desire. We were doing it just to get pregnant.

Finally we stopped just having sex and started making LOVE! We totally put it in God's hand. I stopped looking to see if my friend (period) came. I jumped in my car one sunny evening and just drove and talked to God. I made Him promises, I told Him, "Trust me." I will teach the child The Ten Commandments, The Lord's Prayer and so on. It was a year now and no child. My husband and I decided to go away on a trip to Las Vegas with our family and have some fun. I want you to know WE got pregnant on our trip in Vegas. Nine months later we gave birth to a healthy, beautiful, baby girl!! Glory to God!

I have something for those who have miscarried. Six months later we got pregnant again. I miscarried. Don't get sad and mourn for me. All things work together for good. I was sad and maybe even angry. But God!! God had us to understand that it was better for Him to take that child than to have it come here and suffer! The egg was deformed. You have to pray and really get to know God to understand why. One year later I was pregnant again! Glory to God! I gave birth to a healthy, handsome, baby boy! Just stand and pray and continue to lift you and your spouse up in prayer. He can't help but bless you. Not when you're ready, but when He's ready. Just pray that His will be done!

Your friend in Christ,
Carla

RHONDA C. WHITE

Dear Sister,

When I was a child I had a definite plan for my life. Marry a wonderful man, become a kindergarten teacher and have two children by the time I was thirty. Well, my plan was coming together nicely, Wonderful man, check Kindergarten teacher, check but the two children by thirty was proving to be a little more difficult. This was the time I realized that this was not *my* plan at all. I was really following the plan that God had for me. Having children grow inside my body was the way I saw it happening, but God had another plan, a better plan. It became clear to me that what we wanted to create was a family and if we could not build it biologically we would adopt. Once we began this process things went very smoothly. Our wait was short for our precious son. He arrived just like a Christmas gift on Christmas Eve 1992. We were overjoyed and overwhelmed with the demands of parenthood. We felt and saw no differences between us and our friends who had biological children. *We were a family!* Many people told me, "Now that you have adopted you will get pregnant for sure." I found myself praying that I would not become pregnant. I wanted my children to be able to share their adoption experiences and be able to support each other in a way that one biological child and one adopted child could not. After three years we excitedly began the process to adopt our baby girl. Again, when you follow God's plan things go so smoothly. In just a few short months we received a phone call telling us that our beautiful daughter was in the world and waiting for us. She was like a jewel, sparkly and new. She, in fact, was the crowning jewel to our God-made family. We are now the proud parents of a thirteen-year old son and a ten-year old daughter and our lives are richer, fuller and happier because they are in it.

Commit to the LORD whatever you do, and your plans will succeed.
PROVERBS 16:3 NIV

Proud Mother, Jennifer

JOSHUA'S COMING

Dear Friend:

I am one of those ladies who likes to plan everything out. The plan was to marry, wait two years and then have a baby. So, after we were married about a year and a half, I got off the pill. A few months later I was pregnant. Perfect! God said, "Not so, you didn't ask Me." I miscarried and had to have a DNC. That began the grieving process.

We kept trying and kept trying and trying. Months pass. Everyone wants to know when we're going to have a baby. (Not knowing we're trying.) We want to know too. What's wrong with me? I'm thinking. Why is this taking so long? Am I being punished for past sins? The doctor is very cavalier and tells me not to worry about it. More months pass. What a roller coaster ride. Every month hoping it will be the month. What if I can't give my husband a child? What will he think? What if that abortion was my only chance? Every month I beat myself up over the past. All of this time, both my husband and I were very prayerful. I had a lot to learn about what God's word said about having a baby. I would pray what I learned. It would make me feel better for a while. Then my mind would trip me up again. A year passed on this roller coaster and one day my husband came to me and said God just told him I was pregnant with a boy. Of course I was a professional pregnancy test taker by this point and had plenty in my stash. I asked, "Are you sure?" He replied, "Yes." So, I went and took a test. It said negative. "Am I going to trust that God spoke to my husband or get punked again?" I asked. I chose option number one. The next test I took said positive. David is now three and a half. His life reminds me that God is faithful and just.

When my first son, was a year and a half we began to try for a second child. Within a few months we were pregnant. We went six months and my water bag broke. The hospital said we had to wait a week before they would even admit me. They encouraged us to abort. God didn't tell us to do that so we didn't. My husband was out of town in the Police Academy. I was at my mom's on strict bed rest. No turning on my sides, no sitting up and no bathroom, etc. It was one of the worst experiences ever. I believed God through it all. The baby ended up being stillborn. "God is still faithful and just." We went through another grieving process.

Do we want to try again or be happy with the blessing we already have, (My first son?) My husband said it was up to me. I kept praying and asking God to tell me what He wanted. I couldn't hear from Him. Took "How to Hear from God" in Sunday School. Nothing. Put out fleeces. Nothing. I know God is able but what is His desire for me, I wondered? Over a year passed. I didn't do anything. I kept waiting to hear from the Lord. I'm getting too old. I guess He doesn't want me to try anymore, I thought. I just kept

RHONDA C. WHITE

still. One month I just wasn't feeling like myself. Found out I was almost three months pregnant. My second boy is almost four months.

I've learned so much from my experiences. Mostly being: I am not in control, God is. We're working off of his watch, not ours. God does not hold grudges. He is faithful.

I hope my small testimony will inspire you. God can certainly do for you what He's done for me.

In Christ's love,
Kim

Dear Sistah Friend,

It is unfamiliar to write to someone you do not know personally; but, in life we often share more commonalities than we realize. When Rhonda asked me to share my experience, I was not sure where or how to begin. Then I realized there is no better place than the beginning.

I have always followed the "Good Girl" path in life. That path allowed me to obtain all the trinkets "Good Girls" get. My life's path even took me to meet my husband while I was a bridesmaid in my tenth wedding. While we were watching our friends stand at the altar, we glanced at each other and wondered about our own future. We both did hear something pretty amazing that day. The minister told them, but he was talking to us too, that when people marry, becoming a fruitful/productive couple is more than making babies. He went on to say that God wants us to share our fruitfulness in many ways. We took that message to heart and have incorporated it into our lives together.

Since, before we said, "I do", we began providing support to nephews, cousins, friend's kids and where ever our lives were directed. I even accepted the infant son of my beloved and made a commitment to love him as my own. As we talked about having a baby of our union, I became concerned about how my gynecological history would impact us. I had experienced a long history of missed and absent periods. When we were finally ready to start, I talked to a friend who is an OB/GYN and got a list of questions I needed to discuss with my doctor. I came off the pill and the "games" began. For 6 months we took temperatures and spent a lot of time under the covers . . . NOTHING. I went back to the doctor who then suggested a medication. My husband was against it and knew we could do it on our own. Months later no go. Finally, I started taking medication. I was so discouraged, we told my parents that maybe they would not have grandkids. We even went on to seek out information about adoption. All this time we continued to be active in the lives of the children of our world. One evening at dinner, I told my husband I was tried of trying and said let's just stop. We both agreed that if we did not produce babies of our own, we could still impact the lives of little ones.

Well, that was almost nine and a half years ago. Now, I have a son who is thirteen and I still love him like my own. I know I do because, my twins are eight and a half years old now and I love them all the same. We still stay true to our mantra . . . Being productive and fruitful does not always mean making something one way. It could mean guiding, molding, but most importantly, loving all the kids God sends our way.

As you travel this road in your life's journey, please know that often especially for people who know their way that it is hard not to always be in control or know what is next. For me that time in my life let me know how important loving all of God's children who come into our lives really is. Even the little ones that smile at you in the grocery store or wave from the car. It also helped my faith grow to believe that often, when we think we know what's going on there can be a lot going on behind the scenes that we can only believe and trust in.

Stay Strong my sistah and know that *mustard seeds* are growing everywhere!

Sincerely,
Ann

RHONDA C. WHITE

Dear girlfriend,

I never thought that having a child would be problematic for me. I mean, I come from a family where having babies is just a part of life, and you were more concerned about preventing pregnancy than maintaining one.

I married young and was able to get pregnant right away. I had a problem-free pregnancy and gave birth to a beautiful baby girl. However, there were many problems in the marriage and having other children was not an option at the time. The marriage eventually dissolved and when I remarried several years later and attempted to "be fruitful and multiply" I realized that it would not be easy.

My new husband and I were able to conceive within our first year of marriage. We were doing all the things young married couples should do to prepare for a new baby. My daughter (then seven years old), was excited and so were we. Six weeks into the pregnancy, I miscarried. We were sad, but we realized that things happen for a reason and we planned to try again.

The following year, we conceived again. When we went for the eight week checkup it was determined that we were having twins! What a blessing! Our family was growing by leaps and bounds! Then, at the twelve week checkup, we were informed that the babies' hearts had stopped beating and asked if we wanted to terminate the pregnancy or wait until my body miscarried on its own. We waited and one week later, I miscarried . . . again.

Three years into the marriage and we are pregnant again. Surely the Lord will smile on us this time! We passed the six week point without a problem, and when we hit the twelve week mark and were still okay, we just knew we were out of the woods. We went for a routine check-up at twenty weeks and were told that my cervix was opening and that the water bag was protruding out. This required emergency surgery because if the bag broke the baby would die instantly. The procedure was done and I was sent home on complete bed rest for what I thought would be the next four months. However, within 24 hours, the bag ruptured and I returned to the hospital to deliver a stillborn baby girl. One week later, we buried her and I decided it was over for me.

"That's it!!!!" I told my husband in front of my doctor. "We must not need any more children, because if we did they wouldn't keep dying! I AM NOT TRYING AGAIN!!! I've got fibroids, scar tissue and this weak cervix. Why should I keep setting myself up for failure?" My doctor, a Christian woman as well, listened intently and then said, "All that's true, but you know God can do anything. It won't be easy for you to have a baby, but you pray on it with your husband and don't give up on God."

That was February 2003. In October 2004 the Lord brought forth from my womb a beautiful baby girl, healthy, happy and blessed. Yes, I had fibroids that competed with the baby for space in my uterus. Yes, I had to have my cervix stitched closed at 16 weeks and be on complete bed rest for the remainder of the pregnancy. Yes, I was hospitalized for premature labor and told that my baby was in danger. Yes, we struggled financially because of the loss of one income. Yes, I was at risk for high blood pressure and gestational diabetes because of my weight, age and my forced inactivity. Yes, I'd had abnormal pap smears that the doctor was monitoring for cancerous changes. Yes, I had scar tissue on my cervix that made it dangerous to attempt a vaginal delivery, mandating a Caesarean section. ***But . . . God.***

God didn't see fit to let those things be. We prayed and through it all God kept us and is still keeping us to this day. **Praise be to God, from whom all blessings flow.**

Thank you Lord Jesus,
Shauntel

Dear Friend,

Being in the will of God is not always the easiest place to be—especially when God doesn't tell you what He is doing. I remember crying-out "Lord, oh Lord, I'm still here—you didn't forget about my prayer request did you? You know, the one about me being a mother. You know God, it's been a long time now that you have had me waiting and I think I'm ready for my prayer to be answered. You know Lord, I went through my repentance list *again* and I have even checked it twice to see if I forgot to ask forgiveness for anything because—Hey—once I *really* repent of these things, you can go ahead and give me my baby—Right? Cause, as far as I can see, God, everything else is straight. I'm in good health, I have a nice home, I have money in the bank, I'm even married now, and besides all that, I'M READY!!!"

I mean this is how it's supposed to work—Right? I pray about something that lines up with God's word and then He gives me the desires of my heart—Right? Well why couldn't I get pregnant!!!

It seemed like everyone but me was pregnant. I wanted a baby so bad that if I could have made one myself—I would have. After realizing that there was NOTHING I could do, I surrendered and told myself God is in control. As soon as I gave up the rights I thought I had, my attitude changed and then I began to believe that God's word would indeed work for me too. After ten months of trying we conceived and I gave birth to my firstborn daughter. God then up and did the miraculous and I conceived again approximately seven months later. We now have two beautiful daughters who prove to us on a daily basis that God is faithful.

My friend, God is no respecter of persons. His promises are true and his timing is perfect. God hears your prayers and he knows your desire to be a mother. His plans are to prosper you and not to harm you. His word works even when it does not fall into your time-line. I know it's hard to wait on the Lord, but God wants you to believe that He knows what's best for you. God wants your heart to say it's either "His way" or "No way". God wants you to trust Him at all times.

Be Blessed and Believe,
Lisa

Blessed is she who has believed that what the Lord has said to her will be accomplished!

Luke 1:45 NIV

Dear Friend,

To have or not have children, my choice right? I always thought that the ability to have children was my choice, something that I controlled. I wanted to establish myself in the workplace, acquire a certain amount of financial wealth, material possessions and then fit children into the mix of things. It was supposed to be effortless; after all, the birthing process is not rocket science. That was my plan, but was that God's plan? For a year and a half my husband and I tried to conceive with month after month of disappointment, depression and anger. I sought medical advice, to only be told by countless doctors that all was well with me," you're probably trying too hard," they said. I felt hopeless. I thought I deserve to have children; "it is my right," I cried to the Lord. I finally told God that since he would not allow me to have children, to take the desire away, but the desire grew stronger. I guess God was trying to get my attention. Through sermons and Bible reading, God told me to ask with a right heart and that my desires must glorify Him. Why did I really want children? Because all my friends had some or because others told me it was time? No, I told God that I wanted to please Him and to follow His word that says to be fruitful; that I realized that my body is not my own to have for selfish reasons (having a child is a selfless act). I belong to Him. Sometime after, I was led to see a former doctor, who immediately diagnosed me with a large fibroid tumor. After a surgical procedure for removing the tumor, I was told that my tubes were severely scarred, leaving the possibility of having children very small. I was told that I needed to conceive immediately, before I had another menstrual cycle (as this would ultimately reverse the surgical procedure). Well, I had two more menstrual cycles. However, during this time, I was reading the book *Supernatural Childbirth* and believing the promises shared in the reading, while praying both individually and with my husband a prayer of victory and blessing over my womb. The third month after my surgical procedure, conception had taken place. On July 3, 2000 I gave birth to our first son Immanuel (God with us) and our second son Isaiah (salvation of God) on January 23, 2003. Both pregnancies were extraordinary; I delivered both children vaginally with minimal labor contractions and without medication. God was there and ready, I simply had to check my attitude and myself.

Having Received the Promise,
Tressey

RHONDA C. WHITE

Dear Sister,

My husband and I tried unsuccessfully for 12 years to conceive. For some reason, I was under the impression that I would become pregnant so long as we tried to conceive around the time I ovulated. I quickly discovered that wasn't the case. I didn't realize at the time that we didn't possess the power to create life. Only God does. I discovered that we are merely the vehicles through which life comes. After years of going to baby showers and hearing the wonderful news of friends and family members having babies while my husband and I remained childless, I began to feel hopeless. Some days I was depressed and experienced a myriad of emotions. Nevertheless, my husband and I continued to pray that we would conceive.

In 2000, my husband and I went for an IVF consultation. However, we elected not to attempt it at that time due to the lack of insurance coverage for the procedure, my husband's and my mother's fears and apprehensions, and most importantly, our lack of funds. I had decided to just let the Lord do whatever He wanted. I still believed that somehow I would conceive, even if it were by some miracle. In 2002, my cousin, who is an evangelist, said to me "your baby is on the way" and that there would be an induction. I began thanking and praising God instantaneously. I was so excited and hopeful because I knew that the miracle I sought was imminent. I began imagining how and when everything would take place.

Everything began to unfold in 2003 when a very good friend of ours told us that she and her husband were going through IVF in order to conceive their first child. They urged us to also go through the procedure. Initially, I was very apprehensive because I didn't want to go through the procedure and have it be unsuccessful. Not only that, what if it wasn't God's will? I found that this was a major difference between those who are believers and those who are not. Believers are aware that God's will takes precedence over everything regardless of how much money you have or how many doctors you can afford. Unless it is the will of God that you conceive, it will not happen. In any event, the one thing my friend said that remained with me was that our chances are greater if we try, than if we did nothing at all. I prayed for God's guidance and asked that if this was His will that it be done.

Our first attempt at IVF was unsuccessful, which left me in a depressed state for 3 weeks. Naturally, my husband, parents, family and close friends were very concerned about me. I needed to go through that so I could come to the realization that God's will is what's important, not what I wanted. I struggled those three weeks with turning everything over to God, allowing His perfect will to be done, even if it meant that we would not have a baby. That was the most difficult experience I have ever had. However, God's grace enabled me to do what I normally would not have the strength to do—let it go and trust Him.

We decided to try another cycle at the suggestion of our doctor, family and friends in April of 2004. However, this time I decided not to get my hopes up and prepared for the possibility of our not conceiving again. We found out we were pregnant on June 4, 2004. The enemy tried to discourage and scare us a few times as I was diagnosed with having subchorionic bleeding—bleeding underneath the placenta—after I had an episode where I thought I miscarried. We were also told by our doctor that there was a possibility that we could still miscarry. However, we trusted and believed God. Part one of the word from the Lord had already taken place, "our baby was on the way."

My pregnancy was the most awesome experience I have ever had. I enjoyed every trimester, even the first as I didn't experience morning sickness. I was given a due date of February 15, 2005. God had other plans. On December 30, 2004, I was admitted to the hospital because I was leaking amniotic fluid, a serious matter, which could cause infection and be fatal to the baby. My doctor decided to perform an emergency C-section on the day I turned 34 weeks, Monday, January 3, 2005. On that day, God gave to us our beautiful baby girl, Ryann Mikayla. Part two of the word from the Lord took place "induction" which means the act of causing or bringing on or about. Thus, the emergency C-section.

Although the journey to conceive Ryann was difficult, I thank God for the lessons learned. I was able to place in His hands one of the things I held on to so very tightly concerning conceiving a child—my will. I am confident this whole experience will help me in the future when I will have to again allow my will to become lost in His.

God's word is true, His will is perfect, and His timing is impeccable!

Love ya,
Tracey

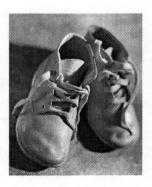

RHONDA C. WHITE

Dear Lady in Waiting,

"First comes love, then comes marriage, then comes Latosha with a baby carriage!" The childhood rhyme may have worked for some people, but that is not my testimony. Oh how I wish conceiving my children had been as easy as the words of this little ditty. Being mad at God does not even begin to explain my disdain for Him many years ago. Don't get me wrong, I blamed myself too. The devil had me beat in the worst way. Through much prayer, I stopped living a defeated life and started believing God would allow me to conceive at His appointed time and not a moment before. This was a hard pill to swallow because I am accustomed to getting and having my way. After all, His word says whatsoever things we ask, and believe, we shall receive. I learned later that God does not give us blessings we are not prepared for. The first years of my marriage were pretty rocky and I believe God did not want a child to complicate matters. Needless to say, I put myself through more turmoil, grief and pain than I wanted to bare. It took several years of prayer, fasting, soul searching and a little medical intervention to deliver a healthy, nine pound four ounce son in July 1998, after two years of trying and a healthy eight pound daughter in October 2004, six years later.

I had been married about a year before we discussed the right time to start having children. Several months turned into more than a year with no positive results. My husband, of course knew he was not the problem because he already had a child from a previous relationship. Therefore, our infertility was all my fault. My mind began to race as to why I could not conceive. I told myself God was punishing me for being sexually active before getting married. This could not be the only reason because I had friends who had premarital sex and were able to conceive right away in their marriages. So, my next reason became my lack of submission as a wife. I'm college educated and did not require financial assistance from a man so what was I supposed to be submissive for? It took many threats of my husband leaving me and years of prayer before I discovered that God's word commands wives to submit unto their own husbands.

To you, my sister going through infertility issues, know that God is faithful. He can bless you just like Sarah, Hannah and any other woman who has walked in these shoes. Sure this is a painful and sensitive issue for couples, but trust that God wants us all to have our own testimony and this is the test He chose for us. If it were not for my test I would not be writing these words to help encourage you. Yes, God allows us to go through storms but He is not doing it to punish us for past sins. Know that Heaven will not run out of little babies before God sends you yours. Walk in faith and begin to prepare your body to sustain a healthy pregnancy via proper diet, nutrition, exercise and good mental/physical health. Pick out a name, maybe two; He may give you double for your trouble. Expect your miracle and it will happen.

God Bless,
Latosha

Dear Friend,

My journey began about ten years ago. After being married for three years, my husband and I decided that we should start trying for a family. After nothing happened for over one year, we decided to speak with a doctor to see what the problem was. My husband was checked out and received a clean bill of health. I was then checked out and also received a clean bill of health. I was told I had no blockage in my tubes and that everything was fine and that we should continue having fun trying for a baby.

Well, after almost another year of nothing, I decided to find a former doctor who I knew would be able to run more tests and answer more questions on what was going on.

After meeting with him, he informed me that he wanted me to be put to sleep and that he wanted to perform an outpatient surgery so that he could peek around in my body to see what he could find. After the exam I was told that I had fibroid tumors blocking my fallopian tubes and that was the cause of me not getting pregnant. It was a good feeling to finally know why it wasn't happening. I was told that if I did not have them removed, I wouldn't get pregnant.

My husband was very anxious, so he reminded me often that I needed the surgery. I had them removed in 1998. Eight months later I was pregnant. After three months of being pregnant, I miscarried. I swore that I would never try again. After much convincing by my husband, family, friends, and much prayer, I agreed to try again.

In 1999 I got pregnant again, I was doing very well. At 8 months pregnant one evening I didn't feel the baby moving. I thought maybe I was imagining things so I didn't worry too much and went to bed. The next day was our baby shower day and I got ready for the shower but still wondered why I hadn't felt the baby move. Well, after the baby shower I finally called the doctor and was told to go to the hospital immediately.

Bad news, the baby died. The umbilical cord had wrapped around the baby's neck. My husband and I were in a state of shock, not believing that this could possibly happen to two strong Christian believers. Well, believe it. It happened to us. We were both basket cases. I was told that I would have to deliver the baby and I did. We had a funeral and buried our baby girl named Kayla.

I was now more determined to have a baby, but really didn't want to try again. I decided the next month that we would adopt and my husband supported the idea one hundred percent.

In June of 2000 we started the adoption process and we prayed to God that He would bless us with a baby for Christmas. Well He is true to His word and He blessed us with a beautiful baby boy in late November and our bundle of joy came home to us in December.

God is truly awesome. Even though those were some to the saddest days of our lives, we both truly believe that trials and storms come to make you strong. We all know that many storms may come, but they must pass eventually.

Love,
A Soldier Singing and Praising and on the Battlefield for the Lord

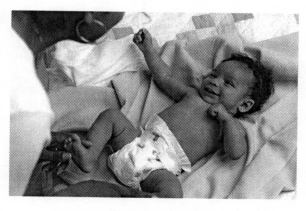

JOSHUA'S COMING

Dear Sisters,

I say to all women facing infertility, there is hope. After five years of trying to get pregnant with no success, I never gave up. My husband Ray and I had tried almost everything, from spending hundreds maybe thousands of dollars on medical procedures, to running from church to church standing in prayer lines in hopes that someone would anoint us and we would go home and become pregnant.

Even though it was hard at times, I remained steadfast and hopeful, still seeking God for a child. Then one day, after seven failed artificial insemination attempts, I heard ever so clearly God's voice saying, "No human being can give life." From that point, I decided in my heart and mind that if I was to become pregnant, I had to change my mind set. Neither I, nor the doctors had control over when and how it was to happen.

When I did that, God blessed us that very same month, through artificial insemination, with our wonderful son DeRay who is now turning four. Ten months after his birth, God blessed my womb with our delightful son Drake, who is now two. Drake came as a surprise, because we were not planning to become pregnant until the following year. Then two years later, God showed Himself strong again by sending us our beautiful daughter Faith who not only was a surprise herself, but has lived up to her name since entering this world in a very surprising way. To every couple who desires a child, seek God for direction, never lose hope, and wait patiently for God to bless you.

Your sister in Christ,
Lynette

　　　　　　　RHONDA C. WHITE

DISCUSSION QUESTIONS

What is behind the misnomer that within the African-American community there are no or few incidences of infertility?

Why do you feel that it is more challenging for African-American couples to discuss their struggles regarding infertility versus other cultures?

Is it contradictory for men and women of faith to attempt to solve their infertility issues through medical intervention?

How do you feel Deanna's control issues affected her faith and her marriage?

How did the Carringtons' infertility cause friction in their marriage and a breakdown in their ability to communicate? Were there any signs early on?

Is what was described in the book as an "emotional affair" as detrimental to a relationship as actual adultery?

Do you think that James' response to his childhood sexual abuse is a normal reaction? Why does it seem to be harder for men to heal from sexual abuse than women?

Do you think in extremes cases like rape that abortion should be considered as a means of terminating the pregnancy?

Would you be able to raise a child that was a product of a rape without any biases?

Why is isolation from friends and family an easy avenue for people to take when they are dealing with serious issues like infertility, abuse or divorce?

Do you think it is possible for men and women to be best friends and remain platonic?

Would you have been able to work on restoring your marriage if your spouse repeatedly was found to be a poor keeper of the family finances or if your spouse left you during one of the biggest storms in your life?

As a reader would you have like to have known who Joshua's father really was? Did it take away from the story not to know?

*May God continue to bless you and know that
whatever you are believing Him for is coming!*

Printed in the United States
100164LV00001B/94-195/A

9 781425 774165